The Last Trollid

Alistair Potter

"Jump into a world that happily offers you a little bit of everything you could want in a grand, sweeping adventure story fit for a king. I was honestly very sad when I reached the end of this story and its sweeping scenery, battles and love. The good news is - it's only the first book in the series!"

- Kathryn Bennett for Readers' Favorite

"The Last Trollid by Alistair Potter is a spellbinding opening to The Sunset of Magic series, a fine blend of sci-fi and fantasy that features magic, battles, unusual creatures, and a quest. Apart from the intense action that permeates the entire story, the author has a gift for humor as well and readers will undoubtedly be hugely entertained throughout this tale."

- Divine Zape for Readers' Favorite

"Great Book! Gripping stuff, well written with a cast of likeable (but also some evil despicable ones) characters. I thoroughly enjoyed it - excellent science fiction / fantasy, top marks."

- Charles Remington – Amazon

"This is a strong fantasy book with almost anything you could want. Epic battles, magical creatures, the last of one's kind, strong female characters, and even a little romance thrown in."

- J. B. Trepagnier Amazon / Goodreads

DEDICATION

Thanks to family, friends and all those who have listened to, read or commented on my work – they have all contributed to making me a better writer.

DISCLAIMER NOTICE

CONTENTS

CHAPTER 1

A flood of freezing air swept into the ruins of an old castle, and to a shrill chorus of alarm the colony of tiny birds harbouring within its walls rose as a twisting black cloud into the spring skies. Seconds later an icy whirlwind formed in the centre of the castle's courtyard, building in intensity until it was tugging and tearing at the long grasses bristling from the uneven cobbles. With a sudden sharp crack, a dark form appeared at the whirlwind's core, and then, like the release of a long held breath, the whirlwind collapsed to reveal a frost coated figure.

Though the terrible cold that surrounded him during his fleeting journey through the void had gone, Wizard Dusswen kept his eyes firmly shut and his hands pressed tight against his face. Only when he was sure it was truly the touch of sunlight on his fingers, did he risk a slow, tentative breath. As the warm air flowed between his lips, he felt a surge of relief; he had survived the journey, the first Harrowen in three hundred years to escape his homeworld Mirt!

Gripping the icy peak of his hood, he forced it back and raised his lizard-like face to the sky, allowing the sunlight to warm his leathery skin. Opening blood red eyes, he found two moons floating above, pale and white against the deep blue of the sky; one large and round, the other small and irregular. He smiled; these were Nal and Ito, the moons of the world Nephus, and the crumbling structure around him was Castle Loden; its forgotten past the key to his mission's success.

Brushing through the tall grasses of the courtyard, he carefully examined the scattered mounds of discarded stone, looking for two with a similar appearance, and set about twenty paces apart. When he found them, he nodded in satisfaction; most would assume this pair of weatherworn blocks were the bases for statues, none would guess their true purpose.

Walking to the nearest, he drew a dagger and scraped a layer of moss from its top. Sheathing the dagger, he took a pouch from a pocket in his robe, loosened its drawstring and sprinkled a layer of grey powder on the stone.

Like parchment laid on glowing coals, the surface of the stone blackened and cracked, peeling back to expose smooth, white marble, and as the concealment fell away, Dusswen's wizardly senses began to alter, the stone's magic dulling his perceptions. This was promising, suggesting the stone still held its power.

There was another simple though unpleasant test. Stretching out a clawed hand he touched the pristine surface, and though prepared, he still shuddered with the shock of contact; it felt like hundreds of tiny needles had pierced his fingertips. There was little doubt now; the magic in the stone was strong.

The temperature within the castle's walls dropped suddenly and Dusswen hastily drew up his hood, turning away as a new void passage began to form. Peppered by an icy hail, and with his robes flapping about him, he waited for the passage to release its cargo, and for the shrill winds to fade before turning back.

A sacking wrapped bundle sat on the ground, a shimmer of tiny ice crystals drifting above it and the grasses around it white with frost.

Without wizardly arts to protect it during the journey, its temperature had plummeted. To approach it so soon would be foolish, instead Dusswen took the opportunity to rub a little warmth into his arms and fingers, and turn to let the sun's heat soak into his body. It had taken many long years to reach this point, a few minutes more would make no difference.

The bundle contained a block of shaped stone; the first of thirty needed to build an arch and form a World Gate. The newly exposed marble plinth was one of the two arch foundations. In order to defeat the human wizards' imprisonment of the Harrowen on Mirt, the block's preparation had required the creation of a new magic. Trapped within the block were the life essences of a host of magic users; older and tradesman wizards, eager initiates, and even children who had shown a magical ability, their deaths now serving the greater glory of the Harrowen Empire.

Seeing that the icy sacking had softened, Dusswen cut away the chords holding it in place, and taking care to avoid touching the stone, folded back the sacking layers to expose a polished block of lustrous grey marble.

One last test remained. If the magics in the plinth and the arch stone failed to blend, the Gate could not be rebuilt; the invasion would fail before it began, and he could never return to Mirt. Reaching out with his mind, he embraced the block, raised it from the ground and moved it towards the plinth. As it approached, he felt the growing attraction between them; an excellent sign, but as he swung the block over the plinth the attraction increased rapidly, threatening to overwhelm his weakened powers.

With sweat beading his forehead, he fought to lower the block slowly, but the closer it came to the plinth, the stronger the attraction grew. He struggled for control, knowing the block could split if it settled too quickly. He should have waited, rested and recovered, but it was too late. A sudden sharp pain lanced through his head, he collapsed to his knees and the block crashed onto the plinth, scattering shards of stone.

Glancing up, he breathed a sigh of relief; block and plinth were intact, and the magics were merging and multiplying, already searching for the next arch stone. The World Gate could be rebuilt.

Staggering to a nearby wall, he settled against it. The next block would not arrive for many hours. Sending him and the first between Mirt and Nephus had taken the combined will of over a hundred wizards, and, like him, they needed to rest before their next effort. On completion, the Gate would be opened, and through the coming months his master, Lord Tekt, would bring soldiers and weapons, building their numbers until he amassed a huge army. Then truly, the invasion of Nephus would begin.

2

Beneath a clear blue sky, reluctant militia cook, Ida Fairweather, waited anxiously on the bench seat of a covered wagon. Her ward, Bort, a giant of a man, sat alongside her, and she could tell by the rippling tension in his broad jaw that his mood matched hers. In front of her, the Silvermeadow militia stood in three neat ranks on the driveway of a modest stone manor house, their steel helmets glittering in the autumn sunshine.

With a rattle, the front door opened and the militia's commander, Baron Endor Caffri, emerged from the manor house. Immediately, his decision to wear his old military uniform caused a subtle stir among the troops. Seldom seen away from the Royal court, it was that of a King's Chosen; a sky blue tabard with the Royal crest of lion rampant in gold thread at the chest. The blue of the tabard was faded and the golden threads had lost their sheen, but that mattered little. The uniform spoke volumes of Endor's long and distinguished career.

As he stepped onto the drive, a barked order echoed from the walls and the militia snapped eagerly to attention.

Endor's manservant, Moleskin, stood ready with his master's horse, but Endor walked by him to approach Ida's wagon, acknowledging her with a friendly nod.

"Good morning, Bort, Ida," he said.

"Good morning, sir," said Bort.

"You look very dashing." said Ida, mustering a cheerful tone.

Endor glanced down at his tabard. "I wasn't too sure if I should wear it, but it's the only thing that felt comfortable. Likely it's the last chance I'll get to wear it."

An awkward pause followed these poorly chosen words and Ida tried to lift the mood. "It looks the part, and the troops seem to appreciate it."

Endor nodded and smiled, and then looked over to Bort. "Ida did a fine job with the uniforms, don't you think?"

"Very fine, sir," said Bort.

Of course Endor had seen to the detail of armour and weapons, but among the many small tasks Ida had undertaken in preparation for this day was the commissioning of the cloth smocks the militia wore over their chainmail vests. They were quartered green and yellow, with Endor's Baronial symbol of a corn sheaf and sickle at the chest.

Endor turned. "Grand sight, eh, Moleskin?" he prompted.

"Yes, sir," said Moleskin, staring uneasily at the assembled soldiers.

Both gaudy and extravagant, Ida thought Moleskin's choice of uniform was ridiculous. He wore a matching doublet and knee britches in a rich green cloth, and with all the hems and cuffs frivolously piped with fine gold braid. Ida had little doubt that the scandalous little man had used Endor's money to buy it, but it wasn't her place to comment.

"Well," said Endor, looking up at the bright, cloudless sky, "daylight's burning. I'd better get them moving."

"We're ready here," said Ida.

Endor smiled. "Of that I have little doubt, thank you, Ida." He turned away to mount his horse, rising easily into the saddle with a vigour that belied his years.

Long ago Ida and Endor had shared a school desk and even a first kiss, and then each had lived quite different and separate lives. It surprised Ida that she even remembered the kiss, but recent events had drawn them together, stirring some very old memories, none of which seemed appropriate for a spinster. Had Endor shown a hint of interest she might have considered revisiting that past, but he seemed oblivious to the possibility.

Endor positioned himself in front of the troop, and after making a show of sweeping his eyes up and down the ranks, his resonant tones filled the air, "Men and women of the Silvermeadow militia, we march to join King Malcor's army, fulfilling a tradition of service and common purpose that has existed in Carolin for over two hundred years. When we fight, we fight not only for our King and country, but also for our loved ones and our homes." He paused. "I want you all to know this; you're as fine a body of men and women as I have ever seen. When we march out, I want you to march tall! March proud! Now, a cheer for the Silvermeadow militia. Hip, hip..."

Ida added her voice to the loud *hooray*, scowling when Moleskin's shout outlasted every other, no doubt carefully timed to appear more enthusiastic.

Endor beamed across at him. "That's the way, Moleskin! Now, best you get mounted up, you wouldn't want to get left behind!"

Moleskin barely kept the sarcasm from his voice as he responded, "Of course not, sir."

Endor called out an order, "Move them on, if you please, Mr. Stamp."

The town constable, Peter Stamp, was now the militia's Master Sergeant. A powerfully built man, with bushy, intimidating eyebrows; he snapped a salute to Endor, arm across chest, and then stepped out from his place on the line.

He turned and swung his eyes onto Moleskin, who had not moved, and his manner hardened. "I believe you've a wagon to mind, my lad?"

Ida suppressed a smile; Peter Stamp had Moleskin's measure.

Moleskin walked to their second wagon, which sat behind Ida's, and she made a point of ignoring him as he went by.

Peter Stamp waited until Moleskin had climbed aboard before giving his order. "Right face!" he barked. "Forward march!"

With Endor at their head, the column marched down the drive.

Ida settled her linen skirt about her knees and ankles, tugged down the hem of her tailored leather jerkin and then nodded to Bort. He gave a firm command, flicked the reins and their wagon lurched into motion, just as a loud cheer came from ahead. The townsfolk were greeting the militia as they emerged from the gates at the foot of the drive.

As Ida's wagon entered the busy cobbled street, a jolly creature with a full waistline and rosy cheeks fell into step alongside. It was Ida's good friend Ephemia Kardy, the butcher's wife.

"Well, Ida," said Ephemia, "I wonder what you've gone and done this time?"

Ida smiled. "We've all got to do our bit, Ephemia."

Peering across at Bort, Ephemia lowered her voice, "Looks like you'll have your hands full. Bad enough you've got to cook for this lot, without having to babysit that big lump."

"That big lump," said Ida, suppressing her annoyance, "is worth his weight in gold to me."

"I hope you're right, Ida."

Bort's sheer size meant he made short work of any manual task, but of course Ephemia meant the unusual events that now found Ida as the militia's cook, and Bort as her assistant.

"It seemed the best decision at the time," said Ida.

Ephemia shook her head slowly. "How you ever convinced the Baron to take him on in the first place, I'll never know."

Ida smiled weakly. She could have argued the point, but Ephemia had very selective hearing, finding only the juiciest tidbits worthy of her interest.

Some months earlier, Ida had convinced Endor to employ Bort as his household cook, with the sweetener that she would train and supervise Bort until he was fully competent. Then the Royal decree had arrived, commanding the town to raise a militia. Quite reasonably, Endor had expected his own cook to take on the duty of feeding the militia, and though Bort's training was going well, he wasn't ready for the task of catering to just over fifty souls from a makeshift kitchen. With no other candidate forthcoming, Ida felt she had no option but to take the job herself. The very least these brave men and women deserved was a decent meal or two.

Ephemia raised her voice, adding sincerely, "I wishes you both well. See and come back safe and sound." She caught Bort's eye. "Bort! You see and look after Miss Fairweather."

He replied with a grin, "Bort will look after Ida, Mrs Kardy, and Ida will look after Bort."

Ida smiled and gave a final wave as Ephemia stepped away from the carriage. Though Ida often despaired at Ephemia's gossiping, she had an uncanny way of getting to the heart of matters. That very morning Ida and Bort had made a pact; no matter what happened, they promised to stay together, and watch out for each other. With such uncertainty ahead, this simple promise held great meaning for her.

The route through the village took them past Ida's prim little cottage. She had missed seeing it in daylight that morning, as she and Bort had risen early to make a final check of the wagons and provisions. The cottage's shutters were closed, and the climbing roses around her front door were gone, pruned back early to keep them neat.

Years before, it had sat at the outskirts of the village, but other houses now stretched beyond it. The place of her birth, Silvermeadow had grown over her lifetime to a sprawling market community, numbering almost four hundred souls. It was a hospitable place, its farms and orchards prosperous, its trades and workshops always busy. She hoped nothing would change in her absence.

She took one last wistful look at her cottage before turning to face forward, and immediately felt a pang of sorrow. Staring at the ranks of soldiers in front of her, she knew that things could never be the same. Without doubt, some of these brave men and women were destined not to return.

Endor's old comrade-in-arms, Otric Moy, Baron of Cadford, was already waiting with his town militia at the main crossroads outside of

Silvermeadow. Otric's troops were resting at the roadside, and as Endor's militia approached they stood and began forming up.

After the briefest halt and a few words of instruction to Peter Stamp, Endor rode forward to join Otric at the head of the column. Following a barked command, the combined militias stepped out smartly. Spotting an opportunity, the drivers of Otric's two supply wagons quickly pulled in behind Ida, pushing Moleskin's wagon to the rear, and the worst of any dust thrown up by the column.

Ida now trailed a column of one hundred and nine fighting men and women marching three abreast. In an effort to make both militias feel themselves part of something bigger, the two uniforms were almost identical, the colours matching to perfection, but with the quartering of the green and yellow reversed. It was an impressive sight

Pushing aside gloomier thoughts of their destination and purpose, Ida resolved to try and enjoy the journey. This part of the countryside was particularly beautiful, with golden fields of ripening corn rippling in the warm breeze.

"You drive well," she said to Bort; it was a new skill he had only recently mastered.

"These are good horses." Bort pointed. "This one is a strong old rascal, and this one is young and smart. Both are good horses."

Ida smiled, marvelling at Bort's insight. "It seems to me that we should think about getting you a job working in a stable, or a coaching house?"

"Bort prefers cooking."

This was true, though the skills had come slowly. Ida remembered a particularly disastrous lesson in Endor's kitchen, involving the overenthusiastic flipping of pancakes, and the later use of a long ladder to scrape them from the vaulted ceiling. On that occasion her patience had grown so thin, she resorted to whacking Bort firmly on the head with a serving spoon. It had improved his concentration dramatically.

"Once this is all over," she said, "I think we can get you back at work with Endor."

"Bort would like that," he said.

His attention shifted quickly to the horses, gathering in a bare handful of reins as he skilfully guided the wagon through a series of ruts in the road.

Not just for his driving skills, Ida was glad to have Bort sitting beside her, rather than marching in front. She hadn't mentioned it to him, but fearful he might be cajoled into joining the militia, she had insisted on having Bort as her assistant. He might seem the ideal warrior, but Ida knew his nature was too gentle for that task.

Remembering Ephemia's parting words, and their pact, Ida smiled. She had little doubt that Bort was serious about his promise, and for her part, it was already a commitment she had made; though in that parental role she might have wished him a bit more forward, even, sometimes, a little more selfish. In many ways he seemed ill-fitted for the world; too big, a little clumsy at times and terribly naive. She knew that others thought him stupid or slow, but she had seen sufficient flashes of intelligence and insight to know this wasn't true. If cook was the life he chose, she was happy with that, but she couldn't help thinking there was more he could achieve. He just needed to find that certain something, and he would shine, but what that was, she did not know.

Endor felt more comfortable than he had for many years. It was good to be marching again with a comrade who understood a world that had been his for most of his adult life, and it wasn't long before Otric produced a flask.

"Fancy a little something to mark the occasion?"

"It's a bit early for me," said Endor, but he accepted the flask and took a good swig. "I say, that's good stuff that!"

"Almost the last of the ninety-one."

Endor passed the flask back. "Good year, the ninety-one."

"That it was." Otric took a drink and then banged the cork in tight.

"I must invite you over for dinner tonight," Endor boasted, "I've got a rather fine cook with me. I think you'll be impressed."

"I heard you signed up Ida for the job." Otric winked. "How'd you manage that, use a bit of the old charm?"

"Well... there was a bit of negotiation involved."

"That's the way to do it. Don't you worry, I'll be there, I wouldn't want to miss the chance of dining in such fine company!"

Endor could have kicked his own backside. "That's not really the arrangement."

Otric looked shocked. "You're not making her eat with the troops are you?"

"I hadn't actually thought about it," Endor admitted.

Otric shook his head in mock despair, and Endor wondered why this hadn't occurred to him before. Ida was a successful merchant and property owner, and probably as wealthy as him; in every way his social equal.

He sighed. "I'll have a word with her, and it would be grand if you could spare some of the ninety-one. Make it a bit of a celebration, first night out and all that."

"Splendid idea, I've a few bottles tucked away."

"Settled then," said Endor. By his estimation that meant at least a dozen bottles. It looked to be a very jolly outing.

"I'd recognise that sword anywhere," said Otric.

Endor gripped its pommel. "Sharpened and ready."

Otric grinned. "Jealous as anything I was, when the King gave you that. Never seen a finer sword then or since. It still keeping its edge like it did?"

"Of course!" Endor pointed. "Is that the old hairsplitter?"

Otric patted the sacking wrapped around the head of a sturdy battleaxe. "Damned mice had got at the shaft, but my smithy cut me a fine new one. Then he polished the head so bright I can use it as a mirror now."

Both men roared with laughter.

This light humour was familiar, a common defence against the deadly serious nature of their profession. Memories of Endor's career flooded back; memories of friendships formed, comrades lost and of all the times he had come close to death. He had enjoyed his share of luck, but mostly survived on his wits and skills. But they had all been skirmishes; intervening in local disputes, dealing with robber bands and the numerous times when a show of strength was enough to maintain the peace. Never in his lifetime had such a widespread call to arms been made.

"I'm wondering who's left of the old bunch?" he said.

"Ah," Otric mused, "who were there, Liff and Etan, Hork and Glar?" He smiled grimly. "And we can't forget Keif."

"Of course not."

Keif had won honours in the pursuit of a particularly nasty bandit who had terrorised a string of villages. His portrait now hung in the King's Gallery, there to be remembered as a hero for all times. But recognition came at a price; Keif had died from his wounds shortly after the action.

If Endor had any regrets about his many years of exemplary service, it was the lack of that one heroic act that might have placed his name in the history books. All soldiers of his calibre hoped for such recognition, but for him it had never come. Still, his days of heroism might be over, but he could inspire it in others. Importantly, he had the skills and knowledge to lead soldiers on the battlefield.

Otric uncorked his flask again. "To Keif." He took a good swallow and handed it over.

Endor held it up. "To Keif." He took a drink before passing it back. "Do you remember our first day?"

"Like yesterday, especially our drill sergeant, Tobias."

Endor smiled wistfully. "Oh yes, the lovely Lena."

Otric paused, the flask at his lips. "We were as green as they came. She soon knocked that out of us."

"And she always had her favourites, as I remember?"

Otric grinned. "I always liked to keep my superiors happy."

Both men laughed quietly.

"I heard you sent your Lizbeth off to fetch her mother?" said Endor.

"Just being prudent. Thought it best if they were both in Cadford."

"And your lad, Grant?"

"Kept him at school, didn't want him caught up in this."

"Of course not, no point in interfering with his education. Likely we'll have this sorted in time for the harvest festival."

"Likely," Otric agreed.

Endor had no wife or offspring to worry about. In a way that was good; no orphans or widow to leave behind should the worst happen. But putting that aside, he was envious of Otric. Endor had never managed to settle back into civilian life the same as him.

Moleskin's wagon rattled along at the end of the procession; his driver gripping the wagon's reins as if he were praying. On the man's head was a battered felt hat that cast such a dark shadow over his eyes, half of the time Moleskin wasn't sure if the man's eyes were open or not.

"Turned out nice," said Moleskin, hoping to relieve the tedium with some light conversation.

"Mmmh," the man grunted.

He tried again. "Nice part of the countryside. Ever been this way before?"

"Mm, mmmh."

Moleskin couldn't decide if this was a yes or a no. "What's that funny noise?" he said. "Is that one of the wheels about to fall off?"

"Mmmh, mmm."

Moleskin feigned concern. "Are you sure?"

The man turned his head and gave him a lazy glower, before returning to his original position.

Moleskin sighed, and then climbed over the bench seat and into the back of the wagon. He wriggled and pressed the top of some bags of dried goods, shaping them into a comfortable bed, and then lay back and stared up at a row of large pots and pans hanging from the iron hoops supporting the wagon's canvas cover. The pots jostled and swung with the motion of the wagon, occasionally colliding to emit a deep clang.

He sat up on his elbows and stared longingly out of the back of the wagon. Bathed in sunlight and with a faint dusty haze hanging over it, the road stretched off in a near straight line. On either side were fields filled with pale yellow corn, waving gently in the breeze.

He glanced forward; his driver wouldn't notice if he slipped out of the back of the wagon and hid in the corn until the militias were gone, and running off would also save him the bother of any confrontation regarding his recent creative bookkeeping, though the careful positioning of the household ledger beneath the leaky tap of a small brandy barrel, would soon render most of the entries illegible.

He patted his waist, feeling the reassuring presence of a money belt hidden beneath his shirt. It was filled with gold coin; enough to buy a seat in a fast coach travelling in the opposite direction, and enough to keep him living in comfort for several months until he found a new position. But his life in Silvermeadow was just too rewarding to give up that easily. Sighing deeply, he lay back and shut his eyes; as long as this present discomfort didn't last, it had to be worth the sacrifice.

3

Just after lunch on the fourth day of marching, the progress of the Cadford and Silvermeadow militias slowed as the road filled with other town militias; they became part of a seemingly endless column of trudging soldiers and heavily laden wagons, all toiling under the sun's heat.

Their journey was almost at its end; from conversations with Endor, Ida knew it was less than a half day's march to the chosen battlefield, just outside of a tiny hamlet called Sollas.

Her duties had kept her busy enough to distract her from thoughts of their destination, but with the journey's end so close, many of her earlier anxieties were returning.

A sharp exchange caught her attention; Peter Stamp was having words with one of the men. She looked around for Endor, whose presence was usually a steadying influence. He was nearby, but rode up slowly, keeping his distance and giving Peter Stamp time to resolve the situation.

Endor pulled alongside and spoke in a low voice, "Good afternoon, Ida, Bort. Any idea what the problem is?"

"None," said Ida, "but this heat has everyone a bit short tempered."

"Let's hope that's all it is."

Endor waited until Peter Stamp had finished, before calling him aside and dismounting to walk with him. They were still close to the wagon, and Ida couldn't avoid overhearing their conversation.

"Bit of trouble there, Mr. Stamp?"

"It's that stupid rumour again, sir. About this army that's coming not being human. It's all anyone's talking about."

"Not that again!"

Stamp nodded, but avoided Endor's eyes.

"Come on, man, not you too!"

Ida watched Endor's face turn red as he fought to contain his anger. The rumour had arrived shortly after the King's decree. Knowing how damaging such nonsense could be, Endor had crushed it immediately, but the rumour had persisted.

Endor shook his head. "This will not do, Mr Stamp! In-human is the word someone will have heard. Soldiers are always saying that about a ruthless enemy. You keep them in line. We'll get this sorted out once and for all when we get to the camp."

Peter Stamp saluted. "Yes, sir."

Endor remounted, and then pulled out his sword and shouted, "A cheer for the Silvermeadow militia. Hip, hip..."

A rousing hooray answered him. In seconds other militias were cheering too, and soon similar shouts were rippling up and down the long column.

Endor nodded in satisfaction and then winked at Ida, knowing that she was shrewd enough to recognise this simple ploy; distracting the troop with good-natured rivalry with other nearby militias.

It was late afternoon when Endor drew his force to a halt at a simple wooden gate, the entrance to a large meadow already half-filled with tents. Further down the road, and just visible in the distance, were the rooftops of Sollas. Warned of the impending battle, its inhabitants had abandoned their homes weeks before.

A scribe with a large book, a bottle of ink and a quill, sat at a table by the roadside. Beside him stood a woman wearing the dark blue tabard of the King's Guard. She was a striking beauty, with superbly toned muscles, short dark hair and a narrow hauntingly familiar face.

She approached, stopped in front of Endor and saluted. "A welcome from King Malcor. Your name and place of origin, good sir?"

Endor dismounted and returned the salute. "Endor Caffri, Baron of Silvermeadow."

The ghost of a smile touched the edge of the woman's mouth, and she gave him a strange sideways look through penetrating green eyes. "How many do you have, sir?"

"Fifty-four, ma'am."

Otric rode up and dismounted just as Endor finished speaking.

The woman looked backwards and forwards between the two men. "Unmistakable," she said, with a gentle laugh. "Endor and Otric. I was told to keep an eye out for you two."

"Our reputation precedes us," Otric suggested, smoothly.

The woman smiled and raised a well-defined eyebrow. "My mother bids you welcome, sirs."

"By the gods!" Endor finally recognised the resemblance to their old drill sergeant. "You're Lena's girl! Last time I saw you, you were no bigger than a kitten."

"Correct! I'm Lineth."

"How is your mother?" said Otric.

"Well, thank you. Might I enquire the strength of your own militia?"

"Fifty-five."

"Hailing from the town of Cadford?" she suggested.

"Yes, of course, Cadford."

Lineth passed the details to the scribe and then returned to the men.

"I wonder," said Otric, "is your mother here?"

Lineth shook her head. "Garrison duties back at Conisby."

"Shame that, would've been good to reacquaint myself."

"I'm sure she would have liked that too." Quickly shifting to a more businesslike manner, Lineth pointed across the field. "If you gentlemen could make camp over there by those trees." She pointed again, indicating a sprawling canvas structure with a bright blue pennant fluttering above it. "And if you listen for the muster call, there's an officer's meeting this evening in the field commander's tent."

After acknowledging her instructions Endor leant close. "Here," he said, in a low voice, "this nonsense about the enemy not being human is still going up and down the ranks. You'd better put a stop to it before it gets out of hand."

Lineth's brow furrowed. "I'm sorry, sir, I'm not at liberty to discuss that. Just make sure you come to this evening's meeting." She saluted smartly. "If you'll kindly move on, there's many more still to be processed. It's been a pleasure, gentlemen."

Endor was stunned by her response. Surely there couldn't be any truth to the rumour? She prevented further discussion by walking quickly away and peering along the road at the militias still waiting, managing to convey some urgency for them to move on.

Endor exchanged a worried look with Otric, who shook his head and glanced at their militias standing close by. It wasn't a good time to continue the discussion. Leaving Otric by the gate, Endor led off, waving his troop to follow him into the field.

His mind quickly shifted to the mundane though necessary task of making camp and he began assessing their given patch, working out the best positioning of the tents, but the encounter at the gate troubled him terribly, and he couldn't get the matter out of his head. He'd been convinced all along that the rumour was just an unfortunate mistake, but had he been wrong? Were they really about to face a non-human army?

Ida was always impressed with how quickly Endor's militia made camp. They were a well-trained and disciplined group, right down to the basics of erecting tents and digging latrines. Having watched them in training, she realised this was entirely due to Endor's diligence and leadership. This was a revelation for Ida; in Silvermeadow he was competent enough at managing the local community, but in public he had always seemed a little lost.

As soon as she and Bort assembled the kitchen, they prepared and served the evening meal. Then, after cleaning and stowing all their equipment, Ida sent Bort to make enquiries about helping with the wounded. The field contained thousands of soldiers, all ready to make the ultimate sacrifice to defend their Kingdom; it was the very least she could do.

Resolving to stay busy, she gathered together Endor's linen and sat on a small stool in the shade of a tree. Unfolding a large white tablecloth, she carefully nicked one edge with her sewing scissors and gave the cloth a tug. It ripped apart with a loud tearing noise.

Moleskin seemed to appear from nowhere. "What are you doing?" he demanded, his voice filled with horror. "Stop that right now! That's my master's finest linen, and those, those are his best bed sheets!"

Ida continued tearing the cloth, removing a long strip. "I'm making bandages."

"What for?"

Ida rolled her eyes. "For treating the wounded, you stupid little man!"

"Do you know how much..."

"I wonder," Ida interrupted, a cold edge to her voice, "if you are actually aware of what's going on? If this battle goes badly, Endor won't need any bed sheets or tablecloths. Haven't you worked that out?"

Bort arrived back with the camp's superintendent, Lineth, the young woman from the gate, just in time to catch the last of Ida's words.

Moleskin stared vacantly at the new arrivals before answering, "Well, yes, of course. Ehm, carry on." He wandered off, mumbling to himself.

"Trouble?" Lineth asked.

"Nothing I can't handle," said Ida.

"Chain of command," Lineth laughed, "let them know who's in charge straight away."

Ida smiled. "Maybe you can give me some pointers?"

"Oh, I doubt that, Miss Fairweather." Lineth nodded towards Bort. "I received your message."

"Yes, Bort and I would like to help with the wounded. I've some knowledge of medicines and healing, and if nothing else we can be two extra pairs of hands."

Lineth pointed to a group of larger tents at the far end of the meadow. "Volunteers are welcome. The King's surgeon has organised a meeting, you'll hear a muster call in about an hour. If you come along, you'll be assigned duties."

Ida nodded. "We'll be there."

"No doubt I'll see you later then, Miss Fairweather. I'm assigned to the field hospital as well." Lineth saluted and marched off.

Ida waved to Bort. "Come and help me with this."

He sat cross-legged on the grass, and once shown what to do, began winding the long cloth strips into neat rolls.

Ida noted that he remained quiet as he worked. "Is something bothering you?"

"Bort is thinking about the fighting."

Ida stopped her work. "Do you know why we have to fight?"

He nodded.

She spoke gently, "Nobody likes fighting, but if we don't fight then we'll have nothing. No homes, no harvest."

Bort nodded again. "When we finish fighting, then everything will be good again?"

Ida looked around at the many tents and soldiers crowding the field. "Pray to the gods, yes."

Among the many unfamiliar faces in the field commander's tent, Endor spotted one he knew and trusted. He marched up and threw out his hand to the powerfully built man.

"Hork! Good to see you."

He immediately snatched his hand back when he saw what hung around Hork's neck; a metal gorget bearing the rank of General. Endor promptly brought his arm across his chest in a salute.

"Sir, it's an honour to serve under you."

Hork grinned, returned the salute and then held out his hand. "And it's good to see you, Endor. Now relax, won't you, we go back too far for that."

Endor shook the offered hand. "It shouldn't really surprise me you made general. You always did have an eye for the bigger picture. Congratulations."

"Thank you, Endor." Hork winked. "You're looking well."

Endor patted his stomach. "Country life is just a little too comfortable."

"Believe me," Hork tapped his forehead, "when it comes to command, it's what's up here that counts. And I don't mind admitting, we're in need of real soldiers like yourself and Otric."

Endor's brow furrowed, but he didn't feel comfortable asking the question that troubled him most. "I did wonder how bad it was."

After checking to either side of him, Hork leant closer. "I've never come across anything like it before, Endor. Nothing we've done has slowed them down."

"What're they after then?"

"We don't know, they refuse to parley. We lost a few heralds trying. Their leader calls himself Lord Tekt, and he doesn't respect any flag of truce. The only reason we know his name is because one of my spies got close enough to hear it. Took an arrow in the shoulder for his trouble, but managed to escape." Hork drew Endor even closer. "And that's not the half of it; they've got blood red eyes, pointed teeth and skin like leather."

Endor was shocked, but this explained Lineth's troubling reaction at the gate. "Damn! Then it's true, they're not human."

Hork's tone was grave. "They're like no human I ever met before."

"You can't be serious! If they're not human, then what are they, where did they come from?"

Hork shook his head. "We've no idea. What matters is that we stop them here."

For a moment Endor was lost for words. But regardless of who their enemy was, fundamental truths remained; his belief in himself and the men and women under his command.

"We'll do it," he said. "You've got a real army to work with now."

Hork stroked his chin. "I had a good look at your militia, Otric's too. Excellent turnout. Are they as good as they look?"

"I believe so."

"That's good enough for me. I plan to spread squads of regulars among the weaker groups; show an example, help keep things tight. I'd like to treat your militias as regulars, use them the same way. Are they fit for it?"

Endor snapped a salute. "The Silvermeadow militia won't let you down, sir."

"Thank you, Endor. I'll have a word with Otric, though I can be sure of his answer." Hork shook Endor's hand again. "When I get a chance, we'll all get together and have a real chat, empty a few bottles."

"I look forward to it," said Endor.

Hork nodded and clapped Endor's shoulder affectionately. He took a deep breath and looked around the tent. "Now wish me luck, Endor, somehow I've got to explain this to everyone, without causing a widespread panic."

Hork walked on, climbing a low podium at the centre of the tent before turning and raising an arm for attention. Endor watched with pride as the room fell silent, all eyes on Hork.

More than an old comrade, Endor knew Hork as a good soldier, a brilliant strategist and protective of his resources. But though strategies and good defensive formations always helped, like all professional soldiers they both shared the same basic knowledge; sometimes it was simply a matter of numbers. Man for man the losses could be the same, and finally, all it came down to was that the army with the greater numbers, and resolve, would win the day. Having seen how far the militias had stretched on the roads leading to the muster camp, Endor had a terrible feeling that the coming battle would be very costly for both armies.

After the meeting, Endor invited Otric to join him for a nightcap, which they drank sitting at a table outside Endor's tent.

They spoke in low voices.

"Damn," said Endor, "I don't know how I'll explain this to the men."

Otric nodded. "I can't believe Hork just came out and said it."

"Only way, much better than all these rumours."

"And they're only a day away," said Otric, "that's not long."

Endor slapped the table. "We'll keep busy with these new drills. Don't give the troops a chance to think on it too much, time enough for that once it's over."

Otric nodded and took a drink from his cup.

Endor looked around the field; groups of soldiers had gathered by glowing campfires and the sweet smell of wood smoke and the gentle melodies of stringed instruments drifted on the night air. Against the background of what lay ahead, it was good to see the troops relaxing.

He sought comfort in the familiar. "Lena's girl, Lineth, she's a fine looking woman."

"She is that, and damned smart too." Otric paused, his voice softening, "She's got her mother's eyes."

Endor grinned but didn't answer.

Otric toyed with his cup. "I remember, Lena never said who the father was."

"You didn't complain at the time." Endor caught the wistful look on Otric's face and added, "And that's best left as it is."

They both knew that Otric was the most likely candidate for Lineth's father, but Endor kept a secret. Just once, at an uncomfortably timely moment, Lineth's mother and he had shared a bed. It was well in the past now, and Lena had never asked either of them to step forward as Lineth's father, quite the opposite. It wasn't worth mentioning now.

Otric drained his drink. "Now, I'd better get to bed. Busy day tomorrow."

Endor stood and stretched out his hand. "Whatever happens, Otric, I want you to know you've been the best friend a man could have."

Otric stood and gripped Endor's hand. "And you too, dear friend, and you too."

The men embraced and then separated.

Endor waited until Otric had left before sitting again. He snuffed out the lantern and allowed the darkness to fold around him, taking respite in the solitude this offered. Apart from the new drills, there was nothing more he could do to prepare the militia for battle; but sadly, he also knew it was impossible to prepare anyone for the real horrors of warfare.

4

From a hill near the field hospital, Ida had a clear view of the battlefield. It was mid-morning, high cloud cast occasional shadows on the lush green landscape, and the air held the faint smells of waxed leather, oiled steel and sweat, all mingling with the sour perfume of trampled grass.

Ida had no ghoulish desire to watch the battle, but felt duty bound to bear witness to the bravery and commitment of the men and women she knew so well. Bort had insisted on accompanying her.

The line of the King's army stretched across the top of the field, with uniforms of all colours dotted among the predominant blue of the King's regulars. Behind the main line, blocks of archers stood ready, and behind them the ranks of cavalry. A large, empty expanse of meadow separated the two armies, but all Ida could see of their enemy was an indistinct mass of black, a single deep rank of soldiers, the width of its line matching that of the King's army.

Bort let out a deep sigh and Ida placed a hand on his shoulder. "We'd better get down, ready to help with the wounded."

Bort nodded slowly and turned to leave.

Ida paused, her eyes lingering on a distinctive patch of yellow and green uniforms. Somewhere among them was Endor. "Be strong," she whispered.

Endor drew up a spyglass and examined the solid line of darkly-clad figures spread across the far end of the field. He had never seen their like before. They had broad flattened features with wide grinning mouths, and most had long straggling hair, woven with beads and trinkets.

As before, there was no call to parley, Tekt's army had simply marched onto the battlefield and formed up, ready to advance. Visible behind the ranked army was a strange square tower, finished in the deepest black. Its purpose had been discussed during the officer's meetings and briefings. This was where Tekt based himself, overseeing his troop movements and observing the battle.

King Malcor's army had assembled at the top of the battlefield just before dawn; Hork identifying this location as one of the few that offered a significant advantage. A gradual rise to a narrowing pass with broken landscape to either side, Tekt's army would have to climb the slope, and if not stopped, would be funnelled into the pass, where they could be contained sufficiently to allow an ordered retreat.

Endor lowered the spyglass and turned to examine his militia. They formed a section of a multicoloured line stretching off to either side. There were uniforms in reds, yellows and greens, others in plain dress, and at regular intervals the deep blue of the King's colours.

The King's cavalry were held in reserve; they had only proved effective in open skirmishes. Previous attempts to use them in battle had been costly, the enemy quickly laying wicked steel traps to snare and maim the horses.

Endor paced along the line of shields, returning frightened looks with what he hoped was a confident, reassuring gaze. He could only guess at the thoughts going through each man and woman's head, here they were, standing on a battlefield facing creatures better found in nightmare or campfire tale.

He spoke with a firm voice, "Well, take a good look. Ugly blighters, I'll agree, but you know what's expected of you. You know your drills. And you're fit, strong and healthy." He pointed over his shoulder with a dismissive waggle of his thumb. "Which is more than I can say for that bunch of mother's mistakes."

This comment raised some smiles.

He continued, "Work together and we'll see this day out. I'll also guarantee you'll have something worth telling your grandchildren about."

A hush fell over Tekt's forces and Endor turned to see what was happening.

As a single entity the enemy began breathing together, making a strange sighing noise, almost like the wind, and a gloomy, oppressive mood seemed to spread across the battlefield.

Endor felt the skin on his back start to creep as cold fingers of doubt gripped his chest. He rebelled against the idea that there were unnatural forces at play, but his concept of what was real and what was fantasy had already been turned on its head.

He had a sudden inspiration. "Would you listen to that?" he roared. "Sounds to me like an army of consumptives!"

His militia laughed. Then the laughter spread down the ranks as his words were passed from mouth to mouth. A few crude jokes were passed back, bringing more waves of laughter. From further up the line, Otric nodded his approval and saluted.

The enemy began wailing and chanting, but this had little effect. The laughter had broken the spell of fear.

Endor prudently stepped through his own line and turned to watch the sky above the enemy. The first likely exchange would be arrow shot. Confirmation came as a grey cloud of arrows appeared, arcing over the field towards them.

"Arrow defence," he shouted.

The ranks around him linked shields to form a protective roof of wood, leather and steel, there was a strengthening hiss and then his ears drummed with the deadly rain of arrows.

Screams came from either side, as poorly prepared squads took losses and suffered casualties.

"Stand firm!" Endor bellowed, anticipating another wave, intended to catch the ill-disciplined as they lowered their shields.

The second wave hit, even as the words left his lips.

There was a sudden loud thrum from the rear, as hundreds of the King's longbow archers released their strings, the hiss of the arrows in flight was sharp, then low as the arrows swept overhead, arcing down towards the enemy. Spotters would range the shot, targeting successive waves to where they could do the most damage.

Endor called out, "Mr. Stamp. Report!"

Peter Stamp was on the front rank. He shouted back, "No more, sir!"

"Frontal defence," Endor shouted, and his militia quickly sheared any embedded arrows from their shields and reformed their original positions. He looked around to assess his casualties. There were none. "Well done, all!" he roared. "Well done!"

Casualties were being removed from other parts of the line, and although Endor felt some responsibility for the civilian militias ranked either side of him, there was very little he could do, setting a good example being the most helpful at this late stage.

What was coming next, more arrows, a charge? Fortunately they wouldn't have to contend with cavalry, Tekt's army didn't have any.

"Sir," Stamp called. "Movement above the enemy."

Endor stared as what appeared to be several large birds rose into the air. As they came closer it became clearer what they were; spinning metal stars with long curving blades. At this range, it was difficult to judge how big they were, but he could guess at their destructive potential. Other than running, there was only one defence that had any hope against this weapon.

"Sloping barrier!" he shouted.

His troop linked and overlapped their shields in a deeply canted wall designed to deflect shot from larger crossbow engines.

The air sang with approaching death, and with an almighty clatter one of the flying stars clipped the rear of Endor's defence, slicing the tops from a few shields and pulling others from their owner's hands.

The huge weapon, each blade the height of a man, buried itself in the earth twenty paces farther on; the blades projecting above the ground still quivering and flexing. The sounds of other impacts and screaming echoed up and down the lines.

"Report!" Endor bellowed.

Stamp called back, "Arrows, sir. Enemy holding firm!"

"Arrow defence," Endor shouted.

The front ranks of the barrier sprang to their feet and angled their shields to complete the edge of the defensive roof. Seconds later it rained arrows.

"Those bloody star-scythe things again, sir," Stamp shouted.

"Sloping barrier," Endor bellowed. He waited until the ranks were formed before calling out, "Thank you for that, Mr. Stamp!"

The rhythmic whirr of a star-scythe grew in Endor's ears, its flickering blades mesmerising as it flew straight towards his militia, seeming almost to be floating on a cushion of air.

He held his breath, sickeningly aware that his contribution to this battle might be about to end, and thought of Ida, hoping she would find it in her heart to shed a tear for him.

At the last instant the star-scythe dipped, the ground trembling as it embedded itself to their front, just paces away.

"Report!"

"All quiet, sir!"

Quiet, it was not! Some of this volley of star-scythes had found their targets, and the steady beat of arrowshot from the King's longbows filled the air. However, Peter Stamp had correctly relayed the information that the enemy had ceased shooting and were not advancing.

"Keep me informed, Mr. Stamp." Endor moved through his ranks, reassuring them and congratulating them on their drills. Though he saw fear in many faces, he knew he had prepared them as best he could. They were ready to fight.

"Movement, sir," Stamp shouted.

Endor pushed his way clear of the front rank and looked down the field. Tekt's entire army was moving forward at a walking pace. "Ready bows," he shouted, then added, "Front ranks kneel."

His own archers now had a clear sight of the enemy, and with so many approaching they were certain of hitting something.

The King's longbows adjusted their range, and the next release flew by, tight on the heads of their own troops, a deep angry buzz that drowned all voices.

Endor knelt down before giving the command to shoot. Most other section commanders ordered arrows released at that moment and a loud hiss filled the air and faded, but the arrows either fell short or flew over the enemy's heads.

"Steady," Endor bellowed. "Archers watch your aim!" He saw a return volley of arrows rise from behind the advancing army.

Peter Stamp shouted, "Arrows, sir!"

"Very well, arrow defence. Front rank closed!" Endor moved under the protective roof and peered from a crack in the overlapping row of shields still presented to the enemy. As anticipated, crossbow bolts came from within the ranks of the advancing horde, thumping into these shields. Then came the deafening cascade of arrows.

"Arrows and Scythes," Stamp shouted.

"Hold this defence!" The flying star-scythes had proved fairly inaccurate, more a weapon of fear. Endor listened for their approach and said a silent prayer. The nearest one whirred over their heads, missing them completely.

"Report, Mr. Stamp!"

"Enemy closing, sir!"

Endor drew out his sword. "Front ranks, loose your swords. Bows, shoot at will. Pikes, make ready."

The wall of shields sprouted long pikes, and a flurry of arrows and crossbow bolts flew into the advancing soldiers, now less than thirty paces away.

This was the true moment Endor had prepared his militia for, and the looks of grim determination on every face told him all he needed to know, they would hold their ground.

Though Endor's militia held against the first charge, the pressure of bodies against their defences forced them backwards. Their pikes and swords dripped with blood, and the archers kept up a constant stream of arrows, straight into the maniacal horde.

Still the enemy advanced, heedless of their losses; flinging themselves over a carpet of their dead and plunging into the thicket of razor sharp steel; pikes splintering and snapping with the weight of their bodies.

"Stand firm," Endor bellowed over the clamour of voices. He had never experienced warriors like them. They came forward with slack grins on their reptilian faces, seeming to revel in the mayhem.

Gradually the militia dropped in strength as some were killed, and as wounded were withdrawn. Each death felt like a knife wound to Endor's heart. He knew them all by name and how much their loss would affect their families.

Endor's fighting came in bursts, the wall of shields would come close to collapse and he would rally his reserves, swinging his sword mightily and felling creature after creature until the gap was plugged. It was the burden of leadership, and he felt that the lives of those still standing were linked with his. If he fought, they would fight. If he faltered, they would falter. It was a terrible responsibility.

He was starting to feel his age, and cursed his stupidity for not exercising more, and his vanity for believing his prowess with arms would be sufficient to see him through the conflict. He was also aware that the whole of the King's army was in near constant retreat. Footstep by footstep the enemy were pressing them back. It was costly though, and this gave Endor hope. He felt sure the enemy couldn't tolerate this level of losses.

Then a creature at least three heads taller than any around him, bigger even than Bort, waded through the Silvermeadow line, dispatching them with cynical ease.

Endor stepped forward, and for a moment they stood eyeing each other, the giant acknowledging Endor's challenge with a gruesome sneer. It was barefoot and wore little armour; a coarse chainmail vest on its torso, and long steel cuffs on its wrists. Its blood-spattered skin was criss-crossed with wound scars; so many Endor wondered if most had been self-inflicted.

With a roar the monster leapt forward, its sword swinging.

The fight raged, Endor pitting his remembered skills against the giant's brute strength. They fought mightily, hacking and thrusting at each other, both taking minor wounds and scratches. Endor's arms burned with pain as he drew on deeper and deeper reserves, shouting out with each sweep of his sword, but it was an inescapable nightmare, too even a contest to be easily won.

Then Endor stumbled on a fallen body, and the giant leapt forward, connecting a glancing blow against Endor's helmet. Stunned, he fell to his knees, barely aware of the giant's sword sweeping up for the killing blow.

Sensing victory, the creature threw back its head and let out a triumphant roar.

Acting instinctively, Endor lunged forward and drove his sword through the chain armour and into the giant's belly.

For a few shocked, silent heartbeats, the giant stared down at its mortal wound, then its eyes glazed over and it toppled forward, pinning Endor to the ground.

Endor's last thought before slipping into darkness, was of the awful stench from the thick, coppery blood draining from the body on top of him.

The stream of wounded from the front line to the sheltered glade serving as the field hospital had been ceaseless. Though appalled by the carnage and misery, Ida assisted with those waiting to be seen by the King's surgeons. She staunched blood flows with bandages and compresses, applied tourniquets and stitched smaller wounds, anything to give the surgeons more time to work. Often all she could do was comfort the dying.

A woman's voice called out, "Listen to me!"

Ida barely recognised Lineth. The blue tabard she wore over her chainmail armour was torn and coated with blood, turning it almost to black.

"Hear me!" Lineth shouted. "We're falling back! Put the wounded in the wagons, quick as you can. Move now if you value your life, the enemy takes no prisoners!"

Ida knew they would need more wagons. Bort was close by, helping to stretcher the wounded to and from the surgeon's tents. "Bort," she shouted, "go and fetch our wagons." She paused; Moleskin's driver had run off on their first night at the camp. Her voice took on a hard edge, "Whatever it takes, Bort, you make Moleskin bring the other wagon."

"Yes, Ida." He set off at a run.

Ida looked down at the dying soldier cradled in her arms. He bled profusely from a wound across his stomach. She touched a wet rag against his lips and squeezed some water into his mouth.

"Thank you, ma'am," he said, his words the barest whisper.

Ida felt his body relax as he died, then a firm hand touched her shoulder, it was Lineth.

"Find a place on one of the wagons, Miss Fairweather. It's hard, but there's nothing more we can do here."

Ida lowered the dead soldier's head to the ground, closed his empty, staring eyes and stood. "I've sent Bort to collect our two wagons. I'll take as many as I can."

Lineth's brow furrowed and she seemed about to object, then she nodded. "Very well, but for your own sake, don't leave it too long."

Ida helped to load the surgeon's wagons with the wounded, all the time looking anxiously for Bort. There were still many who could be saved.

"You must go," said Lineth, finally.

Ida shook her head. "Bort will be here soon. I know he will!"

"Please, Miss Fairweather. There's no more..."

The clatter of wheels and the rattle of harness halted Lineth's words. A pair of wagons appeared from among the trees, jostling along at speed, Bort's firm hands controlling the first.

"Here are the wagons!" he shouted, driving into the glade and manoeuvring close to the wounded. He stopped the horses with a strong pull on the reins, set the brake and jumped down.

The second wagon, driven by Moleskin, drew to a halt beside the first, and Ida could see he was terrified.

"That's both my wagons," she said.

Lineth glanced anxiously back into the woods between them and the battlefield. "Come on then, we'll do what we can."

Ida and Lineth completed the dreadful task of selecting which wounded to save, and were about to leave when a small group of ragged creatures ran into the clearing. Seeing the wagons they screeched and ran forward brandishing their swords.

Ida experienced a moment of shock; they were exactly as Endor had described them.

"Go now!" Lineth shouted as she unsheathed her sword.

Moleskin leapt onto his wagon, cracked his whip and urged the horses into motion.

Ida was steadying a soldier who was climbing onto Bort's wagon, when one of the wounded already aboard suddenly shouted a warning and pointed behind her.

Before she could react, a clawed hand gripped her shoulder and dragged her to the ground. She shouted, "Go, Bort! Go!"

As the wagon moved off the creature leapt on top of her, keening and cackling. Ignoring her struggles it dug its clawed fingers into her scalp; tugging her head back and stretching and twisting her neck. Crimson eyes glared into hers, and a wash of fetid breath reached her nostrils as the beast's lips parted and its mouth gaped open. She stared in horror as its needle-like teeth hovered over her throat, ready to tear into her flesh.

With a loud clang, a big, black frying pan smashed the side of the monster's head. It was struck with such force, it flew through the air, tumbling over and over to land in a crumpled heap.

Bort dragged Ida to her feet. "Ida is safe now!"

Ida coughed painfully and then buried her head in his chest to hug him firmly. "Oh, thank you, Bort, thank you!"

Remembering their predicament, she stepped quickly away to look past him. Both of their wagons were safely on their way, another's hands taking Bort's place at the reins.

Lineth, who had dealt with the other creatures, ran to Bort and Ida. She pointed her sword towards the departing carriages. "We'll not get by that way," she said, quietly. "Look."

Ida's breath froze in her throat as more ragged figures spilled from the woods behind the wagons, their attention fixed on their escaping enemy.

"Quickly," said Lineth, "I know a place where we can hide."

Ida followed Lineth, ducking into cover and pressing through the thick undergrowth.

Lineth stopped and pointed into a heavily overgrown ditch. "Both of you, in here," she whispered. "If you want to live, stay perfectly still and don't make a sound."

In the damp, muddy bottom of the ditch, Ida anguished over each death scream from the remaining wounded, and any who had not escaped. Over the hours that followed the distressing sounds faded, until only silence remained and finally darkness enveloped them.

Ida shut her eyes tight and sobbed silently, terrified that somewhere in the dark, more of the creatures lurked ready to pounce. She had never in her whole life felt so alone and frightened. Then, very gently, Bort stretched an arm around her. As she had offered her protection to him, now he was doing the same for her.

Three years before, she had found him in woods near Silvermeadow; a full-grown man, but cowering like a child behind some bushes, bruised and cut from a beating. A nearby hamlet, frightened by his size and oddly cat-like eyes, had run him off. Under her guardianship and guidance, he'd become a man any would be proud to call son. It was a small comfort, but if they were to die, she was glad it would be in each other's company.

5

One look at the hideous creatures loping across the clearing was enough to convince Moleskin that he was in the wrong place at the wrong time; this was a combination of circumstances he had worked against all of his life. That the wagon he drove was loaded with wounded mattered little, he just wanted to leave as quickly as possible.

Lineth's shout of "Go Now!" was unnecessary. Without a backward glance, Moleskin whipped his horses into motion and the horrors of the glade were soon behind him.

There were a number of advantages to carrying wounded that Moleskin hadn't anticipated. The ragged lines of defeated soldiers he encountered moved solemnly aside to allow him to pass, and at each bottleneck on the road he was passed quickly through. He took full advantage of this and pressed on relentlessly.

Eventually one of the wounded shouted, "Hoy, you can slow down now."

"I need to get you lot to safety," Moleskin insisted.

"No good if we're all dead. Slow down!"

Reluctantly Moleskin allowed the panting horses to slow to a walk.

"Where are you taking us?" the same man asked.

It was a good question. Moleskin had no idea where he was going, or what he would do with all the wounded soldiers. He had just been following the general flow of the retreat.

"I'm taking you somewhere safe," he said, attempting gruff reassurance.

"Where's that then?" the man asked.

"We'll know when we get there," said Moleskin, rapidly losing his temper. "If that's not good enough, you can get out and walk."

There was a rumble of discontent from among the wounded.

"I don't have to do this," Moleskin protested.

"Here, what's that uniform you're wearing?" another man shouted. "You some kind of officer, then?"

"I'm a military attendant," Moleskin replied, haughtily.

There was a gurgle of coarse laughter.

The man who had spoken first said, "How about stopping and getting us some water." He pressed an empty canteen against Moleskin's back. "Some of us are dying for a drink back here."

His words brought more peels of coarse laughter, followed by some uncomfortable coughing and spluttering.

Moleskin thought that for badly wounded soldiers, they had a strange sense of humour.

"Come on, mate," said the first man, "get us some water. There's a stream on the other side of that meadow."

This started a cackle of requests, all asking for water.

"All right! All right!" Moleskin drew the horses up and pulled on the brake. "Give me some bottles."

Three empty canteens were thrust into his hands. He jumped down from the wagon and made his way across the meadow to the stream. After filling the canteens he turned to walk back. The wagon was gone.

"You ungrateful wretches," he howled. He threw the canteens to the ground and jumped up and down on top of them.

Many of the soldiers walking along the roadway stopped to stare and point, some even began laughing.

This enraged Moleskin even further. He turned and waded across the stream, heading towards a nearby hill.

At the top he scanned the countryside around him. On the road, straggling lines of soldiers stretched off in both directions. Tekt's army was not visible yet, but it would only be a matter of time before they arrived. The road was not a healthy place to be, and if he kept going north they would pass him by.

He checked his money belt; it was still heavy with gold coins. Perhaps the time was right for a career change? He was resourceful, intelligent and cunning. It would be easy to start afresh once things settled down, but only if he could stay alive.

After one last dismissive look at the road, he strode purposefully down the opposite side of the hill.

6

Ida was cold and shocked when Lineth coaxed her from the ditch. Dawn had come an hour before, but they had delayed moving until it was lighter for fear of stumbling into any of the awful creatures. Between them they carried little; she, her shoulder bag filled mostly with bandages, Lineth, her sword and a dagger, Bort, his misshapen frying pan, and each had a small water skin. Ida had no idea what to do next, and was content to let Lineth take charge.

Lineth led them carefully through the woods, making her way to the same hill Ida had observed the battlefield from the day before.

As they emerged from cover beneath a canopy of trees on the hilltop, Ida was glad of the warming sunlight, but this small comfort was soon forgotten. She stared in horror at the terrible scene; the whole battlefield was a patchwork carpet of dead.

"So many dead," she said.

"It's been a hard battle." Lineth shook her head. "But not just for us, they lost a lot more soldiers."

As the sun rose a little higher, the shadow cast from their hill crept back, exposing more of the carnage.

Bort stretched out his arm and pointed. "Look, Ida."

The sunlight had struck something that now shone like a beacon among a cluster of green and yellow uniforms.

"It's some of our militia," said Ida.

"Bort must go down," said Bort.

"Don't be stupid," Lineth snapped. "There could still be enemy patrols."

"Bort must go." He set off down the hill towards the battlefield.

Lineth turned on Ida, growling, "Get him to stop!"

"I think he must have seen something," said Ida. "His eyesight is extraordinary."

Ida was shocked by the curse that emerged from Lineth's mouth, but had to forgive her. Bort's behaviour was baffling.

"I have to go down as well," said Ida, apologetically.

With a look of disgust on her face, Lineth drew her sword and set off after Bort, not even glancing back to see if Ida followed her.

Reaching the bottom of the hill, Ida picked her way through the bodies; groups of carrion birds scattering with her approach, only to return once she was by. It was sickening, but there was nothing she could do. At first she had looked for any soldiers that might still be alive, but it soon became clear that this task had already been done, but by those intent on making sure none survived, enemy or ally.

When she caught up with the others, Bort stood over a huge creature that lay face down; sunlight reflecting from the blade of a sword standing erect from its back. The blade should have been coated with blood, but the metal was clean and bright, with no trace of any marking or discoloration.

Bort heaved the giant clear, revealing Endor lying motionless on his back, his face pale and drawn, his body covered in blood.

"Poor Endor," said Ida.

"He went fighting," said Lineth, admiration in her voice. "Just look at the size of this one."

Endor's body trembled, his mouth fell open and he sucked in a deep, rasping draught of air.

"The gods be praised," said Lineth. "He's still alive."

Ida immediately dropped to her knees beside him, searching his body for wounds. She gave Bort a nod of approval; he'd done well to bring them here.

"I can't find any major injury," she said. "I think we can move him."

"Bort will carry master Endor." With surprising ease, he lifted Endor from the ground, cradling him like a huge infant.

"We'll head south," said Lineth. "We can get help for Endor, and once I know you're in safe hands I can rejoin the army."

"North is better," said Bort, and immediately began walking.

Ida was baffled. She had never known him to be so obstinate.

"No, we'll go south," Lineth growled.

Bort ignored her and kept walking.

"What is he doing?" Lineth demanded.

"I have to trust him," said Ida. "You go south, we'll be fine."

"I can't do that!" Lineth's face contorted in anger and she cursed mightily, before apologising again. "Sorry, I'm not used to dealing with civilians." She stooped and pulled Endor's sword from the giant. With a shake of her head, she raised her arm in invitation, indicating they should follow Bort.

"Are you sure?" said Ida.

"I'll not abandon you out here, so it looks like I don't have much choice."

Ida wished there was some way to reassure Lineth that this was the right thing to do, but she was just as confused by Bort's actions.

Even with Lineth's help, by mid-morning Ida was struggling to keep pace with Bort. The terrain had changed from rolling grasslands to fern-coated, steep-sided valleys, and his chosen route took them ever nearer to an imposing mist-shrouded mountain range.

"Lineth, I really need to stop," said Ida.

"Bort!" Lineth shouted. "Stop right there! Miss Fairweather needs to rest."

By the time Ida caught up, Bort had placed Endor on the ground and was giving him a drink from a water skin.

Ida knelt beside Endor. "Where does it hurt most?"

He coughed, a thin smile forming on his lips. "Where does it not hurt might be a better question." His eyes went wide and he gripped Ida's hand. "How did the battle go?"

"We were forced to retreat," said Lineth.

"What of Otric, the militias?"

Lineth shook her head. "Where you lay, there were fallen from your militias, twenty, maybe thirty, I couldn't be sure."

Endor sighed, a look of defeat on his face.

Ida gently released his grip and inspected him more closely. His chainmail armour was nicked and scored, with the metal pierced through in a few places, but as before she found no significant wound. Then she saw the dent in his helmet.

"Take this off," she said to Lineth.

Lineth eased the helmet clear to expose a bloody patch of matted hair.

Ida looked carefully into Endor's eyes, one of them was sluggish to move, and edged with a ring of blood.

"You've taken quite a thump there." She spoke to Bort, "You remember catsleaf when you see it?"

He nodded.

"And meadowshine, and tangles moss?"

"Bort knows them too."

Ida looked around. "You'll find the moss by that stream, and the meadowshine and catsleaf further up amongst the ferns. See what you can gather."

"Yes, Ida." Bort set off at a lumbering trot towards the stream.

Ida and Lineth stripped Endor to his underwear, Ida noting that amongst the newer bruises and cuts were many older scars. Endor never boasted about his years in the King's service, but they had obviously been active and dangerous.

When Bort returned, she had him remove the lining from Endor's helmet; using it as a boiling pot to prepare an antiseptic wash from the catsleaf. While they were cleaning, stitching and dressing the wounds, she gave Endor the meadowshine to chew on, which had properties to combat aches and pains.

When they were finished Bort said, "Ida needs help now."

Ida had ignored the pain across her own shoulder; it came from deep scratches made when the creature in the glade had snatched her to the ground.

"Lineth," she said, "could you wash my wounds?"

"Of course, Miss Fairweather."

Ida took off her jerkin and loosened her blouse, allowing Lineth to draw it down to expose her shoulder and back. The men stared off politely in the opposite direction.

"Oh, Miss Fairweather, you must be in terrible pain." Lineth began washing the wounds. "Some of these are quite deep. I'll need to stitch them closed."

Ida nodded. "Carry on, then."

Though it was a painful experience Ida remained quiet throughout, determined to be no less stoic than Endor.

When Lineth finished, she helped Ida rearrange her clothing, and then announced for the benefit of Endor and Bort, "There, Miss Fairweather, all done."

Ida turned. "Please, Lineth, call me Ida."

"Very well," said Lineth.

They sat around a fire eating fish Bort had skilfully coaxed from the stream, and even though the fire produced plenty of heat, Ida still shivered. The air was turning cooler and grey clouds crept steadily towards them from the mountains.

"We need to find shelter before nightfall," she said.

"I agree," said Lineth, sternly.

"Bort knows a place," he said, quickly.

Lineth raised an eyebrow. "How far away is it?"

He frowned, and Lineth snorted impatiently.

"From now, almost dark there," he said.

"We'd better get moving then," said Lineth.

"Endor, how do you feel now?" said Ida.

He responded slowly. "Oh, yes... much better, thanks to your ministrations," he chuckled, "though a good draught of wine would set me up fine for a march."

Ida scowled. "You old fool, the very last thing you need now is wine." She immediately regretted her harsh words; realising Endor had meant it as a joke. However, she couldn't bring herself to apologise.

After dousing the fire they continued their trek; Endor attempted to walk unaided but faltered after a few paces.

"Bort," said Ida, "could you manage to carry Endor again?"

Without a word, and very gently, Bort swept Endor into his arms and carried him. Again, his pace and choice of direction were consistent, giving Ida some hope that he knew where he was going.

She had never been in this part of the country, and had no idea if there were any towns or villages nearby. The cloud promised rain, maybe even snow, so they needed shelter and warmth before nightfall. She had known people to die from the cold in this kind of weather.

7

Moleskin slept in the centre of a copse of thorn bushes, feeling it offered him some protection from discovery. Although slept was not an accurate description for the restless hours of constant disturbance he endured. Sounds of movement and distant shouts and screams carried on the still night air, and by morning he felt almost as tired as when he had settled for the night.

A cold, damp mist swirled around him, completely obscuring the surrounding countryside, and he was reluctant to venture out, not wanting to risk doubling back on himself.

About mid-morning, by his estimation, there was a noise overhead, like the flapping of sailcloth in a strong wind, and then a peppery odour drifted by, which brought him close to sneezing. This faded, and then he heard a noise that gradually built to a deep resonant chanting. From out of the mist came a line of hooded figures.

He froze in terror. It was more of the creatures he had glimpsed at the field hospital, but these wore long, black robes. They walked in pairs, carrying a pole stretched between them. Hanging from the centre of each pole was a sack containing what looked like a heavy box or chest.

Moleskin was instantly alert. Most likely it was gold or treasure, and though he itched to follow the creatures, to find some opportunity to share in their bounty, even he knew how foolhardy this would be. He kept still and silent for the whole forty minutes it took for the last pair to pass. During this time the mist grew thinner and Moleskin felt less and less confident about his hiding place; pressing himself close to the ground and wishing he could sink into it.

When the last figure disappeared over the ridge of a distant hill, he let out a sigh of relief. He was about to crawl from his hiding place when he heard the flapping noise again. Shutting his eyes tight, he lay perfectly still as the noise grew louder. There was a loud swoosh and a rush of air, then the peppery smell swept over him again, so strong it irritated his nostrils and caught in his throat. He fought desperately to avoid sneezing or coughing.

Finally, there was silence and he opened his eyes. Though overcast and grey the countryside around him was peaceful. Now confident of his direction of travel, he leapt up and sprinted across the grass.

After an uneventful afternoon's walking, Moleskin came to a road. Rutted and marked by coach and cart wheels, he felt confident it would eventually lead to either a village or a coaching stop. Choosing the direction that best matched his previous route, he continued on.

The light was fading when he came upon a coaching house sitting by the roadside. It was a sturdy structure, built from stone and topped with a neat thatched roof. A row of small windows projected from the thatch, indicating it had attic rooms. The sounds of revelry came from within.

He took a deep breath, gathered what little remained of his confidence and pushed the door open.

The room went silent, and a ragged group of shady-looking types sitting around one table examined him from head to toe.

Moleskin feared he had entered a cut-throat's den, but wider examination of the room revealed more respectable types, some even as well dressed as himself.

A large red-cheeked man, wearing a long white apron over his trousers, lurched out from behind the bar counter. "Come in! Come in, good sir. You'll be wanting something to warm your belly, no doubt?"

"I would that, my good man," said Moleskin.

"I've a fine broth on the stove. Would that be to your liking?" The man swept his hand over an empty table.

"That and a pot of your best ale." Moleskin sat and began to relax.

The Innkeeper flicked breadcrumbs from the table, shouting, "Milly! Pot of best ale and a bowl of broth for the gen'lmin." He pointed to Moleskin's uniform jacket. "I see you're an officer, how's that battle gone?"

Moleskin was cautious. "You've not heard anything about the battle?"

"Coach aint due for a day or so. We're always slow in getting the news."

"I'm sorry to be the bringer of bad news, but it was a defeat for the King. We had to retreat."

"Never!" The Innkeeper turned to the others in the room. "You lot hear that, King Malcor's got beat!"

There was a rumble of surprise. Several of the other customers gathered around Moleskin's table, plying him with questions about the battle, though most really wanted to know if they were in imminent danger.

"Now, now," the Innkeeper roared, spreading his thick arms to keep them back. "Can't you see this gen'lmin's had it rough? Sore tired he is. Saved himself by the tip of a toenail looks like." He spoke to Moleskin, "Are they coming our way?"

"No, they're heading west, same as before." He saw no point in mentioning the line of chanting figures, whose destination seemed well away from this one.

"There's a relief," said the Innkeeper. He turned to his other customers. "No need to worry. We're safe enough for now."

A pretty girl with long blonde hair forced her way through the crowd. "Oi!" she screeched. "Out the way! Gent's broth and ale coming through."

She deposited a bowl, a frothing mug and a large bread roll in front of Moleskin. Then she produced a spoon from her apron pocket.

"You looks worn out, sir. You get this down your throat and you'll feel much better."

It was all the encouragement he needed. Tearing off a strip of bread, he dunked it in the broth and pressed it into his mouth, almost weeping with pleasure at the taste.

"You poor thing," she said. "Aint you eaten for a bit then?"

Moleskin's mouth was too full to answer properly, but she understood.

"Clear off, the lot of you! Come on!" She flicked a napkin at the crowd, dispersing them to their seats. Then she came back to Moleskin. "You looks ever so smart in that uniform, you does."

He wiggled his eyebrows and grunted through the food he kept forcing into his mouth.

She winked. "Just you give Milly a shout n' I'll be happy to get you anything else you want."

Moleskin nodded enthusiastically. He could cope with this kind of attention.

Plied with drink by the inquisitive, and given the best seat by the fire, Moleskin enthralled the Inn's customers with tales of the battle. Blood spattered and bedraggled as he was, his retreat in the face of certain death was considered prudent by those around him, no suggestions of cowardice were even hinted at.

His confirmation of the non-human nature of their enemy was met with a mixed response. But Moleskin, a convincing liar at the best of times, was unchallenged when telling the truth. Though he had only a fleeting glimpse of the creatures, he relished the task of describing them, hardly needing to embellish one detail to have everyone in the room silent and hanging on his every word.

The talk turned inevitably to speculation; had the creatures emerged from a deep underground world to claim the lands above, or were they hordes of the damned, unleashed from the fires of hell, or the denizens of an island where lost mariners lived out their lives in torment, the ideas came thick and fast. These were of passing interest to Moleskin, he had already decided to catch the next coach out, and then keep travelling until he was as far away from this part of the world as was humanly possible.

Eventually he retired to one of the attic rooms. After a quick wash, he slid beneath the soft sheets; the bed already warmed by a clay bottle filled with hot water. With thoughts of the true nature of these strange, savage creatures, still troubling him, he drifted off.

A girlish giggle woke him from his slumber.

"Room in that bed for one more?" Milly whispered.

"Rather," he said.

Milly slid under the covers. "Oh, your hands are ever so soft," she said.

Moleskin was in heaven. Milly's company was an unexpected bonus to a very pleasant evening.

However his enjoyment was short lived. They were rudely interrupted by a loud knock at the bedroom door.

"Milly, are you in there?" the Innkeeper called.

"Gods save us, it's my father!" Milly whispered.

"Shhhh," Moleskin hissed.

The knocking became insistent. "Open this door! Come on! If you're up to your old tricks, my girl! There'll be trouble!"

Moleskin panicked. Trouble was the last thing he wanted.

"Don't go," Milly pleaded as he struggled free from her grasp.

"Come out! Both of you!" bellowed the Innkeeper, now pounding on the door.

Moleskin threw on his clothes, grabbed up his boots and climbed out of the window. Sliding down the thatch he landed on a convenient pile of straw.

After pausing briefly to pull on his boots, he jumped to his feet and ran off into the night, only slowing his pace when the loud argument between the Innkeeper and his daughter had faded to nothing.

Moleskin smiled. It had been a pleasant enough experience, while it lasted. Then a sudden terrible emptiness flooded over him as his hands felt for the comforting weight of his money belt. It wasn't there. In his rush to escape, he had forgotten to pick it up.

8

Ida picked her way wearily along the rocky shoreline of a small lake. Luckily the rain had held off, but a cold, damp wind swept by, adding to her discomfort. Though it was a struggle to keep moving, she had found it easier to match pace with Bort on this stretch. The overhanging branches from trees growing along the water's edge were hampering his progress more than hers. Lineth kept to the rear; quiet, withdrawn and clearly torn between two duties. She should be trying to rejoin the King's army, but instead she was minding them.

Bort halted at the end of a small promontory and stared ahead; seeming hesitant to continue. Ida caught up and stood beside him. At the end of the lake a deserted village nestled in a deep stony hollow. It had remained hidden until they were almost upon it.

"How do you know this place, Bort?" she said.

"This is Bort's home," he said.

This revelation surprised Ida; all the times she had quizzed Bort about his past he had always been vague and confused in his answers, as if the memory evaded recollection.

Lineth joined them. "Your home! It looks like nobody has lived here for a very long time."

"Bort did," he said, "and my parents before."

"And just where is this shelter?" said Lineth.

"Shelter is here; good shelter, wait and see."

Bort led them along the last section of shoreline and into the ruined village.

The simple buildings were low stone structures, but most of the roofs were collapsed and the natural vegetation had taken hold; Ida worried that all that remained of Bort's shelter was a memory. Then Bort stopped at what appeared to be a tiny hut resting against a steep rock face.

He pointed. "In here."

Lineth pushed the door open against stiff hinges and entered. Bort went next, carrying Endor, and Ida followed, already confused that the structure could accommodate the others.

The only light came through a small dirt-streaked window next to the door, and it took a few seconds for Ida's eyes to adjust, but the hut was actually the entrance to a cave. The first part was a good-sized chamber with a large wooden table, which served as a living room, kitchen and dining area. Four doors were spaced evenly along the back wall, which she assumed were the bedrooms; and although it was cold, it was dry.

Endor came to as Bort was settling him on a solid rock bench close to a soot blackened hearth. "Where are we, Bort?"

"In a good shelter," he said. "Bort will make a fire now."

"That's an excellent idea," said Ida.

Bort brought an armful of branches from one of the rooms and started building a fire in the hearth.

"We'll need food," said Lineth. "I'll see if I can catch us a rabbit or two."

"Foraged food," said Endor. "There's nothing like it! I'd give you a hand if I could, but I'm having trouble getting these eyes to see straight."

Lineth nodded indulgently and then sat on a chair and started to remove her armour.

Ida noted that Lineth's toes barely touched the ground, and when Ida stretched over the dusty table to pick up a small lantern, the table seemed higher than normal. Clearly the furniture was a better fit to Bort then the rest of them.

Ida lit the lantern and held it up. Seeming to be hewn from the solid rock, Bort's home was a fascinating dwelling, and she couldn't resist the urge to explore it. She went to the first of the back rooms. It was piled high with firewood, probably enough to last a whole year. This was typical of Bort; he seldom did things by halves.

In the second room she found the remains of a baby's crib. She tried to imagine what Bort must have looked like as a child, but found it hard. Something deep inside her hoped that his was a happy childhood. The third room contained two simple beds and a stout wooden chest. She tried the lid, but the hinges were rusted solid.

The last room had obviously been Bort's parents' room.

Carved into the stone on the wall just above the bedhead was a bird with its wings outstretched. Ida leant over and brushed dust from it, and was surprised to find it wasn't really a bird. It was the impression of two handprints, the thumbs linked. One of the hands was smaller, Bort's mother, Ida assumed. She felt tears well into her eyes, and quickly brushed them away.

Neatly laid out on a dresser were a brush and comb, a washbasin and jug, and bottles of toilet water and perfumes. It was just like her own dresser back in Silvermeadow. Running a finger through the layer of dust gathered on the top of the dresser, she couldn't stop herself clucking disapprovingly. It would all need a good clean before they retired for the night.

She felt a flutter of embarrassment when she considered the sleeping arrangements. Ideally she would have liked to sleep near to Endor, to watch over him, but it wasn't really practical or proper. Probably the best arrangement would be if Bort and Endor shared the room with the two single beds, and she and Lineth shared the large bed in this room.

When Ida returned to the main living area Lineth was gone, leaving her chainmail armour draped across the chair. The fire now roared in the hearth, spreading warmth through the room, and Bort had lit more candles and oil lamps.

After checking that Endor was comfortable, she turned to Bort. "It's a lovely home."

He wore a morose, almost childlike expression and seemed lost and uncertain.

She had an inspiration. "Where are your pots and pans?"

His expression transformed. "Bort has good pans, Ida." He went to a small alcove and brought out a handful of dusty black iron pots. "Bort will need to wash them first. Ida will cook a rabbit stew, yes?"

"Rabbit stew," Ida mused. "That's an excellent idea. We'd need some vegetables and herbs for that. I'm sure I saw half a dozen edible plants growing on those ruins, and would there be an old potato patch out there somewhere?"

Bort nodded and asked, "Water first, Ida?"

"Good idea. Always plan ahead, that's the key to successful cooking."

Endor chuckled and Ida scowled at him. "You'd feel pretty silly if you packed for battle and arrived without a sword, wouldn't you?"

"That I would, Ida. Is there anything for me to do?"

"You're lucky tonight; I've taken you off active duty until your head is better."

"I'll maybe not grumble then."

Bort had watched this exchange with a smile on his face, and Ida suddenly felt strangely embarrassed, wondering if it reminded him of similar conversations between his parents.

"You were going to get water," she said.

He nodded. "Yes, Bort will get the water."

Ida set about organising the utensils and pots she needed for cooking the stew, and when Bort returned with the water she found him a big hand basket and sent him out again to search for food. She started cleaning the kitchen area and cooking utensils, resolving to make his home as inviting as it must have been when he was a boy.

The village hadn't changed much in the time Bort had been away. For as long as he could remember, he and his parents were its only occupants, and very few travellers ever found their way there.

Looking about the tumbledown buildings, he had mixed feelings about returning home. He could always picture it clearly in his head; playing as a child among the ruined houses, swimming in the lake and climbing trees in the woods. He could remember the years passing as his parents grew older, content and happy with each other, and always sharing that same warmth and love with him.

Though all these memories remained strong, after leaving the village he had found it hard to visualise how to get back to it. And yet here he was. Sometime during the long, cold night in the ditch, the certainty of where his home was and the urgent need to return had emerged. Possibly his firm knowledge of how safe a place it was had prompted the recall, and part of that was the desire to find a refuge for Ida.

He glanced down at the hand basket. She wouldn't be happy if he returned empty handed. He knew the ground well and quickly collected mushrooms from the woods, an abundance of small white potatoes from an old plot, and an assortment of edible leaves and tubers from all around the village and along the water's edge.

His meandering path seemed to draw him ever closer to a small hill overlooking the village. Eventually he accepted the inevitable and climbed it, pushing through the long, wet grasses. He could probably find the spot with his eyes closed, and soon enough, the grasses thinned and there, set in the ground at the very top of the hill, were two rough stone slabs, his parent's graves.

It came back in a rush; the sadness he felt on the day he left the village, soon after his mother died. Her last wish was that he leave to go and find his way in the world. Dutifully, he had done as she asked.

He heard the brush of footsteps through the thick grasses and knew it was Lineth approaching. Almost more surprising than the memory of this location returning, was his decision to defy her. Something he now felt desperately embarrassed about.

She stepped up beside him and stood quietly for a moment, and he braced himself, knowing she had probably chosen this moment to vent her anger.

"It's a lovely spot," she said.

Her lack of anger confused him. "Bort is sorry."

"For what?" She paused. "Oh yes, I wanted to go south."

"I had to come," he said.

She spoke gently. "Well, if you had to come, then there wasn't much choice in the matter, was there?" She stared at the graves. "To be honest, I can't judge you wrong for bringing us to such a haven."

He nodded and felt relief, he was forgiven. He picked up his brimming basket, and pointed to the two rabbits she held. "Ida will make a lovely rabbit stew with these."

"Sounds wonderful." She made a show of peering into his basket. "And where did you find a market near here?"

"The market is everywhere," he said, grinning.

Ida sent the others to tidy the bedrooms while she prepared the meal. As she worked, she noted again that everything was just that little bit bigger than she was used to. She also marvelled at some of the pieces; cups and bowls that seemed to have been made entirely from stone.

In these favourable circumstances Endor's condition improved rapidly, though one side of his face developed a large, ugly bruise that seemed to change colour by the minute. With the meal prepared and the table set, Ida finally gave him a job. He led the prayer of thanks before they ate.

After the meal was over and the dishes washed and dried, Ida was able to relax. She was well pleased with their newfound refuge. Though it would still benefit from a thorough spring clean, it had achieved that comfortable homely state where the odd patch of dust and dirt was easily overlooked. However, with very little to occupy them, their thoughts soon returned to the defeat they had left behind.

"Now that I know you're all safe," said Lineth, "I should head south and rejoin the King."

Endor nodded slowly. "And I too."

"What nonsense!" Ida scowled at Endor. "You can hardly walk in a straight line, let alone fight. And you, my dear," Ida's voice softened, "what good is one more sword against that enemy?"

"It's my duty," said Lineth. "But I do thank you for your concern."

"Concern won't stop you going off to get yourself killed. At least wait until you're rested."

"I'm a soldier, Ida, I must be with my fellows and mindful of my duty. At most I can stay another day, no more."

Ida could have predicted Lineth and Endor's responses, they were both good soldiers. Other than making sure Endor was fit for the journey, there was likely nothing more she could do to dissuade them.

Endor clapped Bort's huge forearm. "If we had a hundred more like Bort here, we'd soon stop them."

"Bort is the only one left," said Bort.

"What do you mean by that?" said Endor.

Bort puffed out his chest. "Bort is the last Trollid."

Ida was stunned by this idea. The Trollid were found in children's stories; a species who preferred to live underground, who were master stonemasons and who had the ability to see in the dark. It was a ridiculous claim.

Endor laughed indulgently, patting Bort's arm affectionately. "Well I must admit you fit the description." Endor winked at Lineth. "After what I saw on the battlefield the other day, I'm half inclined to believe you, but honestly, Bort, the Trollid don't exist."

Bort wore a puzzled expression. "But Bort is the last Trollid." He rose from the table and went into the room with the two single beds.

Ida heard Bort mumbling to himself, and then there was a protesting screech of rusted hinges. A few seconds later he marched back into the room and placed a heavy cloth-wrapped bundle in the centre of the table.

He stood back and said firmly, "Open it!"

Ida stretched across to untie a woven cord wrapped around the bundle and then folded the cloth back. The material fell away, revealing a large slab of gold, and she let out a gasp of surprise. She had never seen a piece as big before. It had irregular edges, and was moulded to represent a stone slab. Cast into its upper surface were four pictures. The first three depicted a blacksmith's shop, a foundry and a mine. She looked up to examine Bort's features; there was a very strong resemblance between him and all of the busy figures in these pictures.

The last scene was different; it showed a thin man in long, flowing robes. His upturned hands were stretched out to either side of him, and a ball of fire floated over each one. She slid her fingers over several lines of script running beneath the pictures. The strange jagged writing was completely unknown to her.

Bort thumped his chest with a clenched fist. "Bort is the last Trollid."

Ida was not convinced. She pointed to the robed figure in the last picture. "Who's this?"

His brow furrowed. "That is Torven, Friend of the Trollid."

"He looks like some sort of magician," said Endor. "Was he an entertainer?"

Bort grinned. "Yes. Torven is a Magic man. Torven was Bort's secret friend." His chin dropped and his eyes went wide. "Oh, Bort remembers. Bort was not to tell anyone. It was a big secret."

"Not tell what?" said Ida, intrigued and enchanted.

"Torven said not to tell."

"I'm sure he won't mind," said Endor. "We're all your friends here."

Bort sighed. "When Bort was small," he held his hand just below the top of the table, "Torven came out of the wall to play with Bort. Magic and games," his eyes held an inner glow as he remembered, "with pictures and fire and dancing lights."

Ida didn't know what to make of this fanciful idea. "That sounds lovely."

"It was very pretty." Bort smiled. "Torven gave Bort the gold picture."

"You said he came out of the wall," said Ida. "How did he do that?"

"Through the magic door," said Bort, matter-of-factly.

Ida knew how harmless a child's imaginings were, but maybe there was a little truth behind his words. "Can you show us this magic door?"

His face dropped again. "It's not allowed."

"Why not?" said Ida.

"It's a big, big, secret."

"We won't tell anyone else," said Endor. "It'll be our secret too."

"Torven did go away." Bort shrugged. "Maybe Bort will show you the magic door."

"Splendid," said Endor.

Bort stood, walked over to the wood store and pointed into it. "The door is in here."

Ida examined his face carefully, wondering if he was playing some elaborate practical joke.

"That was your play room," said Lineth. "Will we have to take out all the wood?"

Bort nodded.

"There must be a cartload of the stuff," said Endor. "Where are we going to put it all?"

Bort pointed to the room with the crib in it. "In here."

Ida could think of better things to do with their time, but she didn't like to interfere, and it was a harmless enough activity.

It took them half an hour to shift the firewood. Apart from a loose carpet of twigs and pieces of bark, the wood store was almost identical to the room they had just filled.

"Well?" said Ida. "Where's this magic door?"

Bort pointed to the far wall. "There."

She, Endor and Lineth examined the wall, looking for anything that might suggest an opening or secret door. They found nothing. Other than the natural texture of the rock it was blank and featureless.

"It takes magic to open the door," said Bort, nodding wisely.

Ida gripped his arm; the game had gone on for long enough. "I'm sure it does, Bort." She felt a little sad; surely he couldn't believe this was true, there had to be another explanation. "I think we should all sit down and have a nice cup of tea," she said, indulgently.

"Good idea," said Endor, raising his eyebrows in sympathy.

When they were all seated Ida quizzed Bort about his childhood and his parents. The gold tablet had to be a gift from them, and Ida felt sure it was also them who had woven the story of the Trollid around it, possibly to compensate for their decision to live such reclusive lives, but Bort stuck firmly to his story.

"It must be late," said Ida, finally. "We should all turn in and get some rest."

After Endor and Bort had settled for the night, Ida and Lineth sat at the table talking in whispers.

"Is it real gold?" said Lineth.

Ida tried to lift the tablet off the table but couldn't. "It feels heavy enough. I suppose it must be."

"Does he know how valuable it is?" said Lineth.

"I'm sure he does. He knows his coins well enough."

"He's rich. There must be five hundred crowns in it."

Ida stared at the tablet. "He doesn't see it as money. He thinks it's a gift, proof of who he thinks he is."

"He thinks he's a Trollid," said Lineth, "that can't be healthy."

"Does it harm anyone?"

"But surely he'd like to buy things, some land, a farm, he could be very comfortable."

Ida could easily imagine Bort as a successful farmer. She sighed. "This won't be easy."

9

When Ida woke the next morning, she found the table set for breakfast, the kitchen area tidied and a huge fire roared in the hearth. However the gold tablet was gone.

She found Bort in the old wood store, sitting cross-legged on the paved floor, staring at the wall. The tablet lay on the ground in front of him. The only light in the room was the single candle in the lantern she had brought with her.

"Are you all right, Bort?"

"Ida does not believe Bort," he said, in a low voice.

Ida placed a hand on his shoulder. "It would be wonderful to think that the Trollid exist but..." She felt him stiffen and tried another approach. "Bort, if someone loved you and wanted you to feel special, it wouldn't be bad if they told you..."

"A story," he prompted.

"Yes, a wonderful, magical story."

"It is not a story!"

Ida sighed; she hated to be so brutal. "You are a grown man now, Bort. You must let go of these childish things."

"It's not childish, it's true!"

Sadness flooded Ida; she struggled and failed to hold back the tears.

"Ida is not to cry. Bort is not angry. But Bort is telling the truth."

Ida wiped the tears from her face and then gripped Bort's shoulders. "You have to stop it. This is just a dusty old room."

"It's not a dusty old room."

"Please Bort." Ida pointed to the twigs and fine pieces of bark left over from the woodpile. "Look! This is just a home, nothing more."

"It's not dusty," he said, his voice growing stronger.

Ida scowled.

He pointed. "Look, the wall, it's not dusty."

She turned to look and was baffled to find he was right. Except for the wall he was pointing at, all the others were marked and stained from where the wood had lain against them. Puzzled, she picked up the lantern and stepped forward to examine the wall. For a moment she wondered if he had purposely cleaned it, but dismissed the idea immediately. More surprising, at the centre of the wall, and about the width of a door, the debris on the ground had separated from the wall by a gap of about the thickness of a coin on edge. Worried that it was just a trick of the light, she brushed a small pile of bark flakes up against the wall. A thick lump formed in her throat when an invisible force slowly pushed the flakes away.

"Get Lineth and Endor," she said, "and more candles and lanterns."

They inspected the wall again, searching for some mechanism or lever that would release what they all now suspected was a door. But their efforts proved fruitless.

"A fine mystery," said Endor.

"There must be a way to open it," said Lineth.

"Maybe there's only a release on the other side," Ida suggested.

"What use is a door without a way of opening it from both sides?" said Endor.

"Not much use, I suppose," said Ida.

Endor nodded and made a low hmming noise. "So how would you go about hiding the lock or latch?"

"Maybe it's nowhere near the door," said Ida.

"There has to be something." Lineth knelt and placed a hand on the gold tablet. "Maybe there's a message hidden on this."

Bort nodded, and said in a very flat voice, "The message is made from many parts."

"What does that mean?" said Ida.

"Bort does not know," he said.

"But how did you know those words?" said Ida.

He shrugged. "They just came."

"A message made from many parts," said Lineth. "Maybe something to do with all of these pictures?"

Ida stared at the tablet, hoping for a sudden insight, but none came. Then she traced out the jagged script with a fingertip. "If only we could read this language, the answer must be here."

"Yes, the answer is in the writing," said Bort.

Ida examined Bort's placid expression. "Is there something else you want to tell us?"

"No," he said.

"But you think the answer's in this writing?" said Ida.

He nodded. "Yes, the answer is in the writing."

"Here, what's going on?" said Endor.

"Shhhh," said Ida. "It's a message made from many parts, and it comes from this writing. Is that right?"

"Yes, together they make one." Bort blinked with surprise. "Bort did not say that."

Ida felt a growing excitement, someone, maybe this man Torven, had hidden memories in Bort's head. She had seen a similar trick performed by a mesmerist at a harvest fair. "Was it a voice in your head, Bort?"

"Yes."

Ida spoke the words carefully, hoping they would trigger another memory. "A message made from many parts, that comes from this writing, put together it makes one."

Bort shook his head. "No more voices."

"I think I know the answer," said Lineth, breathlessly.

"Come on then," said Endor. "What does it say?"

"It's not that easy." Lineth left and returned carrying a blackened twig from the fire and a length of bandage. She stretched the bandage over the tablet and carefully traced out the characters on the first line.

"I can't see what difference it makes seeing it like that," said Endor.

"If I'm right," Lineth slid the cloth down so that the first line of black marks fell over the second line of marks on the tablet, "we should start to see the message appear."

She traced the second row of characters adding them to the lines already drawn; some of the characters were taking on familiar shapes. When the third row of marks was added, the message was clear, it read; Fit to floor to open door.

"Of course," said Ida, "it looks just like a paving slab."

Bort hefted the tablet up. "Show Bort where to put it."

When the matching slab was found, Bort looked to Ida for her consent. She smiled and nodded, and he placed the ingot on top of it.

Everyone jumped back as a previously invisible door in the centre of the wall pivoted silently aside, and a wash of cool, musty air swept over them.

Ida peered in. A tunnel led away from the door, fading to an impenetrable black.

"I rather think," said Endor, "that I'm inclined to explore this."

"Will it be safe?" said Ida.

Bort thumped the walls with his fist and nodded. "This is strong rock."

"I'd like to see where it goes," said Lineth.

"Decided then," said Endor.

"Bort," said Ida, remembering his words about secrets, "I think you should decide. After all, this is your home."

He stared into the darkness. "Bort wants to see the last home of the Trollid, but outsiders are not allowed." He paused and puffed out his chest. "But Bort is the last Trollid, so Bort can decide! Bort's friends can come too."

"What did you just say?" Endor pointed into the tunnel. "This leads to the last home of the Trollid? You never mentioned that before!"

Bort shrugged. "That was the biggest secret."

"This I definitely want to see," said Endor.

Lineth turned towards the living room. "We'd better be prepared for anything. We'll need food, water, lanterns..."

"Why lanterns?" said Bort.

Lineth pointed. "We won't see a thing in there. It's black as night."

Bort peered into the tunnel. "Not dark." He pointed. "See. At the end, the steps go up."

Ida could see nothing and exchanged a puzzled look with Endor.

"You might not need a light, m'lad," said Endor, "but I do."

Bort beamed. "Bort does not need a light, because Bort is a Trollid."

Endor grasped Bort's arm and pulled him away from the opening. "Well, Mr Trollid, let's get organised. It looks like there's a bit of an adventure ahead of us."

Not knowing what to expect, Lineth and Endor dressed in armour and brought their weapons.

When they assembled back at the tunnel entrance, Ida pushed Bort forward. "As this is your home, I think you should lead."

Grinning, he motioned the others to follow.

The tunnel stayed level for about fifty paces, arriving at a shallow staircase that Bort said ran on as far as he could see. They climbed for about ten minutes before reaching another level path.

Endor, who was wheezing and puffing, stopped and leaned against the wall. "Thank the gods for that. My legs are about to give out on me."

"How are you managing, Ida?" said Lineth.

Ida was feeling the strain of the exercise, and the discomfort of her recent wounds, but was coping. "I'm fine, but I'd like to stop and rest for a bit."

"No point in asking you, Bort," said Endor. "A young fellow like you never needs to... Bort? Bort! Now where's he got to?"

Ida stared into the darkness. "Bort," she shouted. "Where are you?"

"Bort is here," came the answer from ahead.

"We can't see you," said Lineth.

"Bort is coming." His voice was closer, and then he loomed up out of the darkness. "Bort has found a statue." He pointed excitedly along the tunnel. "A statue of Torven."

Endor straightened immediately. "Torven the magician, you say. Lead on then, there's a good fellow."

Ida could have happily sat for another five minutes, but she found Bort's enthusiasm infectious. "Wait for me," she called.

The statue stood in a rocky recess at the side of the tunnel. The sculpting of the life-size figure was fine and precise, but over and around it had gathered a thick coating of dust and cobwebs.

Ida held up her lantern. "What incredible detail." Bort's magic man was a wizened old character with a heavily receded hairline and long flowing hair. His strong angular nose stood proudly from his thin face. She stretched out to brush the face clean, and then leapt back in horror as the eyes blinked open.

"Goodness me!" The statue shook its head and coughed. "I must have nodded off for a bit." Its eyes took in the party, all of whom, except for Bort, had taken a step back.

Endor and Lineth drew their swords.

"Who are you lot?" said the statue. It leant forward and stared at Bort. "Is that you, Latz?"

"No. It is Bort, son of Latz."

"Bort, Bort! No! It can't be! He's only a lad. I was entertaining him with some magic tricks just the other day."

Ida quickly realised that the statue was actually a man, and was cross that he had hidden in the corridor waiting for them. He must have been skulking around all the time they had been in Bort's home.

"That's enough of this nonsense!" she barked. "Just who are you?"

10

Moleskin shivered and pulled the collar of his doublet tight about his neck. The Coaching Inn was well behind him, lost in a damp drizzle, and ahead the road climbed steadily, with thick woodland looming to either side. He had hoped to find a barn or shed to shelter in for the night, but had seen no signs of habitation for some time.

He heard a noise nearby; a scuffle and shuffle of feet in the wet grasses on the verge, and he froze, breathing gently. The footsteps halted and there was silence. Sensing trouble, he ran. Almost immediately the footsteps were there again, but now on the hard pebbled road, and they were running too. Worse, they were getting nearer.

Moleskin ran for all he was worth, but to no avail. A rough hand gripped his shoulder and dragged him to the ground. Then a bright painful flash accompanied an abrupt blow to his head and everything went black.

Moleskin woke with a thumping headache. His hands and feet were bound, and he lay on the ground. Two harsh voices echoed from nearby walls and he remained still with his eyes closed, pretending to be unconscious.

"You said he had a load of gold on him!" said one voice, angrily.

"He did. He must have hidden it," the other whined.

"We'll cut off his fingers, one by one," the first voice suggested. "He'll soon tell us where he's hidden it."

A spasm of fear coursed through Moleskin's body, and a second later he was given a firm kick.

"You awake?" said the angry voice. He was kicked again. "I said, are you awake?"

"I am." Moleskin opened his eyes. He lay near the entrance to a cave and pale moonlight shone from behind two shadowy figures looming over him. One was taller than the other.

"What have you done with all that gold?" said the tall one. He was the angry one.

"I left it at the Inn," said Moleskin, weakly.

"We weren't born stupid," the tall one said. "Where've you hidden it?"

"Honestly," Moleskin pleaded, "I left it at the Inn. I had to leave quickly when the Innkeeper caught me with his daughter."

The shorter man snickered, and was immediately silenced by a thump to the arm. The tall man pulled out a dagger, letting the polished blade flash in the moonlight. "Better tell us now or you're going to start losing those fingers."

"I haven't got any gold," Moleskin wailed.

The tall man cut Moleskin's bindings, snatched a wrist and stretched Moleskin's hand over a stone. He felt the cold edge of the blade press into the skin of his little finger. "Please," he sobbed, "I haven't got any gold."

The pressure increased on his finger.

"I left it behind," Moleskin pleaded. "I'm penniless, it's all gone."

The tall man stood and kicked him in disgust. "I think he's telling the truth."

"What a rotten shame," said the second man. "We came all the way out here for nothing."

The tall man rubbed his chin. "Not quite nothing."

He swung a wooden club and last thing Moleskin saw was stars, and then blackness.

It was daylight when Moleskin woke again, and his head felt like someone had been kicking it around a field. He was shivering with the cold, mainly because his fine clothes were now gone. There were a few small consolations; the robbers had left him a cotton shirt and his underwear, and they had also left him untied.

He staggered to the front of the cave and looked out. It was a bright, frosty morning and the coach road was below him, at the foot of a steep grassy slope. The road wound its way off down a wooded valley; that would be the way to the coaching house. In the other direction it crested a rise and ran off across an undulating moorland.

After picking his way carefully down to the road, Moleskin paused. He had a choice; head back to the Inn or move on. The moorland looked a bit uninviting, but regardless of his condition, he doubted the Innkeeper would give him a warm reception. Also his pride rebelled against admitting to this misfortune, so in fact the choice was simple.

Fortunately the sunshine kept Moleskin warm, but by mid-morning his feet were sore and raw. As he walked, he focused on avoiding the many small jagged stones scattered about the road surface. At that moment he would have traded anything for a pair of stout boots and cursed loudly every time he stepped on a stone, wishing nothing but ill for the robbers.

His grumblings were interrupted by the excited cackle of carrion birds. Looking up, he saw the birds were crowded around indistinct shapes on the road ahead. He walked cautiously forward and the birds scattered.

Moleskin felt nauseous; spread across the road were the remains of the two robbers. He had no doubt about their identities; they were wearing what was left of his stolen clothes.

Other than the seemingly random dismemberment of arms and legs, both of the corpses were headless. Reluctantly, he searched the bodies; gathering back his own meagre possessions and adding anything that might be of use.

His fine uniform britches were useless, since the robber wearing them had only one leg left. He was able to replace them with a much shoddier pair he found in the man's backpack. Luckily Moleskin's jacket was intact, though it was liberally spattered with fresh blood. He found his boots spread some distance apart, with the unfortunate robber's feet still in them.

He took inventory of his new possessions; he had clothing and money, though not a great deal, and also food and water. Tucked into his belt were a wooden club and a pair of daggers. In reality, he was slightly better off than when he had left the Inn.

He wondered if he should bury the robbers, but thought better of it. Best to move on quickly; it seemed unlikely, but this had to be the work of the strange cloaked creatures he had seen the day before. This road was not as safe as he first thought, and he had to get off it as soon as possible, but the moor was too open and desolate to offer any safety.

Ahead on the horizon, a dark line of trees promised shelter.

It took an hour of fast marching to reach the trees, and even though it felt safer, he kept up his pace, wanting to get as far away as possible from the dead robbers and who or whatever had killed them.

The road wound on through the woods, and about mid-day he saw smoke lingering over the treetops ahead. It had to be a village. He picked up his pace in anticipation, but faltered when he heard distant screams and the loud roaring of what sounded like a wild animal. He left the road and approached warily through the trees, until ahead he saw a tiny village; just a scattering of cottages to either side of the road.

From a hiding place in thick bushes, he watched a huge winged creature stalk the road between the cottages. By every description he had ever heard or read, this was what a dragon looked like, but it was something he had only believed to exist in stories.

A small leather-clad figure sat astride the dragon's back, screeching with glee as the dragon tore off a thatched roof and reached inside to select a victim, a man still wearing his nightshirt. After a fierce bite, and a shake of its jaw, the dragon tossed back its long, pointed snout, throwing the unfortunate man's head high into the air.

The dragon repeated its cruel sport with the man's arms and legs. Finally it cast the bleeding remains aside and began looking for another victim. Without doubt, this is what had happened to the robbers.

A man tried to scurry across the street behind the dragon, but it turned quickly and pounced with cat-like precision. The man's dying screams of fear and pain carried to Moleskin, thin and distant.

The ghastly work continued for a few minutes, and then the rider dismounted and wandered through the remains; seeming curious, rather than looking for anything in particular. Meanwhile the dragon settled to gnaw at the corpse, which it held delicately between its foreclaws.

Moleskin wanted to look away, but couldn't; it was such an awful and unusual sight.

Finally the rider remounted, and the dragon was urged to extend its wings. With powerful rhythmic beats, it rose into the air and Moleskin began whimpering when it flew directly towards his hiding place. He squeezed himself beneath the bushes and shut his eyes. There was a sudden swoosh of air as the dragon's immense shadow passed overhead, and then a familiar peppery smell; the dragon had flown over him twice before! He lay perfectly still, praying it would not return.

After about ten minutes, Moleskin finally found the courage to venture into the ravaged village. Once he was sure there was no one still alive, he quickly searched the cottages, gathering food and winter clothing for a trip through the mountains to the north. With the invaders sweeping through the lands to the south, and the coach road no longer safe, this seemed the least hazardous choice.

His route came from a map he found, and he was soon hurrying along a well-worn track away from the village and towards the mountains. It was a popular drover's path, confirmed by the evidence of sheep and goat droppings. It would eventually lead to the safety of some remote villages dotted along the coastline on the far side of the mountains. Though cold and bleak places in the winter months, they were still habitable.

As he marched, the bright sunlight faded and low cloud began to obscure the mountains. This far north and so high up the snows came early and soon small, wet flakes were falling, melting into the ground and turning the track to a sticky mess of mud. Moleskin pressed on, stopping only to pull on a woollen hat and fur lined mittens.

Late in the day he came to a flat pasture; summer meadow it might have been, but a thin, white carpet of new snow covered the grass, and it was fast becoming a harsh and desolate place. A drover's shelter was marked on the map, and it didn't take long to spot its soot blackened chimney projecting from a snowy mound. It was a timber-lined hut with a sod roof and walls, and was mostly sunk into the ground.

It had everything Moleskin needed; a bed, a stove, a table and a chair, but as he tidied and organised the small, dusty room, he felt a strange unease. Understanding of this came gradually as he lay in the bed, the tiny stove bathing him in heat. For the first time in his life he was completely alone; his comfortable, safe world had fallen apart and all that remained was this lonely little nest of warmth. Closing his eyes, he tried to pretend he was safely back in his bed in Silvermeadow, but the terrible images of the dragon's brutality kept appearing in his mind.

He fought to avoid contemplating that death for himself, but the thoughts wouldn't leave him, and his body, though warm, began to shake with fear. Welcome release came when exhaustion finally submerged him in sleep.

In the world outside, the remains of King Malcor's army fell back, their initial rush becoming more disciplined as the squads of regulars and militias reformed, and as the chain of command was re-established. Quickly the order came down, that the next battle would be fought from within the walls of the King's seat at Conisby, and all were to rally there.

Cavalry bravely probed and harried Tekt's army, slowing their advance and giving the foot soldiers and wounded time to retreat. Wagons loaded with engineers aided their efforts, scurrying across the countryside to collapse bridges and harvest timber from forests.

All the villages that might be vulnerable to Tekt's army, or its foraging parties, were cleared; their peoples, provisions and livestock moved to safety. Anything that might serve the enemy was either removed or destroyed.

11

With slow, jerky motions, and to an accompaniment of painful grunts and complaints, the dust covered man stepped out of the recess.

Ida shook her head in contempt as he continued with his pantomime, but said nothing.

"Dear me, my old joints have gone a bit stiff." With an audible creak the man stretched his neck from side to side. "That's better." Taking note of his appearance he began brushing the dust and cobwebs from his clothing.

Ida, Endor and Lineth were forced to shield their faces as clouds of fine dust rolled over them. When Bort stepped forward to help, brushing away the dust with careful reverential strokes, Ida was appalled.

"Thank you. Very decent of you," said the man.

"Who are you?" Ida demanded.

"As I remember," said the man, "I was the first to ask that question. Now this young fellow," he pointed to Bort, "claims to be Bort, son of Latz. A claim I will be very pleased to have confirmed. But regarding yourselves, this is not a place I would expect to meet outsiders. Your presence will require some explanation, or I will be obliged to ask you to leave."

"Now just a minute," Endor brought up his sword, "there's no need to be like that."

The man raised an arm; his loosely curled fingers holding something that pulsed and glowed, shining red through the skin of his hand. "Stay yourself, sir! I have, as yet, no reason to bear you ill-feeling. I suggest you do nothing to change that opinion." The something in his hand glowed fiercely, punctuating his last words.

Ida was relieved when Endor lowered his sword. She didn't believe in magic, but she knew of many dangerous alchemic substances that could burn and poison.

"Introductions first," the man suggested. The glow faded and he opened his hand to reveal it to be empty.

Ida shook her head; she'd seen similar tricks with coins and other small objects.

The man stretched out his hand. "If you are Bort, I'm pleased to meet you again. Can you remember my name?"

Ida's mouth fell open when Bort knelt and gently took the offered hand.

"Torven," said Bort. "Your name is Torven."

"That's quite correct." Torven smiled and pulled Bort up to stand. "Yes, you're the son of Latz and Janna."

"They are both gone," said Bort.

Torven nodded slowly. "It has been a while then. Fine folk they were." He raised his eyebrows. "And these uh... companions?"

Bort turned to Endor. "This is my master, Baron Endor Caffri."

"The Trollid know no master," said Torven, a harsh edge to his voice.

Bort shook his head. "No, no, master Endor pays Bort to cook for him."

"Ah, your employer! Nothing wrong with an honest day's work for a fair day's pay." Torven held his hand out to Endor. "Pleased to meet you, Endor. A King's Chosen, I see?"

"Formerly, sir," said Endor. "Called out of retirement by recent events..."

Torven raised a hand to silence Endor. "More of that later. Bort, I'd be pleased if you would introduce me to these two fine ladies."

"This is Miss Fairweather, Bort's uhh... friend."

Ida hesitated, then, out of kindness to Bort, she curtsied.

"Very pleased to meet you, Miss Fairweather. I see Bort chooses his friends well." He seemed to examine the air around Ida. "More than a friend, I'd say. You've taken the lad under your wing?"

Ida reasoned that, like all good tricksters, he'd made a good guess at their relationship, but she wasn't about to be swayed by a little charm.

"It's Ida," she said, abruptly. "And yes, Bort is my ward."

Torven's brow furrowed. "Miss Fairweather, Ida, I sense you are injured. Have you had treatment?"

Ida was confused, she was sure she hadn't displayed any weakness or signs of pain. "A minor wound," she said, "it seems to be on the mend."

"Hardly minor," said Torven. "But I'm glad it's healing well."

As Ida wondered how Torven knew about her wound, Bort continued with his introductions.

"This is Miss Lineth," he said.

Lineth slipped her sword into its scabbard and snapped a smart salute. "I'm Lineth Tobias, a Lieutenant in the King's Guard."

"Pleased to meet you," said Torven, bowing graciously. He turned back to Bort. "Let me see you, lad." He held Bort at arm's length and looked him up and down with obvious affection. "I must say you've turned out a fine looking man."

Ida's mood softened when Bort cast his eyes down in embarrassment.

Torven laughed gently and then slid his arm through Bort's, drawing him along the passage. "Do you remember the games we used to play?"

"Yes, Bort remembers."

Torven paused and looked back over his shoulder. "If you are all here by Bort's invitation, I can hardly turn you away. I don't suppose you'll want to stand there all day." He pointed a finger towards the ceiling and said, "Light."

A faint yellow glow shone from the rock above, strengthening until the full extent of the tunnel was visible.

Ida felt a surge of panic. What she had just witnessed with the light was impossible, but beyond any doubt it had happened. She was also surprised by what the light revealed. The tunnel shrank off into the far distance in a perfectly straight line.

"As you can see," said Torven, "we've a way to go. Best we don't delay."

The old man Torven was talkative enough, but Ida quickly grew frustrated with his answers. He flatly denied any subterfuge, clinging to his story about falling asleep, and it disturbed her that Bort was so easily taken in by this trickster. Were it not for the constant and sincere affection he showed to Bort, she would have found it hard to stay civil.

Finally, they approached the end of the tunnel and were faced by an impenetrable, empty blackness. Ida waited, wondering what nonsense Torven would entertain them with next. She couldn't have been more surprised when Bort's face lit up with rapture.

"What is it," she said, "what do you see, Bort?"

"He's home," said Torven. He stepped onto the edge of the blackness and his voice boomed out, deep and resonant, "Behold, The City of Garn, the last home of the Trollid."

He swept his hand in a broad arc, and as he did so a pale orange glow radiated from his fingers, revealing a wide avenue running away from them, flanked either side by fluted columns bearing statues of the Trollid.

The glow strengthened in an expanding wave of light that fell on broad curving staircases, elevated walkways and tall spires dotted with black shadowed windows. The underground city was huge, stretching far into the distance, with massive pillars of intricately carved stone supporting the vaulted roof of the cavern.

Everything was coated in dust and strung with cobwebs, but as the light touched the cobwebs they began collapsing and dissolving away.

"By all that's holy," said Endor.

"It's beautiful," said Lineth. "So beautiful."

Bort's eyes were bright with pride and tears trickled down his smiling face.

Ida placed a hand on his shoulder. "Oh, Bort, I'm so sorry I ever doubted you."

"Come away then," said Torven. "My cottage is near. You'll need to eat and rest after that trek."

Ida could find no rational explanation for Torven's abilities, unless one accepted that they were truly magical, which was deeply troubling.

As they walked, the cobwebs continued to collapse and fade to nothing and Ida knew that any house-proud woman, or man, would love to know the secret behind this particular phenomenon.

"What is happening to the cobwebs?" she said.

"The city is self cleaning." Torven pointed up. "It's the light, it has a special property."

It seemed such a simple explanation, but what was this special property? Ida noted that Torven's robes, which had been dark grey with dust, were changing colour and becoming lighter. In fact her own clothes, which had suffered terrible neglect over the last few days, were becoming cleaner too.

As the dust and cobwebs disappeared, the gemstones and precious metals that were a part of many of the city's structures began to glisten and shine, reflecting a rainbow of colours. The city seemed to be coming alive, which made the absence of dwellers more noticeable.

When they arrived at the cottage, Ida shook her head in amusement. Torven called it a cottage, but it was much grander than that, more like a villa. She stroked the intricately carved stone roses appearing to grow up the walls either side of the front door and thought of her own cottage, and the careful pruning needed to keep the blooms returning. These roses never needed pruning.

Every element that was familiar was different too, with most of it painstakingly carved from stone. The roof looked like a solid sheet of stone, detailed to resemble straw thatch, and the glass in the windows was seamlessly fused to delicate stone astragals. A too familiar garden bench sat beneath one of the front windows, almost the twin of one sitting outside Ida's cottage, but of course this one was crafted in stone. Even the front door was stone, worked to represent wood, exquisite in the detailing of knots and wood grain. It even had a small diamond-shaped window inset fussily at head height.

"What do you think?" said Torven.

"Wonderful," said Ida. "Such detail."

"And yet," said Torven, "these were considered simple tasks in the eyes of the Trollid. This is nothing compared to some of the wonders they achieved."

Ida glanced over at Bort. He was wide-eyed and his mouth hung open, as awed by the experience as she was. She felt sad, had he still been part of this community, he might have learned these incredible skills.

Torven swung the door open and beckoned them in. "Please, may I share my simple dwelling with you?"

The room was pristine, more magic Ida assumed, and familiar beyond reason. From within the cottage, they could have been anywhere above ground. Some trick of the glass threw shafts of what resembled summer's sunlight into the room, and looking out, the Trollid city appeared to be in daylight.

Torven's robe was now a pristine white. "A cup of tea first, maybe some scones?" he suggested. "Then I'll find you all beds for the night."

"Scones!" said Ida.

"Yes, why not, I have all the ingredients here. Bread might take a little longer; I'd need to prove the dough."

"Bort will help," said Bort.

"Grand," said Torven.

The tea and scones Torven prepared tasted fresh and full of flavour. Ida asked about this and he demonstrated the airtight properties of the container the tealeaves and flour were stored in, but she doubted that this was a good enough explanation. If she allowed herself to accept Torven had stood in the tunnel for all these years, this meant that the food had lain in storage for the same time. Food kept for so long would not survive without losing some of its flavour or rotting to dust. Even more it convinced her Torven was a trickster, though she had to admit he seemed pleasant enough.

Once they were settled and allocated sleeping quarters, Torven suggested they might explore the city. Bort, Ida and Lineth set off at a brisk pace, and Endor and Torven strolled gently behind, quickly becoming separated from the others. Soon they were alone, pacing a silent street that was easily broad enough to take six wagons abreast.

Endor was baffled and confused; in all his years of soldiering there was little that could have prepared him for what he encountered on the battlefield at Sollas, and nothing could have prepared him for the events that were now unfolding before his eyes. He clung desperately to the notion that it was all some form of science or trickery, but if it was trickery, it was tremendously accomplished and entertaining.

He shook his head. "I never thought that the Trollid actually existed. I always thought they were just stories. Someone should pinch me hard; I'm probably still lying there on that infernal battlefield with my head split open."

Torven smiled indulgently. "Regard it a great privilege, Endor. Had the Trollid still been here, you would not know of them. Sadly their time has passed; a different time has come upon the world."

"They must have been a fine people. The world would've been a better place for their knowledge and skills."

"In many ways it is. As the Trollid population fell, some left to embrace the world of light, spreading their gifts throughout humanity. But sadly, many of the higher forms of their art have been lost."

Endor paused at the threshold of a stone bridge that spanned a wide crevice; the passing of many carts had worn grooves into its surface.

"They were here for a long time," he said. It was a question as much as a comment.

"A very long time," Torven agreed. He led Endor forward.

Endor peered over the parapet. Far below he saw a ribbon of glowing red. "What is that?"

"Molten stone," said Torven. "Have you ever seen a volcano?"

"Heard of them, dangerous things surely?"

"They can be if you get too close, nature in one of her more destructive moods."

"I've heard the rock flows like a river."

"Exactly that! What you see below is a molten river of stone. Among their other accomplishments, the Trollid found ways to tap the natural energy in the molten rock, producing some of the heat and light you now experience."

"Smart fellows, then?"

"Undoubtedly. Don't let their appearance or manner fool you. As a race, they have talents and skills you could only dream of."

"Makes me ashamed, just employing Bort as a cook's assistant."

"Not at all, Endor, he seems happy enough."

"Well he was, we all were, until this damned Tekt appeared."

"This conflict," said Torven, "tell me about it."

Endor explained, trying to describe the creatures, and his confusion and disbelief when he first saw them.

Torven's face quickly lost colour; any hint of humour fading from his eyes. He probed Endor with more and more questions, until it became clear that they were very directed.

Endor grew suspicious. "You know who they are!"

"I may well do," Torven raised an open palm, "but I'd have to see them to be sure."

"Who are they?" Endor demanded. "If you know, you have to say."

"A little patience is all I ask." Torven pointed over Endor's shoulder. "I see the others."

Endor turned. Bort, Ida and Lineth were standing on a distant street corner. He looked back to Torven, wanting to pursue their conversation, but it was clear from the expression on the man's face that it would not happen.

"Patience, you say?"

Torven nodded. "I promise you, it will be rewarded."

Endor felt excitement; Torven's hinted knowledge of the enemy, his mastery of the incredible science evident all around in the Trollid city, and his promise, all pointed to the possibility that he could be a powerful ally.

"Very well, patience it is." Endor turned away and waved, shouting, "Ho there!"

A faint echo of his voice came back a few seconds later. Then Lineth waved, and the two parties started towards each other.

"Ah yes," said Torven. "There's something along this way that you might find interesting."

Ida and her party joined Torven and Endor, who waited at the foot of a broad stone staircase that led up to a temple-like structure. She craned her neck to examine a tall spire rising from the top of the building, it reached up to touch the roof of the cavern. There were support columns all over the city, but this was much thinner and didn't appear to be one of them. She wondered what purpose it could serve.

"What is this place?" she said.

Torven started to climb the steps. "It is known as the Palace of Visions."

Pausing in front of a pair of tall doors with a huge golden eye embedded into them, he turned the door handles and pushed them both open, splitting the eye in two.

"Come in," he said. "It's perfectly safe."

He called for light, revealing a tiled hall that led into a small theatre. Staggered ranks of curved seating rose steeply around a modest circular stage, which was made from a single slab of white marble. The light over the stage was subdued and dim.

Ida assumed it was a place for entertainment. Musicians or dancers would occupy the stage, their audience all around them on the seats. It seemed a very civilised arrangement.

Torven climbed into a pulpit overlooking the stage and grasped two of three long metal poles hanging down from the ceiling.

"Watch the table," he said, and an intense spot of light appeared at its centre.

Torven had described the stage as a table and curious of this, Ida walked to its edge and rested her hands on the smooth surface. The bright spot grew suddenly bigger, quickly expanding to cover the table and she snatched her hands back in alarm. Now sitting on the table was a blurred picture of a mountain, its snow-covered peaks shrouded in cloud. The image sharpened to show the finest detail and then rotated, as if the observer were turning on his heel to see all around him.

"Weather's on the change," said Torven. "That's a snowstorm coming in from the north-west there."

Ida gasped in shock. This wasn't a simple picture; it was somehow looking outside the mountain. She felt a moments dizziness as the view on the table appeared to plummet into a valley, and then flinched as the valley floor loomed closer. Hesitantly she stretched her fingers out to touch the edge of the image.

"Don't worry," said Torven, "it won't harm you, it's just light."

Ida stretched her hand into the image, and then turned it over and stared into her palm. She appeared to be holding part of the picture, and on the table was a shadow matching the outline of her hand. She stared up, squinting against a sharp point of light on the ceiling.

"Just light?" she said.

"That's all," said Torven, "quite harmless."

"Wonderful." Ida spread her fingers, almost expecting the picture to drain from her hand, but it didn't.

"Ah... that valley will be thick with snow soon enough." Torven centred the image on a smoky chimney projecting from a low hump in the snow. "That's odd," he said. "Normally the pasture is only used during the summer. But whoever's in there will be warm enough, it's a fine little hut."

Ida stared as the image moved on, taking in more and more of the landscape, and then flaring intensely as it focused briefly on the evening sun. She felt disappointment when it shrank again to a white spot and faded to nothing.

The chamber was silent for a few seconds, and then Endor clapped his hands enthusiastically. "What a wondrous thing! I've never seen anything like it before. How does it work? Surely it's not..."

Torven interrupted, "Simply the application of scientific principles. There is no magic in this, my friend. A lens gathers the image, which is then reflected through mirrors until it is focused onto this table. I can show you how to operate it if you wish?"

While Torven demonstrated how to control the machine to Endor, Ida sat with Lineth and Bort, all watching the table.

Ida wondered what Bort made of all of this, his heritage, the city of his ancestors. He seemed at ease, a contented look on his face. But if he truly was the last of this race, then this must be a terribly poignant experience for him. She hoped he felt great pride for his people's achievements, but she also knew there would be great pain too. The city spoke of a vibrant, powerful culture, but somehow it had all disappeared. She wished he could have been here when the city was alive with people, his own people.

12

By morning the fire in Moleskin's small hut had burnt down to ash, and the air inside was cold enough to fog his breath. Pulling the blanket around his shoulders, he swung his legs clear of the bed and pushed his feet into his boots. He knelt to remake the fire; raking out the ash and preparing a pile of kindling. He had just lit it when he noticed a flicker of movement through a thin crack in the door's planking. Curious, he went to the door and peered through the crack.

His heart thumped and his breath froze in his throat. Directly in line with his view, and about a hundred paces away, was the dragon. It lay with its glossy, grey body shivering and twitching in the early morning sunlight.

He leapt to the stove and pulled out the kindling, smothering the flames with his blanket and splashing any embers with water from a small blackened kettle. By the time he finished, a thin smoky haze lingered in the hut.

He crept back to the crack and looked out. One of the dragon's eyes was open and it seemed to be staring directly at him. It suddenly rose onto all four legs, stretching its wings wide, and a shudder of horror ran up Moleskin's spine; it had seen the smoke and was coming to tear the roof off.

But the dragon's head turned, and from the edge of Moleskin's line of sight, its rider strode into view. Relief flooded him, the dragon was just responding to the rider's approach. He let out a slow wavering breath, he was still safe.

Rider and dragon met, and the dragon nuzzled its huge mouth against the rider's shoulder, as any horse might greet its rider.

Close too, the rider was less menacing, tiny by comparison to the creatures in the glade at Sollas. Shorter even than Moleskin, its thin, wiry body was clad in a close-fitting leather suit, and angled across its back was a sheath containing a short narrow sword. Its dark hair was neatly braided into a long ponytail, and as it moved the braid swung hypnotically from side to side; there was even something about its gait that suggested femininity.

Moleskin watched it make ready to leave; harnessing the dragon and gathering up its small camp into saddlebags hung around the dragon's neck. It then paused to draw a pair of gauntlets over its delicate clawed hands, pressing them on by scissoring its fingers together.

Finally ready, the rider called out and the dragon crouched, its tail coiling and whipping sinuously against the ground, throwing up puffs of powdery snow. The rider strode nimbly up one of the dragon's forelimbs, and it let out a deep rumbling growl as the rider settled in the saddle. It then slapped the side of the dragon's neck affectionately and in response, the huge creature rocked its head, emitting another long growl of pleasure. Moleskin was caught between fascination and terror.

The rider had the dragon stand, ready for flight, and the beast unfolded its wings, stretching them to either side. The wings then beat against the air, and in a great swirling cloud of loose snow, and haloed by a bright rainbow of colours, the dragon rose majestically from the ground and flew off.

Moleskin slumped to the ground, his back resting against the door. He would probably never experience such a wonderful sight in his life again. What kind of creatures were these dragonriders to master such fine beasts and fly them about the skies like the birds? They must own wonderful castles, and castles required staff, a lot of them. Surely they could use the services of a skilled retainer like himself?

The fantasy of a life in the service of these extraordinary creatures took shape in Moleskin's head. If only there were a way to talk to them, convince them of his undoubted talents and skills. The fantasy dissolved rapidly as he remembered the ravaging of the village; he was more likely to end up as a meal for the dragon, than a servant to its master.

Moleskin emerged from the hut and looked carefully around. The drifted snow had saved him from detection; smoothing the contours around the hut, and hiding it. This had been a matter of luck; if the dragon and rider returned he would certainly be found. The spot was too exposed, and the sooner he left, the better.

By midmorning Moleskin was on the move again, fleeing for his life. After the meadow, the track rose into the mountains. At first the going was easy, the path well marked and gently sloping, but soon it became slippery and treacherous, winding its way up through a narrow cut in the rock.

Despair came in waves as the day progressed; the sky darkening steadily as thick cloud gathered overhead. At times it seemed that the landscape was about to open onto another pasture, but a sharp bend and a twist in the path would quickly draw him back into the dark corridor of rock. The sky became ever distant above him, sometimes appearing as only the thinnest line of pale light, and late in the day snowflakes began drifting down. There was one consolation; the way was too narrow for the dragon.

He was so cold and miserable when he stumbled onto a high pasture, he didn't at first realise the rock walls no longer hemmed him in.

A storm was building, and thick, heavy flakes swirled around, confusing him and hiding the pasture's details. He searched for shelter, eventually stumbling into a low wall. Quickly laying out his sleeping roll, he arranged an oilskin over himself, sealing its edges by tucking them beneath the bedroll. Sleeved in this protective layer, and sheltered by the wall, he settled to sleep out the storm.

His world had shrunk again to the tiny space around his shivering body, and again the dreadful feelings of loneliness came to him. His future seemed so hopeless; he almost wished that he would freeze to death before morning.

That night in a shallow cave, dragonrider, Nitha, and her mount, Whisper, rested easily. Whisper was impervious to the cold and his body served to seal the cave-mouth, protecting Nitha from the elements.

Eyes glowing red in the ember-light of a small fire, Nitha pondered her options as she drew an oilstone along the edge of her rapier in a slow, repetitive motion. A few humans carrying the Agnem mark had fled the battlefield at Sollas. The mark was a sure sign of Trollid activity, and could, if Dusswen was right, lead to the Trollid City. She grinned, one in particular had chosen an interesting though troubled path. This particular human seemed to act with great determination, but had then fallen foul of robbers.

Hoping to set the human back on its path, Nitha had aided it by killing the robbers, and then, to coax it towards the mountains, she had lain waste to the next village. After leaving to search for the other marked ones, she had returned and settled for the night in clear sight of this one's shelter; a complete coincidence, but tremendously entertaining.

She cackled as fleeting images drifted into her thoughts; mind-linked to the dragon, she often shared its dreams. She closed her eyes and was there, on dragon back. The ground, distant, glimpsed through ragged cloud, and then the thrill as they plummeted, the cloud whipping by and the ground racing ever closer, only to shrink away as Whisper's great wings beat the air. The breathtaking swell of his primal thoughts was intoxicating, but distracting. She blinked her eyes open and took a deep breath.

If, as she now suspected, the human continued to skirt the mountains, then it was obvious it had no knowledge of the Trollid city. If that happened then Whisper could feast on it; a special reward for all his hard work. The marked ones had a certain aromatic delicacy, appreciated only by a dragon's palate.

13

Endor woke, eager and refreshed, but was disappointed when Torven said he had important business to attend to elsewhere, but promised to return that evening. Endor's only consolation was the hope that this *important business* was connected to defeating their enemy. He started his morning with the others, wandering around the Trollid city, but it proved an increasingly frustrating experience. At each new destination he hoped to sweep open a door to reveal a powerful arsenal of weapons, or even a library with a dusty text describing the origins of their foe would have been useful, but it was all just empty buildings. The city had been swept clean of every single artefact.

After lunch they separated, Bort with Ida and he with Lineth, each pair setting out to explore the city again. Endor tried to remain positive, but his mood was in decline. Regardless of how finely decorated or grand the architecture, by late afternoon he'd grown weary of entering yet another empty building.

His interest was piqued as they rounded a corner and approached a low monolithic structure, which appeared as solidly built as a castle's walls. It seemed only to have a single storey and was made from huge interlocking blocks of deep red stone.

Lineth gripped the handle on a heavy wooden door, turned it and pushed, but nothing happened.

"Endor, I think this door's locked."

Endor was instantly alert. "You sure it's locked?"

Lineth turned the handle a few times more and then squinted into the gap in the door frame, next to the handle. "The latch seems to work well enough, it's just locked."

Endor stood back and examined the building. If it was locked it meant there was something inside to protect. Endor's conscience fought against the desire to hack the door open, and he looked to Lineth for a hint of consent, but her face mirrored his own thoughts; they shouldn't do anything to offend Torven.

Endor attempted humour. "We'll have to ask him what he's hiding in here when he gets back."

Lineth nodded. "Yes, best if we do that."

Endor looked to either side of the door; there weren't even any windows to peer through.

He sighed. "Fancy an early tea?"

Torven did not return that evening, and with no sign of him when Endor woke the next morning, Endor went to the only place that gave him any connection to the world outside the mountain, the Palace of Visions.

The unnatural silence of the place was broken when Lineth joined him.

"Morning, Lineth," he said. "I couldn't wait to try this contraption again." He struggled with the controls, revealing only a patch of white snow with a sheer rock face nearby. "Haven't quite got the measure of it though."

Lineth stared at the table and shook her head. "Did you have breakfast?"

"Breakfast, I quite forgot about that." Endor patted his belly. "I'm sure I can miss the odd meal, it's not like I'm wasting away."

Lineth produced a small bundle; a napkin she unfolded to reveal a serving of sandwiches. "I think you should eat something. Eat when there's food, sleep when you can, in the fight for life, let the weaker be damned."

Endor recognised the creed from his army training and smiled. "I'll not argue with that." He took a sandwich and they sat close to the viewing table as he ate.

"That's Torven back," said Lineth.

"Good, maybe now we can get some answers." Endor stared at the sandwich, sighed and took a mouthful. He had an awful suspicion that Torven wouldn't be any more forthcoming than before.

"It makes you think," said Lineth.

"Eh?" Endor mumbled between mouthfuls.

"All the things we were told of as children, the Trollid, Harrowen, Nitmin, Wizards, Dunnit Sprites and all the rest. How many of them used to exist, even still do exist?"

"It's a sobering thought," said Endor, cautiously.

"Those creatures on the battlefield, could they be Harrowen?"

Endor hated to openly admit that he had already considered Lineth's suggestion. The physical appearance of their enemy did match that of the terrible mythical creatures of so many campfire stories.

"I don't know," he said, "but I've no doubt that Torven does."

Lineth nodded grimly. "And what about Torven, the way we found him? Do you think he's a wiz..."

Endor interrupted. "Theatrical nonsense and parlour tricks. The old fellow must have heard us coming and hid in that dusty corner."

"But..." Lineth began.

"But nothing! This lot, the Trollid, Torven said it himself, there's nothing magical about them. Why, our world is covered in peoples of all different shapes, sizes and colours, whole tribes of men and women half our size. And Harrowen, next you'll be telling me you believe in dragons! I don't know where this Lord Tekt and his foul army came from, and frankly I don't care to know. I'll be happy when every one of them is dead and in the ground, and we can get back to the way things were. "

"But what about the way all those cobwebs..."

"I'll not hear it!" said Endor, firmly. He was a soldier, first and foremost. He knew how to take orders and how to give them. He knew the craft of warfare and how to organise a community. A world so different from the one he knew, and always had known, seemed unthinkable.

He rose to his feet and returned to the controls. "I'm starting to think there's very little in this city that can help us when we get back to the fight. Maybe this thing can at least let us see what's happening out there!"

Endor stared down at the table in surprise. A shambling figure had staggered into view. "Here, Lineth, look at this poor fellow. He looks done in."

Lineth peered over the table. "Endor, I think I've seen him before."

Endor struggled with the controls. "I'll... just try... to get this a bit clearer."

The figure grew in size, almost filling the whole table, but the image was fuzzy and unfocused.

"Damned machine," he cursed.

The image fell starkly into focus just as the stumbling figure raised his face to the skies.

"Goodness!" said Endor. "It's Moleskin!"

"Don't touch anything," Lineth cautioned. "I'll fetch Torven. He'll know where Moleskin is. We can go out and fetch him."

Endor nodded, but kept his eyes fixed on Moleskin. He raised his voice, "You're in a sorry state, Moleskin! Where are you?"

"Endor, he won't hear you."

Endor looked up at Lineth. "What? No, hmm, I suppose not."

"I'll go and fetch Torven."

"Right, right, good idea." Endor turned back to the image. "Don't you worry now, Moleskin, we'll come and fetch you. I'll not see you suffering like that..."

Ida was appalled when Torven refused to go and rescue Moleskin. Instead he gathered them all in front of the fireplace in his cottage.

"I'm sorry," he said, "but we must leave him where he is."

"That's monstrous," Endor roared. "We can't leave him out there to die!"

Torven turned his back on Endor and stared into the empty grate. "It's not such a simple matter, Endor."

"You can't say no," said Ida, firmly. She didn't relish Moleskin's company, but she couldn't condemn him to death.

"I can say what I want, madam!" Torven spun around to face them, a deeply troubled expression on his face. "What you ask is too much. That you came with Bort is just about acceptable, after all you helped him find the way. But now this other..."

"Show us the way out," said Lineth. "We'll leave, and never come back."

Bort had remained silent throughout. "Bort will go too."

Torven shook his head in disbelief. "You as well, Bort?"

"Bort wants to help Moleskin."

"What is so special about this Moleskin?" said Torven.

"Nothing." Ida scowled. "Other than he's another human being. And if you can't care enough about that, then I pity you."

Torven glowered. "If you knew the facts, madam, you would never dare say that to me."

Ida bit back a reply. What could trouble Torven so badly that he was willing to condemn Moleskin to death?

Bort began collecting his possessions, making ready to leave.

"Don't go, Bort," said Torven. "There's nothing out there for you now."

"Moleskin is out there," said Bort, calmly.

"Damn and blast! Very well! I will rescue this, Moleskin person. But you will all remain here until I return. I must have your solemn promise on that."

Ida was glad that Torven had finally seen sense. "Thank you," she said, as sincerely as she could.

Torven left without another word, and Ida watched from the cottage window as he walked by a little later, pushing a narrow handcart. He stared straight ahead, refusing to acknowledge her obvious presence.

Two hours later she heard the cart's wheels rattling towards the cottage and rushed out to meet Torven. Moleskin lay on top of the cart, bundled in blankets and with only his pale face visible.

"How is he?" said Ida.

"He'll live," said Torven.

Moleskin's eyes fluttered open. "Is that you, mummy?"

Endor leaned over Moleskin. "Poor fellow's deranged. It's me, Endor, remember? Endor, Miss Fairweather, Bort, we're all here."

"I'm dead then," said Moleskin. "Am I in heaven?"

Torven choked back a laugh.

"Are you a god?" said Moleskin.

"No I am not a god!" Torven spoke to Ida, "Are you sure this one was worth saving?"

Ida gave Torven a sharp look of disapproval.

Moleskin snapped upright, a look of terror on his face. "The dragon!" he shouted, and then fell back in a dead faint.

Ida ignored the shocked expression on Torven's face. Had he known Moleskin better, he would know this outburst was just some nonsense the stupid little man had contrived to gain their sympathy.

"I hate to see a man in this state," said Endor.

Lineth shook her head. "The poor, poor, man."

Ida sighed in frustration; Moleskin had taken them all in.

"He'll live," said Torven. "Best if you get him inside, take off his wet clothes and tuck him up in bed."

Once inside, Ida began removing Moleskin's damp clothing. Regardless of his villainous nature, he still needed a healer's care.

"I'll get some hot soup," said Lineth.

"Not too hot," Ida cautioned. "The shock of it could kill him."

"I see you have some knowledge of the healing arts," said Torven.

"It's true; I've tried to gather a knowledge of healing." Ida waved Bort over. "Bort, give me a hand here. Endor, would you prepare a bed for Moleskin, and take the chill off it with a bed warmer."

From the corner of her eye, Ida watched Torven as he stood back to let them work. He seemed withdrawn and desperately troubled. What was causing such concern?

When morning came, Nitha searched for the marked human, eventually coming upon a high plateau, a low wall and a hollow in the snow. The human had slept here, but it was gone.

From the air she searched along the track, up and beyond the highest pass, well beyond any distance the human could have covered on foot, but there was no sign of it. The human could had fallen into a deep crevasse, or been eaten by wild animals, but there was another tantalising possibility; it had entered the mountain to seek refuge in the Trollid city.

She flew back to where the human had slept and waited as Whisper's wide, leathery nostrils flared, drawing in a massive lungful of air to absorb the scents on the snow-covered ground. He let out a long growl, fogging the early evening air with his hot breath and a rush of expectant pleasure flooded Nitha.

"You have it! Well done, my sweet."

The beast growled again and his body trembled. Stretching his long neck, he turned his head to catch Nitha's eye.

"Take the trail, Whisper." Nitha kicked at Whisper's flank. "Follow it, my sweet, follow and find."

The great creature's snout fell to the ground and he crept forward, his long tail cutting a deep groove in the snow.

Eyes closed, Nitha bathed in Whisper's excitement. "Follow and find, my Whisper. Follow and find."

14

Fearful that he might take a sudden turn for the worse, Ida kept a close watch on Moleskin, though there was little more she could do; he was warm, recently fed and safe. Endor joined her, bringing a cup of tea.

"How is he?" he said.

Ida finished mopping Moleskin's brow before turning to speak, "Much better, but he's still talking complete nonsense. He keeps going on about dragons and other awful things."

Endor nodded. "I've seen that before. Happens when they've been pushed too hard, seen too much, they retreat into their heads. By the looks of his clothes, all that blood, he's been in amongst it."

"Apart from a few bumps on his head, he hasn't been wounded," said Ida, suspiciously.

"He's been lucky then." Endor smiled. "Makes me proud, he must have fought like a man possessed."

Ida suspected the whole performance was an act to gain their sympathy, right down to the fantastical mention of a dragon. She had seen the blood from the creatures at Sollas, and saw enough difference in it to know that the blood on Moleskin's clothes was human. Rather than as the result of fighting, it more likely came from the wounded he had handled after the battle. She hoped that his actions had been honourable between leaving the battlefield with a wagon full of injured, and arriving by himself some days later on the side of a mountain. The horrible possibility that he had dumped the men off the wagon and used it to flee seemed too awful to contemplate.

Torven came into the room and walked across to Moleskin's bedside. "How is he now, Ida?"

"He's fine." Moleskin looked small, pale and childlike; uncharitably Ida thought of a viper huddled in its nest.

"He looks well enough to be left for a while?" said Torven.

She nodded.

"Come, I have something I need to show you all."

"What's that then?" said Endor.

"It will soon be clear," said Torven.

The bitter tone in Torven's voice worried Ida. She followed with the others, her heartbeat quickening as they approached a low stone building that she immediately recognised from Endor's description.

Apart from its odd shape and lack of windows, it was the only building any of them had found that was locked.

Torven produced a large brass key from the folds of his robes and unlocked the door. He waved them forward into a dim entrance hall, which had shelving to either side holding rows of hand lamps.

"Don't they have that fancy roof light in here?" said Endor.

"Not all Trollid buildings have that light." Torven gave a lamp to each of them. Bort declined, but Torven insisted, adding, "The colours are much improved with the addition of a little light."

Intrigued, Ida inspected her lamp. It had a handle set behind a polished reflector, and to the front of the reflector was a glass cylinder filled with a green fluid. She couldn't see how it would work as there was no wick.

Torven moved around the group, uncapping the cylinders and placing a drop of clear fluid into each. Almost immediately the green material began to glow, emitting a warm yellow light that quickly grew brighter until it was sufficient to see by.

It was a strangely familiar light, and Ida wondered if Torven had found some way to harness and distil the light from glowflys.

Torven picked up a lamp. "We use these because the fabric of what I am about to show you can be damaged by harsher light."

"Lead on," said Endor.

After descending several flights of stairs, Torven paused at a side passage. "Please do not touch the walls, and also avoid brushing against them." He walked in and pointed to either side. "This is a part of the history of the Trollid. It was kept in this form to recognise both their origins and to make the history available to even the youngest mind."

Ida shone her lamp on the wall. There were brightly coloured images of the city, its streets busy with Trollid. It seemed very peaceful.

Endor, who was a little ahead, gasped. "You must see this."

Ida walked forward and examined the scene; it depicted Trollid warriors fighting darkly-clad figures. "They're the same as the ones at the battle," she said. "Who are they?"

"These are Harrowen," said Torven.

"Then they do exist?" said Endor.

"Yes," said Torven, "the Harrowen are very real. They almost wiped out the Trollid."

"No, it can't be!" Lineth stood a little further down the corridor.

"What is it?" Ida had never heard Lineth so animated.

Lineth pointed to the wall and spoke to Torven. "This can't be real, can it?"

"This is the history of the Trollid. Everything you see in this corridor happened."

"But this," said Lineth, "it's a..."

"Yes," said Torven. "It is a dragon."

"Let me see that." Endor pushed forward. "Gods, that's an ugly creature."

Ida added the light from her lantern. The dragon held a Trollid warrior in its foreclaws, tearing the unfortunate man apart. Other dismembered bodies littered the ground. It was shocking, and now Ida understood the reason for their visit to the bunker. "You think Moleskin really has seen a dragon?"

"I fear so," said Torven, "and if there is a dragon about we are all in terrible danger. Dragons are fearsome in battle, but the Harrowen also use them as trackers." Torven turned to the ghastly scene on the wall. "A long time ago my kind found a way to isolate the Harrowen, trapping them on their world. It seems they have overcome those measures."

"What do you mean by *their world*," said Lineth.

Torven spread his arms wide. "Much as this whole world is like an island floating in the emptiness of the void. There are other worlds, complete and separate, with their own continents and oceans, and peopled by many different beings. These worlds would never know of each other were it not possible to harness the energies of the void and travel between them."

"Like continents separated by oceans," said Ida, breathlessly.

"Very apt, but no known vessel can survive the journey across these oceans."

"How do they do it then?" said Endor.

"By a powerful magical device called a World Gate, there were several on this world, but most have been dismantled. Once it was possible to travel to many hundreds of worlds."

Though struck by the awesome magnitude of what Torven described, Ida had only one question, "What do the Harrowen want here?"

Torven stroked his chin. "The most obvious reason for them coming to Nephus is simply the distance between this world and theirs. Unfortunately, though the distances are vast beyond imagining, Nephus is the nearest world to theirs." Torven's brow furrowed. "And now that they are here, I imagine they have two objectives. No doubt they intend to reopen the Gate at Conisby to strengthen their position."

"Always west," said Lineth. "It makes sense now, they march on Conisby."

Torven nodded. "Conisby is the site of a Master Gate. If they can use it, it will allow them almost unrestricted access to this world."

"You mentioned another objective?" said Endor.

Torven looked up towards the dark ceiling. "Originally the city of Garn was nothing more than a place to house the Trollid workers who built another structure, the Library of Banna. The Library holds an immense storehouse of knowledge gathered from a hundred different worlds, a thousand different cultures."

Ida stood in uneasy silence, struggling to absorb his words.

"Without doubt, their other objective is the Library." Torven stared at the wall for a few seconds and a pained expression appeared on his face. "Those of my kind are forever in debt to these Trollid workers and warriors for denying them that goal last time."

"What last time?" Ida knew enough of Carolin's history to know there was no mention of these strange and horrible events.

"A little over 300 years ago, just before the Isolation, the Harrowen attacked Garn. It was only by sheer physical bravery and sacrifice that they were repelled." Torven looked to Bort. "During that awful time, the Trollid homeworld Hamman was just one of several worlds the Harrowen invaded. They laid waste to everything, killing every man, woman and child."

Lineth cleared her throat nervously. "Is that what the Harrowen intend for us?"

"Most likely," said Torven. "When the Harrowen had finished their foul work on Hamman, almost the only Trollid left alive were the workers and their families living here. This became their new home. It saddens me forever that those remaining few were then asked to sacrifice even more of their number in that final terrible battle to close the Gate here in Garn. If the Harrowen had captured the Library, not one of the known worlds would have been safe." Torven looked uncomfortably around the group. "The same is true now."

"Was that why you wanted to leave Moleskin outside?" said Ida, softly.

Torven sighed. "Yes, Ida. Terrible though that sounded, it seemed the best choice."

Though Ida understood Torven's reasoning, she knew she couldn't have abandoned Moleskin.

Torven's eyes suddenly widened. "Quickly now, we must go to my workshop. The ways into the mountain are well hidden, but if an Agnem trail has been left for the dragon to follow, we are sorely at risk of discovery."

Torven's workshop lay beneath his cottage, and was reached by a descending flight of steps alongside the building. At the bottom of the flight he gestured with his arm and a door opened in the blank stone wall.

Ida followed, entering a large barn-like room, and was immediately baffled by row after row of strange apparatus made from polished copper vessels, glass tubing and masses of twisted pipes. All around, the walls were decked with shelves, which were lined with hundreds of jars filled with liquids, crystals and powders. Faint alchemic odours lingered in the air.

"There's something familiar about that smell," said Endor.

Ida sniffed and scowled. "It smells like a distillery."

Torven was already halfway across the room, and called back, "True, but most of what I distil would not sit well on the palate."

Torven waved Endor towards a small wooden hut, ushering him inside and closing the door. He took the others to an observation slit, which he slid aside. Ida could just make out Endor standing uncertainly in the dark.

"What should I do?" said Endor.

"Just stand still," said Torven.

Torven pulled a lever on the wall of the hut and Ida heard a little door in the ceiling creak open. Immediately Endor's hands glowed a ghostly blue.

He held them up, the glow strong enough to pick out his worried features. "Here, what's up with my hands?"

"It is as I feared," said Torven. "You have the Agnem mark."

Endor rubbed his hands on his britches, but it had no effect, the blue remained. "How do I get rid of it?"

Torven opened the door and waved him from the room. "It's quite harmless, but once marked you cannot lose it." He pushed Lineth into the room. "Quickly, we must see how many of you are marked."

Lineth's hands shone blue, but Ida was relieved to find that she and Bort were unmarked.

"There's a puzzle," said Torven, "what do you handle in common that neither Bort nor Ida do.

"Endor," said Lineth, "it must be your sword."

Ida nodded. "Bort and I have had nothing to do with it."

"There's nothing wrong with my sword!" Endor protested.

"Of course not," said Torven. "But it is very likely the source of the mark. Can you fetch it here, Lineth."

When Lineth returned with the sword it was placed in the room. It shone a brilliant vibrant blue.

"Now don't be telling me it's a magic sword," said Endor, sceptically.

"There is a kind of magic in everything," said Torven. "Some might say it is a magic sword because it holds its edge so well, and because it is lighter and stronger than many baser weapons. Others might say it is a product of science and holds no magic at all. Each must decide for himself. You will have noticed it can cleave armour?"

"I never liked to test that too much," said Endor. "I didn't like to risk damaging the blade."

"You won't damage it," said Torven, "not with base armour. The sword is made from Agnemite, a metal highly prized by Trollid metalsmiths. It is very hard to find. You are a King's Chosen, Endor, and it is indeed appropriate that you should become the weapon's keeper. Only Trollid warriors of the highest calibre were awarded such an honour."

Ida looked with new respect at Endor, King Malcor would not have known it was a Trollid sword, but would definitely have known its quality when he gave it to Endor. His service in the King's army must have been exemplary.

"What causes the glow?" said Lineth.

"Agnemite has an energy deep within its structure that radiates into the skin."

"Sounds nasty," said Endor.

Ida suppressed a laugh and Torven scowled.

"As I said, it's quite harmless, more of an unfortunate side effect. I doubt it is worth testing Moleskin, he must have handled the weapon often?"

"Yes," said Endor. He recovered his sword and brought it out of the room, inspecting the blade from end to end. "A Trollid sword," he said, with relish.

Torven drew on a pair of cotton gloves and held out his hands. "May I see it?"

Endor handed the weapon over.

Torven inspected the blade. "Many Trollid weapons will have found their way into the outside world, but very few of them will have been worked with Agnemite." He pointed to a mark on the hilt. "Ah yes, the work of Hano Lat. This is indeed the finest of weapons. There were a great deal of ceremonial procedures observed in the handling of these swords. All aimed at making sure the warrior never touched the blade with their bare skin. All forgotten now, of course."

"Is it a fine enough weapon to fight a dragon?" said Endor.

"The weapon would stand the job, but the match of man and beast is too uneven."

Ida knew where this whole conversation was leading. "So we come to the basic fact that the dragon can find us."

"Yes," said Torven, "there are a number of trails it could follow. Fortunately they do not last. The mark left by your passing will have faded by now, and in time Moleskin's trail will fade too. But if he was close enough to see the dragon, then it was aware of his presence. I fear it and its rider may have been following him in the hope of locating the city and the Library."

"What can we do?" said Lineth.

Torven returned the sword to Endor. "We need to destroy the dragon and its rider."

"But you just said we couldn't fight it," said Endor.

"That is correct. I can think of only one way that might work." Torven's eyes went up. "We could drop the roof of the cavern on top of it!"

Ida was appalled by Torven's calm decision to destroy the city. She glanced towards Bort, noting the sad expression he wore. "Is that the only way?" she said.

Torven looked to Bort, "I'm sorry, but I can think of no alternative."

Bort nodded and sighed deeply. "Garn is empty, nobody lives here anymore."

"Now," said Torven, "I'll need a few words with Moleskin."

Moleskin's eyes fluttered open and he stared at the unfamiliar ceiling for a few seconds, trying to remember where he was.

Endor squeezed his shoulder. "Hullo, Moleskin. Glad to see you looking a bit better."

Moleskin turned his head, finding Endor sitting in a chair by the bedside. "I'm terribly sorry, sir," he said, attempting to rise from the bed. "I must have slept in..."

"Lay still, man." Endor held Moleskin's shoulder, and then called out, "He's awake."

Moleskin looked around; it was a small, tidy bedroom with evening sunlight shining in through the window. One after the other, Ida Fairweather, Bort, Lineth and an old gentleman with a narrow face entered the room.

"Where am I?" said Moleskin.

"You'll see soon enough," said Endor, "but you're safe now. Can you remember where you were before you came here?"

"Yes, I was lost in the snow. What happened?"

"We found you and brought you here." Endor turned to the old gentleman. "I think he's well enough to answer your questions."

The old gentleman came over. "Moleskin's your name?"

"Yes, sir," said Moleskin, immediately. Something about the man's manner commanded instant respect.

The man placed a hand on Moleskin's forehead, and Moleskin's mouth fell open in shock as the fatigue in his muscles drained away. This man was no ordinary healer.

"Indeed yes," said the man, "you are recovered. Come, sit up."

Moleskin was amazed by how different he felt. It was as if he had enjoyed the best night's sleep ever. He sat up in the bed.

"Thank you," he said, and then noted the suspicious expression on Ida Fairweather's face. She and the others were unaware of what the old man had done to him, and likely Ida would think he had been faking his illness.

"Freely given," said the old man.

Moleskin could tell by the grudging tone and stern expression on the man's face that there was nothing charitable about the act. He gathered his thoughts, ready for the inevitable questions.

Under probing scrutiny, he gave a carefully edited account of his misadventures since leaving the battlefield; how he relinquished his place on the wagon to more needy wounded, became lost when escaping from Tekt's horde, his sighting of the strange column of paired figures, and how, after a brief stay at the Inn, he nobly elected to carry word of the King's defeat to the next village. The robbery and the events that followed needed no editing. He neglected to mention the gold in his money belt, as most of it had been embezzled from Endor.

The old man, who gave his name as Torven, was mostly interested in the description of the dragon.

"The dragon is quite young," said Torven. "The rider is a Shil, a special breed of Harrowen, slight of build and gifted with peculiar mental powers." Torven examined Moleskin briefly through narrowed eyes and shook his head. "We must make haste with our preparations. I will return shortly." Without another word he left the room.

"What's wrong?" said Moleskin.

"Nothing for you to worry about," said Endor.

But his manner was a little abrupt and Moleskin feared his lies had been too transparent. Did they know more of his misadventures than they had said?

Bort came over and gave Moleskin a huge grin. "Moleskin is better, that is good."

Moleskin felt instant relief, and was genuinely touched. "Thank you, Bort."

Ida left, returning with a steaming bowl of broth. With a snort of contempt she handed over the bowl. "Here, you'll need to get your strength up."

Moleskin said nothing and began eating. After a few uncomfortable minutes, Ida and Endor left, leaving just Bort and the woman Lineth. Moleskin sensed that the gloomy atmosphere had something to do with him. When he asked about this, the woman Lineth explained.

"Oh, I see," he said. "If you'd left me to die, you'd all still be safe."

"Nobody's blaming you," she said. "It was unlucky, that's all."

Since leaving Silvermeadow, Moleskin's life had been a series of misfortunes. Even now, having avoided certain death, it turned out that it might only be a temporary reprieve. Whatever plans the others were making, he had no desire to hang around and let a dragon rip him to pieces. He spooned the soup down greedily, resolving to make best use of this new situation before leaving.

15

General Hork waited impatiently in the audience hall for King Malcor to finish his business. As he paced, he looked down at the solid sheet of natural stone that made up the floor. The walled city of Conisby was old, built as much from quarried stone as the natural rock it stood on. More than anything else, the fundamental structure of the city gave him hope that they would survive this conflict. He knew its details intimately. He had to, his was the job of defending the city and protecting its occupants; soldiers, citizens, nearby villagers and all the militias that had taken refuge here, many thousands more than normally sheltered behind its walls.

The city was a complex structure of concentric walls and ramparts. From the main gate, which guarded the top of a long cobbled ramp, its streets spiralled and criss-crossed their way up through the jumble of houses, stables, yards and markets of a garrison city, all leading to the King's castle at its peak. The city perched on a rocky spire at the edge of foothills, which rose in steep undulations to the north towards a range of mountains. To the south and east were wide plains covered in grasslands and forest, and to the west the sea and the harbour town of Conisby Port.

The city's scarred battlements had withstood the ravages of many great battles, survived the passing of dynasties and witnessed great acts of heroism and sacrifice. Now Hork prepared for another battle. One that was greater than any fought in living memory, even greater, he suspected, than any fought in recorded history.

At last, King Malcor approached; a lean man of middle years with long greying sideburns.

Hork saluted. "Sire, you wish to speak with me?"

The King waved Hork towards a doorway with a balcony beyond it. "Come, tell me how your preparations are progressing."

Hork followed a pace behind, through the door and onto the balcony. It was bright and warm, but a fresh breeze tugged at his cloak.

The panoramic view took in most of the north, east and southern aspects. Hork motioned the King to the balustrade and pointed down to parties of woodsmen and engineers who were busily clearing the ground outside the city. Most of the timber was heading into the city, but there were also numerous bonfires, trailing dense streamers of woodsmoke.

"The work is almost done," he said.

The King was not a warrior, but had understood Hork's harsh tactical suggestions to clear the land. Tekt's army would find little of use in the way of cover or resources when they arrived

The King nodded. "Very well, Hork, and the nearby villages, the Port?"

"All cleared, Sire."

The King shook his head. "I do not relish this siege, are you sure it is our best course of action?"

"Their commander seems careless of his troops," said Hork. "Let them fall in waves against our walls. Once they see the futility of their venture, they will surely retreat."

"You are that confident of our defences?"

"The walls of this city have never been breached, Sire. I'd rather be in Conisby than any other place at this time."

"And if they don't attack, but choose to wait?"

Hork knew that their food supply was limited. It would mean terrible hardship, but carefully managed it could last several months. "If we can hold them here for the winter, it will give the many friends we have in other Kingdoms time to gather armies and, the gods willing, let them come to our rescue. At the very least we will preserve the lives of our remaining soldiers, and allow them time to rebuild their strength and spirit."

The King nodded, and then turned to Hork. "Why are they here?"

"Sire, I do not know. In truth I am just a simple soldier, I find it easier to judge my path if I put aside these questions."

The King gripped Hork's arm. "You say you are a simple soldier, but I value your counsel as much as I would the learned discussions of any of my advisors. I doubt that their fancy words can provide a solution to our problem. It may seem like a terrible responsibility, but we are all in your hands."

Hork's thoughts were for all the men and women who had already fallen, and for those that would surely still sacrifice themselves. He took a deep breath. "And, Sire, in the hands and hearts of thousands more like me."

Nitha sensed Whisper's disappointment; he growled in frustration as he swept his head backwards and forwards in front of a vertical wall of rock.

"What is it, Whisper," she said, "have you lost the trail?"

Whisper pressed his broad forehead against the rock, his foreclaws furrowing the snow and earth as he strained and pushed.

"Steady, Whisper. Settle." The prey had been lost, but a greater prize might have been found. Hardly able to contain her excitement, Nitha climbed from the saddle and slid across Whisper's broad back to the ground. She pressed her hands against the rock and concentrated, using her mind to feel beneath the surface.

Impatient, Whisper nudged at her shoulder with the edge of his nostril.

"Steady, Whisper. There's no mistaking it, this is a Trollid door. The very thing we were sent to find." Nitha stood back and stared up at the featureless rock face. "It's a tricky one, Whisper, built by those tricky Trollid. We'll need to find another way in, won't we now?"

Whisper snorted, sending a fine spray of sticky mucus onto the disturbed ground.

Nitha turned and patted Whisper's broad snout. "Here's a fine job for you, Whisper. Can you find another door?"

The dragon stretched back its head, letting out a long resonant roar that echoed in the surrounding mountains.

Disturbed by the noise, a flurry of loose snow trickled down the rock face and landed on Nitha's head. Laughing, she knocked the snow off, and then darted up one of Whisper's thick forelegs and onto his back. She clung to his neck, bathing in the glorious mixture of vibration and emotion radiating from him. She shouted through the continuing roars, "Come, Whisper, we must return to Lord Tekt with our news."

Ida watched in disgust as Moleskin helped himself to even more of the biscuits Bort had baked, and then settled to eat them at the dining table with a large mug of tea; with his health improving, it hadn't taken long for his true nature to emerge.

She now suspected that Torven had speeded his healing, and judging by the contempt Torven showed Moleskin, she doubted it was a humanitarian act; he had simply done what was necessary to allow Moleskin to be questioned. Still, were her thoughts not so prejudiced, taking ample nourishment is exactly what she would have recommended for his recovery.

Torven entered the cottage, carrying a handful of lanterns and with two canvas holdalls sitting crosswise over his shoulders. After unloading his burden he called for everyone to gather at the table where Moleskin sat. He gave Moleskin a barely disguised look of contempt before sitting, and Ida found it reassuring that they shared the same low opinion of the man.

Once all were gathered, Torven began, "I will help you with this conflict against the Harrowen, but before I can consider the situation in the world outside, we must first destroy the dragon. To that end it is I who must ask for your help."

"Of course," said Endor. "Just ask; we'll do whatever you ask."

Torven nodded. "Thank you. But first, you must all prepare yourselves to leave at a moment's notice. If we have to flee this dragon, we should only take what we can easily carry." His eyes lingered on Moleskin. "Take only the essentials. I know it is close to nightfall, but we have important work to do. Ladies, if you will wait here, on my return I will assign you tasks at the other end of the city. If the rest of you will come with me?"

Taking one of the bags and three lanterns, Torven left with Bort, Moleskin and Endor, and returned by himself about twenty minutes later. At a fast pace, he then led Ida and Lineth in the opposite direction.

Torven allowed his pace to slow a little as they passed through one particular district. "Ida, I think you will find this area of interest."

She had noticed a subtle change in the nearby architecture; most buildings were graceful and airy, with few built more than two levels high.

"Somehow," said Lineth, "it seems very restful."

Torven smiled. "Precisely that, my dear. Sick Trollid were brought here for treatment by the finest surgeons and healers. Their knowledge was impressive; they knew the medicinal properties of minerals, herbs and plant substances. They also had an excellent understanding of anatomy and surgical procedures. But their wisdom in healing stretched beyond that, they knew how to harness the natural energies that exist all around us."

"That kind of knowledge would be very useful," said Ida. "Has it been saved in the Trollid Library?"

"Oh yes," said Torven, "that and a great deal more. But remember, the Trollid only built the Library, and their achievements are only one tiny part of what is contained there."

"There must be so much of use," said Ida. "I'd love to see it."

"I'm sorry, it would be unwise for me to allow that."

Ida was stunned by this response. "Whyever not?"

A troubled expression came over Torven's face and he sighed. "My apologies, Ida. I merely intended to give you more of a sense of who the Trollid were, and yet I have exposed one of my greatest shames."

Ida exchanged a puzzled look with Lineth. "I don't understand."

"Few would," said Torven. Seeming close to tears, he stared around at the buildings. "I will try to explain. You have heard what Bort calls me; *The Friend of the Trollid*. Well, I was their friend, but in many ways I think I was their worst enemy."

"I can't imagine what you mean," said Ida.

Torven shook his head. "I was too much of a friend. The Trollid had a strong, vibrant culture, but they came to rely on me more and more for the answers to their problems. I was such a fool. It was flattering and it happened so slowly, I didn't understand it. You see, Ida, I took something away from them, something essential, I took away their sense of self-worth. I couldn't tell you exactly when it happened, but they lost the will to expand and take on new challenges. In short, they stagnated."

Ida had imagined Torven to be old, but he talked as if he had been present for the whole of the time the Trollid had lived in Garn.

"Just how old are you?" she said.

Torven's eyebrows went up, and he managed a weak lopsided grin. "My dear, I commissioned the building of the Library. I have been its custodian for all these years."

"Nobody can live that long," said Lineth.

"My kind age slower than yours, and I can prolong my life by resting, much as you found me in the tunnel."

Ida struggled to believe that the man standing before her had outlived generations of her ancestors. Like the magic, it was difficult to accept, but the proof seemed inescapable.

"So, how did it all end? Where did they all go?" she said

"The younger ones, and those who still had a bit of fire in them, left to make their way in the outside world. Those who remained grew smaller in number. Then one day, they were all gone."

"Except for Bort," said Ida.

"Yes, except for Bort. But he came along long after the city was empty. His parents, Latz and Jana, must have been one of the last pure Trollid couplings. Trollid often seek isolation and they must have been delighted to find the cave dwelling in that deserted village. I visited a few times and they welcomed me. Neither of them knew the history of their people, or their heritage. As Trollid, they should have seen the door in the cave, but I hid it from them. I left them alone mostly, but watched over them, and when they had Bort, well, I was delighted."

"It must have been very lonely," said Ida. "In this city, all by yourself."

"Yes, and I knew that one day Bort would be alone too, so I gave him a gift."

"The gold tablet?" said Lineth.

"Partly." Torven smiled. "But the real gift was the memory of who he truly was, buried deep, so that if one day he needed me, he could return."

"That explains a lot," said Lineth.

Ida smiled, remembering Bort's refusal to follow Lineth, and her most unladylike cursing. Lineth had reluctantly gone beyond the call of her duty to care for them, but in return had become part of something most extraordinary.

As if reading Ida's thoughts Lineth returned her smile and Ida couldn't help thinking how lucky they were to have her as a companion.

"When I think about it," she said. "I can see the physical aspects of the Trollid in many men and women I have met."

"Yes," said Torven, "but when I ponder what they had…"

Ida interrupted. "That's the reason you won't let me see the books?"

"Yes. I have had a long time to think about this, a very long time. Part of me is happy to share this knowledge, but there's another part that keeps saying it will only weaken you as a race. I doubt you'll understand."

"Like a child," said Ida. "Coddled and spoiled by its mother. It always clings to her skirt."

"How very apt," said Torven, bitterly. "How very apt indeed. I coddled the child so much it withered and died." Torven stared up at the empty windows of a nearby building. "It's all gone now," he said, quietly, "and soon there will be nothing left." He turned to Ida. "I'm sorry, I find this quite hard…"

"We'd better get on," said Ida, tactfully.

"Of course," said Torven.

The light was that of a late evening when they arrived at a small, ornate park, criss-crossed by paths and raised flowerbeds. The beds were bare, holding a layer of dry, dusty soil; without gardeners to tend and water them, nothing remained.

The base of one of the cavern's support columns stood in the very centre of the park, and was covered in a delicately-carved stone frieze, depicting rural scenes. Though immense in proportions close to the roof, at ground level the columns were slender by comparison. Were they all to hold hands, they could almost have linked arms around it.

Torven pointed. "All these panels have to come off. We need to uncover the crystal beneath."

"Crystal?" said Ida, intrigued.

As Torven inspected the panels for a suitable place to start the work, he explained the history of Garn and the purpose of the crystal.

The city was only ever intended as temporary quarters for the Trollid workers. First they built the city, and then they built the Library. With this intent to later demolish the city, its design had included blocks of immensely strong crystal at key points in the supporting columns. Sounding the right tone would cause the crystal to shatter, removing the support of the columns and allowing the cavern to collapse.

When Torven found his spot, he waved for Ida and Lineth to stand back and placed the tip of a large chisel into a crack between two panels. He hammered the chisel with a big blocky hammer and once the tip was well in, struck the chisel sideways to lever the panel free. After a few blows, the panel jumped out and crashed to the ground, breaking into several pieces. The exposed crystal was smooth and glassy.

"Strike here," he said, demonstrating the placing of the chisel between the exposed edge of the next panel and the face of the crystal. He handed the chisel to Ida and the hammer to Lineth. "Work together, quick as you can until all this has been removed."

"Won't we damage the crystal?" said Lineth.

"No. It's very tough. The only thing that will break it is the right tone." He pointed. "Once you've done this one, there's two more columns over that way. Please complete this as fast as you can."

"What if the dragon comes before we are ready?" said Ida.

Torven shook his head. "Just pray that it doesn't come to that."

The picture of the Trollid warrior being torn apart flashed into Ida's mind and she felt a terrible pain well up in her chest. It was a far from satisfactory answer.

"Torven," she said, "I know this may sound like a drastic measure, but if we destroyed the Library instead, surely that would make a difference? Maybe if there was no reason for the Harrowen to be here, then they would leave."

Torven's eyes opened wide with shock. "It's not quite as easy as that, Ida. Even without the Library the Harrowen would still seek conquest. Other than to record the achievements of many different races and civilisations, there is another reason for the Library's existence. I don't know quite how to explain it."

Lineth's voice was hard. "Considering part of the reason our world has been invaded is because you chose to build the Library here, I think you should try."

"Very well." Torven looked backwards and forwards between Lineth and Ida. "We wizards try not to involve ourselves in how races interpret the fundamental truths of how living things exist and interact, but a very long time ago we discovered that all things are connected. We cannot explain how this is, but we have learnt how to use these connections, and also learnt that the progress and development of all races occurs faster if the knowledge fundamental to that progress already exists somewhere. Does that make sense?"

Ida was confused by this logic. "But you said you won't share the knowledge in the Library."

"Not directly. But because it exists, and because all things share a collective connection, then the knowledge will emerge in some form or other. Some individuals are more receptive to this process than others. Often the seed for their ideas comes from the most ephemeral of places; a lucid dream, a sudden insight while watching the waves lap on a beach, even from observing shadows on a roughly plastered wall. Their skill, talent or genius comes in snatching these ideas from the ether, and nurturing them into reality. I promise you, without the Library, this would be a far slower process."

Ida struggled to follow what Torven was saying, and stared deep into his eyes, finding only conviction. She did not truly understand his explanation or his motives, but clearly he believed everything he said, and without him there might be no way to defeat the Harrowen.

She turned to Lineth. "We'd better get busy then."

"Thank you, Ida." Torven frowned. "I apologise, to both of you, I was maybe a little abrupt before; I have already taken measures to warn us of the dragon's approach, and my next task is to spread some false trails to confuse and delay it. But there are too many possible ways for it to reach us and it would take too long to visit every one and prevent their use. I cannot be absolutely sure, but I am confident we are not in immediate danger. Were that so we would not be standing here."

Ida nodded her thanks. "We'd better not delay you any further."

16

Draped across his throne inside the black tower, Lord Tekt stared out over a sea of twinkling campfires and torches. The audience chamber's flush wooden sides were pivoted up at present, serving as awnings over a balcony that ran around the whole of the tower. Were he to turn his head, he could view all the lands around him.

The sounds of revelry and song drifting up from the camp were reassuring, and he could not have been happier with their progress. Though losses were high, the next group of reinforcements and supplies would soon be arriving from Mirt.

Tekt heard laboured footsteps on the wooden stairs leading up to the chamber. Dusswen, most senior of all his wizards, paused at the top of the steps to bow deeply.

"My Lord?" he said.

Tekt waved him forward. "Come, Wizard Dusswen."

Dusswen leant heavily on his staff as he made his way across the polished wooden floor. Tekt could have commanded him to hurry, but the wizard had won his respect and admiration. His epic journey had finally freed the Harrowen, and his wise council had aided Tekt's rise to power. The laboured pace was an annoyance, but easily forgiven; previously in his prime, Dusswen's brave passage across the void had aged his body noticeably.

Dusswen stopped in front of Tekt and bowed again. "Death is life," he said.

"Life is death," Tekt responded. "What brings you here at this late hour?"

Dusswen pointed with his staff. "The dragon returns, my Lord."

Tekt's ears twitched, searching for the beat of the dragon's wings on the night air. Pulling himself from the throne, he walked eagerly to the balcony. Looking up, he scanned the cloudless sky, and then saw the glimmer of moonlight on the dragon's glossy skin as it started a long, graceful glide that brought it to the foot of the tower.

He smiled. "Excellent. Now we will see if your investigations have been fruitful."

After landing, the Shil rider, Nitha, settled and calmed her beast, making it lay full length on the ground. Its tail whipped idly from side to side, coming so close to a campfire, the soldiers sitting around it retreated to the opposite side. Tekt chuckled; even though the soldiers dwarfed this young dragonrider, none of them dared complain.

When Tekt heard Nitha's light footfall on the steps to the audience chamber he returned to his throne.

Nitha entered, her head erect but her eyes cast downward, and the pace of her walk just urgent enough to confirm her recognition of Tekt's power. The Shil were almost a breed apart, regarding themselves above most Harrowen, but answering the call to battle when required. She prostrated herself elegantly at the foot of the dais.

"Your most humble servant, Nitha, begs audience with Lord Tekt."

Tekt waited a second before answering. "Rise, Nitha. You have brought us good news I hope?"

"My Lord." Nitha stood, her eyes fixed on Tekt's feet. "I do bring good news."

Tekt was pleased, not just with the promise of good news, but with her conduct. Many of the Shil, though diminutive, were haughtily mannered and showed little respect for their leaders. "Speak it then."

"One of the marked ones led me into the mountains, and then disappeared..."

"What!" Tekt roared. He sprang to his feet, his hand resting on the hilt of the dagger at his waist. "Have you lost your wits? You call this good news?"

Nitha dropped to her knees. "A Trollid door, my Lord. The trail ended at a Trollid door!"

"Ah, I have been hasty." Tekt settled back in the throne, waving her to her feet again. "Tell me of this door?"

"I could not open it, my Lord, but there will be other doors," she added, quickly.

Tekt nodded slowly. "The young dragon, Whisper, has he the skills for this?"

"He does, my Lord."

"Good. And you, Nitha, what of the door? Was it beyond your art?"

"I knew its like, my Lord. Few could have entered that way. I will find another, I promise."

"Be careful of promises! Many have died by a promise they could not keep."

Tekt saw a tremor of fear run through the girl and knew he was being too harsh; she had done well, and likely a wizard would manage the door. He walked to a large map hanging on a vertical panel and spoke with a gentler tone, "Come, Nitha, show us where this door is to be found."

Nitha accepted a wooden pointer from Dusswen and then indicated a place at the edge of a mountain, well to the north of their position.

"My Lord," said Dusswen, "this is excellent news."

Tekt examined the map closely, the mountain range was extensive and the Trollid city could be hidden anywhere within it.

"Nitha," he said, "you will return and search for another entrance. I will send a party to meet you in the mountains. It will take three days for them to reach you. Either at the first door, or another, you will place a marker stone to guide them. You will wait for them there. Is that understood?"

Nitha bowed. "Yes, my Lord."

"If your promise holds true, you will have found an entrance by the time they arrive. Together you will enter the city and claim the Library in my name, and for the Emperor and the glory of all Harrowen."

"Yes, my Lord," said Nitha.

"You may go." Tekt waved his hand in dismissal.

Bowing constantly, Nitha walked backwards to the steps, and then scurried out of view.

Tekt returned to his throne. "So, Dusswen, if the old texts were right, the Trollid City of Garn is here."

Dusswen smiled. "Yes, my Lord, and somewhere nearby the Library of Banna."

"You hope much of this Library. Can it truly contain knowledge of such great value?"

Dusswen held himself erect. "By all accounts, the Library of Banna contains the massed knowledge of many races; lost magic, wondrous sciences and war machines of incredible destructive power. With them the Harrowen will be great again."

"And what of these tales of a guardian?"

"Only one reference was found, Torven, an ancient wizard. If he still lives he will be as nothing."

"And your champion, Wizard Amrax, is he ready?"

Dusswen inclined his head. "He is, my Lord. If Torven still lives, age will have diminished his powers. Truly, Amrax will best him easily."

Tekt laughed. "And sweet Tukkle and his merry sewer rats will deal with any other resistance. It will be a pretty conquest."

"It will, my Lord."

Tekt strode to the balcony and looked out. Dawn light gathered on the horizon, and below, Nitha was coaxing the dragon into the air. He watched her fly into the distance and inhaled deeply. He was in the midst of history. What would the historians call it; *The Time of Rebirth? The Awakening?* No doubt they would find a suitably epic description to match his deeds.

He thumped his fist on the balcony. "Yes, Dusswen, this is a fine world. A fitting place for the Harrowen to rebuild their Empire." He paused, his clawed hands curling around the timber railing. "We wasted long months at the first gate, Dusswen. Conquest cannot be achieved with those restrictions. Once we have the Master Gate at Conisby, this whole world will be ours."

Dusswen sank to his knee. "Lord Tekt, with your leadership it will be a great conquest. It is you who will obliterate the shame of past mistakes. It is you who will make the Empire of the Harrowen feared and mighty once more!"

Tekt stared out over the camp and nodded. Humankind's day was almost done, an older and fiercer breed, his own, would soon be masters of this world.

17

Bort sat patiently on a bench at the front of Torven's cottage. The city cavern was brightening, matching a clear daybreak in the world outside the mountain, and the decorative claddings on the highest towers and spires were already sending shafts of rainbow light across the cavern's roof.

Like the others, he had spent much of the evening and early night time hours preparing the columns, returning just after midnight for a late supper and a welcome bed. Reassured that Torven was taking measures to delay the dragon, he was able to sleep away the remainder of the night.

When Torven came up the steps from his workshop; he looked tired, with grey shadows beneath his eyes, but his manner seemed bright enough.

"Ah good, you're ready. Come, Bort, it's time."

Bort stood and lifted a heavy canvas tool bag as if it were a feather pillow.

"We work on the bell tower next," said Torven.

"The bell tower," Bort echoed.

Torven led off and Bort followed.

Their destination was a tower at the very centre of the cavern. From far enough back it was possible to see a huge bell sitting in an airy cloistered chamber just below the vaulted roof. Its pealing would shatter the crystal in the support columns, but first the bell's striking mechanism had to be unlocked.

As they approached the tower Bort looked up, it was thicker than most of the support columns, and uniformly round, though the perspective made it appear to taper. Other than at the top, it had no windows or openings of any kind.

"There is a spiral staircase inside," said Torven. He stopped in front of a section of wall. "The entrance is here, can you see it?"

Bort peered at the gently curving wall of interlocked stone, it all looked the same. He shook his head. "I don't see it."

Torven placed a hand on his shoulder. "Let your mind start to see with true Trollid eyes, Bort." He pointed to a particular stone block. "Here is the key. Can you see how this stone is subtly different?"

As Bort stared he began to notice a difference in the stone. There was also a faintly annoying pain developing at the back of his eyes. When Torven removed his hand from Bort's shoulder the pain vanished.

"Little by little," said Torven, with a smile. He pressed his hand against the stone and a door swung outwards, the sides of the door following the stepped lines of the mortar joins between the blockwork. It revealed the foot of a spiral staircase. Torven waved for Bort to follow and started up the steps.

Bort hesitated. Torven had done something to him. Not something bad, but something quite extraordinary. He moved his hand from block to block, sensing that every stone was different, not because it was a different shape, but because the material within the block was different. He also saw that every block was positioned within the wall to make best use of its inner strengths.

Torven called back, "Little by little, Bort. Don't try too hard."

After about a minute of climbing, Bort turned a corner to find Torven resting on a step.

"I'm sorry, I'll need to stop here a moment," he said.

Bort sat on a lower step.

Torven wiped sweat from his forehead. "I haven't had this much exercise for a long time."

Bort smiled, but said nothing.

"You're keeping very quiet," said Torven. "I know there's something bothering you, what is it?"

Bort shrugged. Torven was exactly as he remembered him, but Bort had always talked to him as a child to an adult, it was hard to find the words he needed to say.

Torven smiled. "Speak up. You can say what you want to me."

Bort's brow furrowed. "This is the last Trollid city," he said, quietly.

Torven sighed. "I should have brought you here sooner. It must seem terribly cruel to finally see it, only to have it snatched away like this, but for all its wonder, this is only a place where people lived. It's not a place but the people that make a home or a community; Silvermeadow is your home now, among fine people like Ida and Endor."

Bort understood this, but he still wished he had known and been a part of his own people. Though he had no relish for fighting, his ancestors were very different. He looked up; Torven wore a kindly and sympathetic expression.

"My people, the Trollid, they were strong, fierce warriors, and very brave."

Torven clucked. "Yes, yes, the strong, brave, fierce ones were! But not all Trollid were like that. Many, many more were just like you, Bort. And many of those brave, fierce warriors started off just like you, but changed to defend themselves and their families. If you choose to be brave and fierce, do it for those reason, not because you feel you have some Trollid traditions to uphold."

Delivered with such passion, Bort took great comfort from Torven's words.

Torven smiled. "That's better; and know this, Bort, I see a true Trollid sitting before me. One who carries all the strength, wisdom and compassion of his race. Never doubt that for a second." Torven reached down and gripped Bort's shoulder. "Now, we've a job to do, best we get on with it."

Bort felt much better, and did feel himself part of something bigger; maybe the last, but the last of something very noble and worthy.

As Lineth swept her sword down, Endor heard a telltale hiss of breath through her teeth. Instinctively, his sword came up, deflecting hers, and again he swung it quickly around to rest against her unprotected flank.

"Damn it!" she growled. She shook her head. "I feel like an idiot."

"A very lethal one, if I may say so," said Endor. "You just need a few more pointers and you'll match the best of them."

"I'm not so sure," said Lineth.

Having completed all the tasks asked of them, Endor and Lineth had thought it wise to practice and hone their skills. Staying close to their base, they were on the street outside Torven's cottage. Ida was busy indoors preparing lunch.

Endor withdrew his sword and rested the flat of the blade on his shoulder. "You're a product of standardised training. Don't get me wrong, you've been trained well, but you lack finesse."

Lineth shook her head. "I'm not sure what you mean."

"Here," Endor raised his sword above his head, "first you've got to know the weapon, know its weight and how fast you can make it change direction. But know it without the need to think about it." He stepped back and began a series of twisting exercises, which had his blade weaving and flickering in circles and figures of eight, narrowly missing his body as it swept by him. "See, and all the time I'm teaching my body how to keep the blade's energy whenever possible." He brought the sword to a halt above his head.

"Show me that again," she said, "but slowly to start with."

After a few minutes practise Endor said, "Now try again."

Endor was pleasantly surprised when Lineth began her attack. She was a very quick study. There was more fluidity and economy to her motion, and she soon had him under greater pressure.

"Ho, ho," he gasped. "That's better, much better."

She pressed forward against his defence until a sudden discordant metallic ringing stopped the contest. Endor halted his sword uncomfortably close to Lineth's neck. Her sword, which should have blocked the sweep, was useless, snapped through just below the grip.

"Damn!" she cursed again.

"Bad luck that," said Endor. "Blade must have had a weakness."

"You're hurt!"

"Now that you mention it," Endor examined a cut on his forearm, "I've got a scratch here needs a bit of patching."

"I'm sorry," said Lineth.

"Nonsense! Not your fault at all."

"I'll get a bandage, you wait here."

Endor sat on a bench while Lineth went inside. She returned a few seconds later, announcing, "Ida's bringing her bag, she'll be out presently."

Lineth joined Endor on the bench while they waited. It was one of those inevitable moments when seasoned soldiers discussed their old wounds and compared scars, a contest Endor was easily beating her in. Though there was no hiding how young and beautiful she was, he found it easy to look past that, treat her as he would any other comrade, and it was good to make this connection.

When Ida emerged from the cottage, she found Endor and Lineth resting on the garden bench sharing a joke. Lineth immediately stood to allow her to sit next to Endor, and took charge of the bowl of warm water Ida had brought from the kitchen.

Ida examine Endor's wound. "Not quite a scratch," she said, "it'll need a few stitches."

Endor shrugged. "Can't be helped sometimes."

Ida cleaned the wound and then applied a salve to slow the bleeding and numb the skin, all the time uncomfortably aware of the warmth and energy pouring from Endor. Hot from his exercise, he seemed more alive and vital than she ever remembered him being in Silvermeadow, and it took some effort to focus on her task.

Torven arrived just as she was threading a needle.

"Is that another scar for your collection, Endor?" he said, leaning close to examine the wound.

"I'm afraid so," said Endor, "blade of Lineth's sword broke off and caught me on the way by."

Torven peered more closely. "Doesn't look that bad, I'm sure Ida's got everything under control."

"Where's Bort," said Ida, noting his absence.

"Oh, quite safe, Ida. He went to have another look at the Trollid history."

Ida nodded gently. Of course; he'd want to know more about his people, and what better way than by examining the pictorial history.

Torven held out his hand to Lineth. "May I see your sword?"

She gave him the two pieces. "I don't think it can be repaired."

Torven fitted the parts together, and then separated them to examine the broken ends. "Nothing wrong with the metal." He smiled. "But it's about what I'd expect against an Agnemite blade. You'll be needing a replacement?"

"Yes," said Lineth.

"Well," he said, with a twinkle in his eye, "I might have something in my workshop that would do."

Ida saw Lineth's excitement, and felt uncomfortable that this emotion was for a weapon designed to kill and maim. But putting that aside, she hoped Torven would gift her a blade similar to Endor's. They left and Ida brought her attention back to his wound.

She concentrated; using neat, precise stitching to draw the skin shut.

"I doubt any King's surgeon could manage it better," said Endor, softly.

Ida didn't know how to respond; the growing closeness she felt for him was troubling, but in the midst of such uncertainty it seemed foolish to acknowledge or pursue her feelings. She should really make conversation, thank him for his compliment, but instead she kept quiet

Lineth and Torven returned just as she was applying the bandage.

Lineth drew and displayed her new sword; obviously delighted with the narrow, gently curving blade.

"Looks like a fine replacement," said Endor.

Ida tied off the bandage and Endor thanked her. She scowled and busied herself tidying away her healer's bag, probably leaving Endor struggling to think what he had done recently to annoy her. It was maybe unfair, but she was too weary to pursue an explanation.

Lineth provided a distraction, passing the new blade to Endor for him to look it over.

"This has the looks of an Agnemite weapon?" he said.

"It is," said Torven, "and a blade worthy of its recipient. Don't you think, Endor?"

"Without doubt! I'll have to be careful, or Ida here will be patching me up for the rest of the day."

Not wanting to spoil the mood, Ida smiled indulgently.

Torven cleared his throat. "There's another matter I've had some thoughts on. Now that we've prepared the cavern, it's time we concentrated on a plan to help you defeat the Harrowen."

Ida was immediately alert; finally Endor's patience and effort would be rewarded.

"If you'll come with me," said Torven, "we can take another quick look at the Trollid history."

"Excellent," said Endor.

"Now," said Torven, "where has that fellow Moleskin got to?"

"He's inside sleeping," said Ida.

"Rouse him up then. He'll be able to confirm something for me."

Torven led them back to the history building, collecting Bort on their way to a new corridor of wall paintings. Torven stopped at one particular scene and waved Moleskin forward.

"I'd like you to have a look at this."

"That's exactly what I saw!" said Moleskin. "Yes, they were in pairs, carrying something between them."

"It is as I thought," said Torven. "These are Harrowen wizards."

"Wizards," said Ida, doubtfully.

"Yes, Wizards. Ones capable of performing magics of the foulest sort."

Ida sighed; she was still struggling to accept the reality of magic.

Torven noted her mood. "Magic is a thing of the mind, Ida, it draws on the most fundamental energies of the world; some so subtle they are invisible. Wizards are merely trained practitioners in the art of concentrating and manipulating these energies."

Ida wished for the simpler world she knew before the battle at Sollas, before Bort's Trollid revelation, before meeting Torven, but she knew it was long gone. It served little purpose to fight what was now obvious and almost commonplace.

"What are these Harrowen wizards doing?" she said.

Torven marched along the corridor. "I'll show you."

He stopped at a scene showing the wizards unloading their burdens. The looked like simple stone blocks. In the next image the wizards were building the blocks into a curving structure, but without any formers or scaffold, which looked precarious. Further along the corridor, the structure was complete, an archway.

Torven pointed to the picture. "This is a World Gate. This is how the Harrowen have come here."

"A simple stone arch?" said Endor.

"No ordinary stones," said Torven, "each one is permeated with magical energy, and each stone multiplies the power of the previous one. The Gate links this world and theirs. Without a Gate they will be unable to bring reinforcements. And yes," he said, pre-empting Endor's next question, "those that remain can be defeated by strength of arms."

"If we knocked it down, would that do it?" said Endor.

Ida smiled; he did always look for the simplest solution.

Torven nodded. "That would work, but only if the stones were then dispersed or destroyed, and no one could put the arch back together again. They will have brought extra stones, but remove or destroy enough of them and the Gate will not function."

"Where is it then?" demanded Endor.

"I've been thinking about that," said Torven. "The Gate must be erected on foundation stones. Come, it's best if I show you what I mean."

Torven took them to what looked to be the oldest building in the Trollid city; its ponderous and timeworn architecture holding an air of brooding darkness about it, and Ida immediately felt the charged air within the building.

Torven stopped in the centre of the hall. "This was once the site of a World Gate." To either side of him stood two stone plinths, smooth topped and with a gap between them large enough to fit four wagons side by side. He swept an arm over his head. "It was dismantled and the arch stones scattered and hidden." He pointed to one of the plinths. "Again, it's best if you experience this for yourself. Touch the stone. Its effects will surprise you, but do not worry they are only fleeting."

Endor and Lineth went first, Endor snatching his hand back and shaking it. "Damn, it's hot."

"No," said Lineth, cradling her hand against her chest, "it was cold, like gripping ice."

"Nonsense!" Endor touched it again. "It's hot!"

Hesitantly Ida tried, giving a yelp of surprise and pulling her hand away quickly.

"Well?" Torven said.

"It felt hot, but it also felt as if my fingers were sticking to it."

Bort touched the stone momentarily and then rubbed his forehead. "Sore, like a cut, and it gave me a headache."

"Ah," said Torven. "Then I'd advise against repeating the test."

Moleskin screamed, leapt away from the stone and then danced around shaking his hands furiously. "My fingers," he howled, "they've gone to sleep. I can't feel a thing."

"Ah yes," Torven nodded and grinned, "an excellent demonstration of how the magic in the stone responds to a person's inner nature."

"Well," said Ida, mischievously, "dishonesty has its own special rewards."

"Madam, I take offence to that remark." Still nursing his hand, Moleskin turned his back on her and strode away to sit in the shadows at the foot of a thick column.

Ida felt a little remorse, after all Moleskin had worked as hard as any of them to prepare the Trollid city for collapse, but it was not enough to make her apologise.

"Could this be used again?" said Lineth.

Torven nodded. "In theory, yes. Were the Harrowen wizards to bring their arch stones here it would work. But there are other sites scattered here and there on this world. The most important of these is the Master Gate at Conisby. It was never destroyed; instead it was hidden by stone and strong magic. If the Harrowen replace the arch stones with theirs, they can use it again. After that nothing will stop them."

"What is so important about a Master Gate?" said Ida.

"The other Gates can only function at certain times, sometimes less than once a day and only for a short period, minutes in fact. But a Master Gate can be used more often and for longer. If they can use the Conisby Gate, the Harrowen will be free to come and go very much as they please."

"And their dragons?" Endor asked, in a worried tone.

"Interestingly, bringing a dragon across is no easy task. It needs the presence of many wizards on both sides of the Gate. The effort leaves the wizards drained and vulnerable for many days. Without a Master Gate, the chances of success are very low; this dragon and its rider are very likely the only survivors of many attempts."

Endor rubbed his chin. "I don't know if that's any comfort."

"Deny the Harrowen the use of their Gate," said Torven, firmly, "and you will have no fear of dragons."

"Very well," said Endor, "but where is the Gate they are using now?"

"The Harrowen came from the east, so most likely they used the Loden Castle Gate at first. From Moleskin's observations, it is clear that they have abandoned that foundation and brought their stones forward."

"Lines of supply," said Lineth. "I've heard of Loden Castle, it's right on the eastern edge of Carolin. It's now too far away to be practical. Where is the site of the Gate they are using now?"

"I will need to confirm it, but there is only one place I can think of, an old city called Domidia. It lies quite close to us, to the east of this mountain. It has been abandoned for many years."

"Is there a map we can look at?" said Endor.

"Yes, but I will need to fetch it from the Library." Torven turned and looked around. "Now where has that fellow Moleskin wandered off to?"

Moleskin had quickly lost interest in the discussion. With his larcenous instincts strangely heightened by the contact with the foundation stone, he was too easily tempted when a twinkling light beckoned from the far end of a cloistered walkway.

He came to a tall door and grinned when he found that the eyes of a grotesque bronze face set into the door's ancient timbers were crafted from glistening gemstones. They were rubies, each the size of a chicken's egg. Cautiously he touched one of them, almost expecting the same unpleasant shock as before, but it felt cool.

After a furtive glance over his shoulder, he produced a short dagger and began working the stone loose. The aged bronze disintegrated rapidly under his determined attack and a short time later the first ruby dropped into his hand.

He felt its weight and inspected its surface, it was a perfect specimen. Working quickly, he soon had the second stone free.

The stones were no sooner hidden than his name was called. Smiling secretively, he rejoined the group.

It hadn't taken him long to recover his wits and orientate himself to this new situation. His instincts for self-preservation and personal gain had quickly attuned to the many possibilities the city offered. This most recent find was a welcome addition to his steadily-growing horde of treasure.

18

Nitha's natural talents for reading the landscape, combined with Whisper's heightened senses, had brought them to a sheer face of smooth grey rock. Fresh snow lay about the ground, and a chill, gusty wind snatched at her ponytail.

The last rays of the dying sun barely warmed her back as she pressed her hands against the rock, but she was beyond caring about physical discomfort, they had found another door.

"Well done, Whisper, well done."

He bobbed his head and made small growling noises of pleasure.

"It's a fine Trollid door, Whisper," she said, caressing the rock. "And I have the feel for this one."

Her brow furrowed as she concentrated; her mind adapting to the structure of the rock and delving inwards, searching for the mechanism to release the door. She sensed the latching device and gradually realigned the energies gathered around it. With a nudge, it shifted. The rock door shuddered and swung open to reveal a large, dark corridor leading into the mountain.

Fatigued by her effort, she staggered back, falling onto Whisper's broad snout. Immediately his intense desire to continue the quest overwhelmed her senses, and she began to walk forward. Losing the connection, reason returned quickly; her instructions were to wait for Wizard Amrax and Tukkle to arrive.

Whisper nuzzled into the back of her head, and again the strong desire to go forward swept over her. The sun was almost gone behind the nearby mountaintops, and the shadows around her were turning to the deepest blue. Amrax and Tukkle were still two days away, and with storm clouds gathering, the poorer weather would surely delay them further.

She felt an indignant surge of anger; the task was hers, as was the glory. She was Nitha Corrt of Family Tulst and the Clan Barok; dragonrider and worthiest of the Harrowen. Why should she share this honour with the common ground-dwelling Harrowen?

From inside her tunic she produced the two halves of a marker crystal, allowing them to snap together to form an almost perfect sphere that immediately began to warm her hand and pulse with magical energy. She placed it on the ground and pressed it into the snow with her heel. Clapping Whisper's jaw firmly, she stepped aside to clear the way for him.

"Come, Whisper," she said, "find us the way."

In answer, a fierce burst of pleasure flowed from the dragon. Without hesitation, the great beast pressed forward, the passage barely wide enough for his bulk.

Torven had gone to collect a map and Endor waited impatiently for his return. He sat on the bench outside the cottage; the light just starting to fade to its nighttime level, and the air warm, like a balmy summer's evening.

Lineth joined Endor, presenting a mug of tea before sitting alongside him.

"Easy to forget we're inside the mountain," she said, sipping from her own mug.

"It is. Funny how quickly you get used to it. No hot sun, damp mists, or chill breezes."

"Or biting gales," said Lineth, "it's snowing hard outside."

"Back in Silvermeadow we'd have the shutters closed, and the curtains drawn by now."

"Just the same in Conisby, but I might have had the night watch. You'll not be missing those?"

"No, that's a duty for you youngsters." Endor smiled and flexed his arms. "Mind you, I've not felt this good for many years. Rattling about in my manor house, I was turning into an old man before my time."

Lineth smiled. "Mother always talked about you and Otric."

"Oh, yes," said Endor, cautiously.

"She said you were two of the finest she'd ever trained."

"Maybe true once, but the years have caught up with me, I'm afraid to say."

"I hadn't noticed."

"You're very kind."

"Otric..." Lineth began.

"Yes?"

"He's not my father."

Endor paused, experiencing panic and unsure how to respond.

Lineth's eyes sparkled with humour. "Mother told me all about her and Otric, but she chose someone else, a gentler man. She hoped I wouldn't follow in her footsteps."

"A worthy goal," said Endor, relieved that she couldn't be talking about him. "Did you know him, your father?"

"No, but that was mother's way. She said he was a scholar visiting from another kingdom." Lineth laughed gently. "Mother led him astray."

Now certain that Lineth was not his daughter, Endor was finally able to relax. It was a small change, but strangely Endor couldn't help thinking that had she been his daughter he would have been very proud of her achievements.

"Some of those scholarly ways must have rubbed off," he said.

"I suppose so. I've a head for figures and the sciences, but soldiering was always what I wanted to do. Mother was never keen."

"Soldiering's a fine life, but it's not for everyone."

"When I was small she left me with a nanny, but I always snuck away and went down to the barracks to watch her. She was my hero, all dressed up in her uniform and ordering everyone around. When I was big enough, I practised with her sword. Eventually she gave in, but she made me study, so I'd join as an officer."

Further up the street, a figure appeared. It was Torven, but he was running at a fast trot.

Seeing them, he shouted, "Quickly, gather the others, we need to go now!"

Fighting exhaustion, Ida had gone to her room to doze on top of her bed; she was woken by Lineth, her face grim.

"The dragon?" said Ida.

"Yes, we must leave now."

Ida gathered up her pack and joined with the others at the front door of the cottage. The cavern was still light, but it was dimming fast.

Torven quickly decided on a single file order; placing Ida behind him, then Moleskin, Bort and Lineth, with Endor at the rear.

"Come, we must hurry. Stay close to the walls and be as quiet as you can," he said, then led off at a brisk pace.

They had gone no more than fifty paces when they heard a distant echoing roar. Moleskin pushed past Ida in panic, stumbling into Torven.

"Take care," Torven whispered, angrily. "You will bring it to us. Now get back in line!"

Ida fought the urge to chastise Moleskin further; harsh words would just as likely attract the dragon.

After less than a minute's walk along the shadowy edge of a broader street, Torven turned sharply down an alley between two buildings, stopping at the mouth of a black tunnel. He gave one end of a rope to Bort and positioned the others at short intervals along it. Groping inside his robes he pulled out a rolled up map and thrust it into Endor's hand.

"Listen carefully," he said. "The Gate the Harrowen are using is definitely at Domidia. I've marked it on the map."

Ida felt an immediate tremor of fear; did Torven doubt he would survive his next task? Of course, if there was the smallest chance he wouldn't, it made sense to share what he knew. She hoped this was prudence rather than desperation

"You said these gates had limitations, how often can this one be used?" said Ida.

"Very good point," said Torven. "Once every twenty hours, and maybe for two minutes, though it is not an exact process."

"It's bound to be well defended," said Lineth.

"We can discuss that later," said Torven, "but I'm sure there are ways to overcome the problem of numbers. A significant advantage is that proximity to the Gate and even the individual Gate stones confuse a wizard's senses. The Harrowen will not detect our approach."

The dragon roared again, and Ida looked back along the length of the city chamber. In the weak light she saw a flicker of movement above the buildings; the dragon was aloft at the far end of the cavern, arcing gracefully backwards and forwards. The size of the animal put her in awe, and she judged the length of its head alone was greater than Bort's height. The rider was just visible, a small black-clad figure tucked tight against the dragon's back.

"Incredible," Lineth whispered.

"Surely, that's a fearsome looking beast," Endor said, softly.

Ida hoped that both of them knew the futility of fighting this creature, she could easily imagine how uneven a contest it would be.

Torven cleared his throat gently to get their attention, whispering, "We really do need to move on. Now, don't bunch, and don't pull on the rope. Keep a good hold of it though; you'll get lost if you let go." He waved to Bort. "On you go, straight over to the exit on the other side. Follow the tunnel to the chasm, and then the path to the gate. Don't wait for me."

With a nod to the group, Torven strode back along the alley, quickly turning the corner.

Bort headed into the tunnel and Ida let the rope draw her forwards. After about twenty paces, the feeble light from behind faded and she was surrounded by blackness. She could still hear Bort's steady footsteps ahead, and the footsteps of the others behind her, but she sensed there was nothing close by, and judged they were negotiating a huge, empty chamber.

After about four hundred paces, she heard a slight echo from nearby walls, and then another twenty paces on she flinched when a large hand pressed on her shoulder.

"Almost there," whispered Bort.

Ida allowed herself to be led again; meandering backwards and forwards through a large winding tunnel, and with a sulphurous smell growing stronger with each footstep. Eventually Bort stopped and lit a lantern, handing it to Ida. As the others shuffled closer, he busied himself lighting more lanterns and handing them around.

Beneath Ida's feet was a neat cobble-paved road, which continued on from the tunnel mouth for about five or six paces before stopping abruptly. To either side were iron railings; the section of road and the railings were the partial remains of a bridge that was long gone. Ida crept to the lip of the road and peered down. It was a deep chasm with a thin line of glowing red lava at its base.

She held up her lantern and stared into the gloom. The opposite rock face was about fifty paces away and the blocky stone corbels and matching ironwork remains of the same bridge projected from its face, though the tunnel opposite was sealed with brick. Above, the vertical walls stretched up into blackness.

Ida remembered Torven's mention of a bridge, but this couldn't be it, and she hoped Bort had taken the right path.

"Where do we go now?" she said.

Bort had just finished coiling the rope; he walked to one of the side railings and swung open a gate. Turning to face her, he stepped through it and climbed down a ladder. Ida shuffled forward; he now stood on a path that ran under the bridge. She hadn't noticed it before, and felt a little foolish. It was about the width of his shoulders and angled down to their left, along the face of the chasm. It was an adequate path, if one ignored the chasm's depth, and the occasional yellow flare of hot gasses bursting from the surface of the lava.

"You can't be serious," said Moleskin, in a panicky voice. "We'll fall to our deaths."

"The rock is good." Bort jumped up and down. "Very safe."

"I won't do it," Moleskin protested.

"Bort will carry Moleskin." He climbed back up the ladder and stretched his arms towards Moleskin.

"No! No! Stay away!" Moleskin backed off until he came up against the tunnel wall, sliding down it until he was a crumpled heap on the ground.

Ida knew of a quick cure for hysteria, but hesitated, wondering how Moleskin would react to a good, hard slap.

Endor beat her to it, gripping Moleskin's lapels and dragging him to his feet. "Pull yourself together, man! You're making a fool of yourself. Come on now, it's perfectly safe."

Just then the tunnel echoed with the ominous pealing of a huge bell. It rang on and on, until a deep rumble obscured the noise. The ground shook and a few seconds later a rush of dusty air blew down the tunnel.

"He's done it," said Lineth. "He's collapsed the cavern."

They heard footsteps approaching and Torven appeared.

"Why are you still here?" he said, anxiously.

"Moleskin was worried about falling off the path," said Endor, "but he's fine now. Aren't you Moleskin?"

Before Moleskin could answer, a distant deep roar echoed down the tunnel.

"Damnation," Torven snapped, "the dragon is still alive. Quickly, you must move on!" He turned to Moleskin and clapped his hands together, illuminating Moleskin's face with a flash of blue light. Moleskin blinked a few times and rocked unsteadily.

"What have you done to him?" said Ida.

"Nothing much," said Torven.

"Nothing much," Moleskin repeated, in a flat tone.

"The path is safe, and I am not afraid of falling," said Torven.

"The path is safe, and I am not afraid of falling," repeated Moleskin.

"Bort will lead the way and I will follow," said Torven.

"Bort will lead the way and I will follow," said Moleskin.

Torven lifted the top flap of the large knapsack Moleskin carried, looked inside and snorted in disgust. "I won't need my pack," he said.

"I won't need my pack," said Moleskin.

"Best if I throw it away," said Torven.

"Best if I throw it away," said Moleskin.

Moleskin unshouldered his pack, stepped up to the end of the bridge and threw it into the darkness. As it tumbled out of sight, a cluster of shiny objects spilled from it.

"That's better." Torven ignored Moleskin's echo response and turned to Bort. "Quickly, Bort, take everyone to the other side of the bridge. I'll try to delay the dragon here."

Bort turned and led off down the ladder. Without a moment's hesitation, Moleskin rattled down the rungs and strode confidently after him. Ida went next, and Lineth and Endor brought up the rear.

Fearful of tripping, Ida kept her lantern held low and avoided looking into the dizzying depths of the chasm. It was nightmarish, but the thought of being caught by the dragon urged her on.

"Here is the bridge," said Bort, finally.

Ida paused, steadied herself and looked up. The bridge was a single slab of natural rock, leading to a dark tunnel mouth on the opposite side of the chasm. At the start of the tunnel was a metal gate. Though it had no handrail, the bridge was a lot wider than the path.

With her heart beating furiously, she kept her eyes fixed on Moleskin's heels and followed him over the bridge. She was almost across when a series of lightning-like flashes lit the rock around her. She stopped and turned to stare back along the chasm.

The dragon lay in the tunnel mouth, stretching around the end of the bridge and trying to reach down to Torven with one of its clawed forelegs. Torven stood on the path, just beyond its reach and with his arms outstretched; an intense jagged flame coursing from his hands and curling around the dragon's glistening hide.

The creature writhed and twisted, trying to shake off the flame, but finding no relief it retreated into the tunnel.

Torven immediately turned and ran along the path. Seeing them still on the bridge, he waved his arms frantically, signalling them to move on.

There was a blur of motion in the tunnel mouth, and a shower of loosened cobbles tumbled free as the dragon arced into the air.

Torven stopped and turned, raising his arms to send another fiery blast towards the riderless dragon as it swept by.

"Quickly, now!" Endor herded the group off the bridge. "Nothing we can do here."

From inside the tunnel mouth Ida watched the battle continue, the dragon sweeping backwards and forwards, constantly attempting to snatch at Torven as it passed. But the narrowness of the path acted in Torven's favour, and the creature's wings brushed the crevasse wall if it came too close.

When Torven reached the far end of the bridge he called over, "Bort, make ready the gate."

Bort positioned himself by the gate, ready to swing it shut.

Torven edged his way across the bridge, the dragon swooping and diving above him. He was close to the centre when he stumbled and the dragon swept by, a stretched claw just missing his back.

"Come on, man," Endor shouted, "get up!"

Ida's heart leapt when Endor drew his sword and began to move forward.

Torven lifted his head. "Stay!" he commanded.

Endor stopped as if he had run into a wall, and then staggered back towards the tunnel.

Throwing up a cloud of dust with its fast, rhythmic wing beats, the dragon landed at the opposite end of the bridge. It seemed little injured from the collapse of the city roof, with only a few scratches on its glistening hide. It hesitated, its long neck sweeping from side to side, its huge yellow eyes fixed and staring. Stretching out a forepaw, it gingerly tested its weight on the bridge before slowly advancing.

Torven staggered to his feet and turned to face it, his hands hanging loose by his side. He twisted his head a little, but kept his eyes on the dragon. "Close the gate, Bort."

"No!" Ida protested.

Bort drew Endor back into the tunnel mouth and threw the gate over, making a loud resonant clang.

With a triumphant growl, the dragon stalked forward.

"Fight, man, fight!" Endor pleaded.

As the dragon drew closer, Torven's head tipped back until he was staring almost straight up, the creature's massive jaws towering above him. Then Torven drew himself erect and stretched his arms out to either side; a red ball of fire forming in the air above each open hand.

"Just the same as the gold tablet," Lineth whispered.

Ida pressed herself against the bars, horrified by the unfolding scene, and for a moment the only sound was the dragon's coarse, rasping breath.

Torven spoke, as if directly to the beast, but his calm words weren't for it. "You'll find a key by the door. Bort knows how to use it."

Ida's hands gripped tight on the gate's bars and she held her breath in anticipation, hoping Torven had some way to defeat the creature without sacrificing himself.

The creature spread its wings wide and opened its jaws, revealing rows of huge pointed teeth. Then it plunged its head down.

The cavern erupted in a blinding flare of light and an immense blast tumbled Ida backwards along the tunnel. Crawling back to the gate she pulled herself upright. Blinking through the bright blotches lingering in front of her eyes, she peered out; the bridge was gone, and with it Torven and the dragon.

Bort joined her; large, wet tears flowing down his face, his thick fingers gripping the gate.

"Torven is gone," he sobbed.

"No, I'm not," Torven's weak voice answered.

Ida looked down; Torven clung to a lip of stone just beneath the gate.

Endor eased Ida aside. "Damn it, man, well done!"

Bort quickly unlatched the gate and stretched down, hoisting Torven into the tunnel. His clothing was scorched and torn, and his hair singed and smoking. After dusting himself down, he pulled the gate over, closing it firmly, and then turned to the group.

"You had us all fooled," said Endor.

"Always good to have some sort of backup plan," said Torven. "I wasn't quite sure how it would work, but I had to convince the beast I was on my last legs."

There was a sudden scraping at the gate, and a long set of claws snapped through the bars and wrapped around Torven's waist. With a scream of pain he slammed backwards against the bars.

Ida staggered back in horror, and was quickly pushed aside by Endor, who swung up his sword and began hacking at the claws, but they seemed almost impervious to his blows. Lineth joined Endor, but with little effect.

The dragon's wings were gone, with only thin tatters of skin clinging to a skeleton of bleeding bone, but the remainder of its torso and limbs seemed undamaged. It gnawed at the gate, its huge teeth trying to close on Torven's head; the only thing protecting the wizard was the thick metal of the bars. Then, with a sudden discordant creak, the gate buckled, straining against its fixings.

Coughing a spray of blood, Torven called out, "The eyes! The eyes!"

Endor gripped his sword overhand and leapt against the bars, stabbing at the dragon and searching for its eyes.

The top hinge groaned, and Ida shouted an anguished warning as it tore free and the gate tipped away from the tunnel mouth, carrying

Endor with it. He quickly steadied himself and knelt alongside Torven, his attention focused on the dragon, who still clung to the underside of the gate.

Feeling helpless, Ida crept to the edge of the tunnel, just in time to see Endor plunge his sword deep into one of the dragon's eyes.

Mortally struck, the creature writhed furiously, screaming and roaring, and Endor hung on desperately as the gate shook and bucked. Then the light seemed to fade from the dragon's remaining eye, and with one last screech, it tumbled into the chasm.

Endor immediately threw his arm around Torven, to prevent him from sliding off the gate.

"Throw them the rope, Bort," Ida pleaded.

Instead Bort moved her gently back and gripped the bottom of the gate. Pulling steadily, he tore the lower hinge from the wall, and taking short juddering steps, shuffled slowly backward into the tunnel, dragging Endor and Torven to safety.

Ida immediately knelt beside Torven and began peeling blood-soaked hair away from his face.

His hand came up to grip Ida's, and he glanced between her and Endor. "Not such a good plan after all." He coughed a mouthful of blood. "I'm sorry, but you're in charge now, Endor." His words came in short panting breaths, "Let Bort be your guide to Domidia. The Library has what you need; you just have to find it. Good luck to you all."

Then Ida heard a too familiar sigh as the last breath left Torven's body. She pressed a finger into his throat, searching for the heart's pulse in the large blood vessel on the side of the neck, but there was nothing. He was dead, and Endor's bravery had counted for nothing. Torven was one more casualty in the fight against the Harrowen, and with such a determined and ruthless enemy, Ida prayed that his last words would bear fruit. If this Library did not hold the answer to defeating these invaders, then they were all doomed.

Resting a comforting hand on her shoulder, Endor said, "I'm sorry, Ida, there's nothing we can do for him now."

Fighting to hold back her tears, she nodded and stood. If Endor had chosen to take her in his arms she wouldn't have fought him.

Instead he turned to the others. "It might seem callous, but it won't help us staying here any longer. Gather your packs, we're moving on now." Noting Bort's pained expression he added, "Don't worry, lad, he'll get a good and decent burial. But there'll be time for that later."

Ida nodded, accepting Endor's wisdom. When they returned for that unpleasant task; they could clean up the body before burial, and let Bort's last memory of Torven be as agreeable as they could manage.

Lineth lifted Endor's sword from the gate and presented it to him. "Don't forget this."

Endor thanked her and then gently moved them on, sending Bort to the front.

Ida fought the threatening tears as she followed him along the tunnel; but the terrible scene she had witnessed played over and over in her head. Torven's death and Endor's incredible, foolish bravery were all mixed together in a terrifying blur. And what lay ahead, some book-filled repository of knowledge? How could that help them now?

After about five minutes of walking, Bort stopped and moved aside. Ida held up her lantern, finding a stout wooden door blocking the way. A large brass key hung on a hook near the lock, and it seemed odd that the key should be so readily available.

Endor pushed forward and took the key from its hook. He held it out for the others to see. Apart from the handle, which was a simple ring, it was a featureless brass rod.

"Odd looking key," said Lineth. "There are no teeth sticking out."

Endor handed the key to Bort, saying gently, "Old Torven said you'd know what to do with this."

Ida waited expectantly; Bort was subdued, grief stricken, and when he looked at her she offered an encouraging smile and nodded.

With little enthusiasm, he inserted the key in the door's lock and turned it backwards and forwards, but it rotated freely without engaging the mechanism. Wearing a pained expression, he handed it back to Endor. "Bort does not know how the key works."

"We're stuck here," Moleskin moaned. "We can't go back and we can't go forward. We're going to die here, aren't we?"

"Shut up, Moleskin!" Endor barked. "You're behaving like a damnable coward."

"We're going to starve to death," Moleskin continued, "we've only enough food for a few days. I've got hardly any in my... my... where's my backpack?"

Endor gripped Moleskin's shoulders and shook him firmly. "You dropped it. Now pull yourself together, man!"

"Dropped it! Where? When? But it was full of my, uh... things."

Endor pushed Moleskin aside roughly. "Not another word," he growled.

Ida just shook her head in contempt and turned her back on Moleskin. Torven had said Bort would know how to use the key, but as before, he might need some prompting. She held out her hand to Endor. "Can I see the key?"

Endor passed it over.

Ida set her lantern on the ground, removed her shoulder bag and sat down. As tormented as she was, she had to take charge. "I know we're all very upset by what happened, but we need to calm down and approach this rationally. I think it's another hidden memory. Bort must have it stored in his head and we have to find a way to release it. We'd all better sit down and see what we can think of."

Lineth nodded and sat beside Ida.

Endor glowered. "Can't we just knock the ruddy door down?"

"What with? Your thick skull?" Ida immediately regretted her words.

Endor harrumphed, stifling an angry response.

"Bort can knock it down," Moleskin ventured.

"Nobody's knocking anything down," Ida snapped. "Now let's all sit down and think this through."

Endor glowered at her before turning to Bort. "Well, Bort, fancy a crack at it?"

"Sit down, Bort," said Ida.

Bort looked backwards and forwards between Ida and Endor, torn by his loyalties.

"Now, Bort!" Ida barked. Though it looked like a simple wooden door, she very much doubted it would respond to force of any kind. Torven would not have left the Library so vulnerable, and an attempt to force their way in would probably prove fatal.

Avoiding Endor's eyes, Bort sat down on the spot.

Endor threw down his pack and paced off along the tunnel, grumbling angrily to himself.

"You too, Moleskin, sit!" said Ida.

Moleskin sat.

"Right," said Ida. "There is a door in the wall, it is locked, and we have the key." She looked expectantly at Bort, but he just shrugged. "The key," she continued, "is made from brass. It has a round handle, but does not have any teeth." She stopped again, but all she heard was Endor muttering to himself from further along the tunnel. Bort turned to look, but Ida snapped her fingers. "Pay attention, Bort."

Bort nodded. "Yes, Ida. Of course, Ida."

Endor must have kicked a rock, and it scuttled noisily along the tunnel.

"I wish that stupid man would stop his nonsense," said Ida, sharply and loudly. She was having enough trouble controlling her own emotions without Endor behaving like a child.

"Maybe I should go and have a word with him," said Lineth.

"You will do no such thing," said Ida.

"I just thought…"

"Trust me," Ida snapped.

Lineth closed her mouth.

"Now," Ida showed the key to Bort, "what am I holding?"

Before Bort could answer, Endor shouted from down the passage, "I'll not be made a fool of, not by anyone!"

"I asked you a question, Bort," said Ida.

"I'll not be spoken to like that," Endor shouted, his voice becoming more distant.

"Bort! Pay attention!" Ida clattered Bort's forehead with the end of the key. "How does the key work, Bort? How does it work!"

Bort's huge hand closed on the key, and for a second Ida thought she had gone too far.

Gripping the key's shaft, Bort rotated the handle and a row of teeth folded out from the end, snapping into place with a click. Bort handed the key back. "The key works like that, Ida."

Stunned, Ida held up the key. "As easy as that," she said in a weak voice. "It was as easy as that."

"I'll fetch Endor," said Lineth.

"Yes, of course." Ida turned to Bort. "I'm so sorry, I shouldn't have hit you. It was wrong, I lost my temper."

Bort nodded. "Bort is fine. Bort will answer quick next time, and not make Ida angry."

His words humbled her. Then it was all too much, their escape from the Harrowen, the horrors on the battlefield and the death of Torven; the tears flooded out.

"Do not cry," said Bort. "Ida did not hurt Bort."

Bort's attempts at consoling her only made Ida feel worse.

"What's all this then?" said Endor, arriving back at a trot. Immediately he took Ida in his arms. "There, there, m'dear, don't cry."

When Endor's arms encircled Ida, calm descended. She suddenly felt very safe. "Oh, I'm so sorry," she sobbed, "it's all been a bit too much."

"I know what you mean, Ida. I felt like crying myself when old Torven died. Damned awful it was. I've been acting the fool as well. I'm sorry. I should've listened to what you said."

"But if I'd asked in a reasonable way, you wouldn't have got so upset."

"All forgotten now," said Endor.

Ida sniffed back the last of her tears, took a deep breath and eased herself out of Endor's arms. She pulled out a hanky, blew her nose and quickly brushed the tears from her eyes. "Yes, of course, thank you, Endor."

Endor sighed. "Best we get on then."

Bort unlocked the door and as it swung noiselessly open, a waft of clean, fresh air drifted by. Staring into the dark, Bort's eyes opened wide with surprise.

Ida remembered the same expression from when they first arrived at the Trollid city. "What can you see?" she said.

19

Lord Tekt stared out over the jumble of tents surrounding the command tower. Daylight was fading fast, the sun's last rays cutting through the haze of wood smoke lingering over the camp.

In this idle moment his troops were relaxing; dancing and singing to loud dissonant music, and off in the distance a new column was approaching, bringing reinforcements and supplies. Everything Tekt saw was as it should be, but not all matters were as well ordered.

He spun around to glare at the group of six small leather-clad figures prostrated on the floor of the audience chamber. Attendants and supporters to Nitha and Whisper; none dared to meet his eyes. He paced across and leant over their leader, Stol. Like all the male Shil, he was clean-shaven and wore his hair in a long braided tail; his was peppered through with grey. On his back was the thin rapier blade they all carried, halfway between sword and dagger. Stol had his eyes screwed tightly closed.

Tekt growled through clenched teeth, "The dragon is gone, there is no doubt?"

"None, my Lord," came the weak reply.

Tekt drew Stol's own blade and rested the tip on the nape of his neck. "Death is life," he whispered.

"Life is death," Stol whimpered.

Stol convulsed as Tekt plunged the blade into his brain.

Tekt withdrew the blade and threw it aside. "Get out! All of you!" He kicked Stol's lifeless body onto its back. "And take this refuse with you."

There was a scurry of movement as the remaining Shil grabbed the corpse and dragged it from the audience chamber.

Tekt shouted after them, "Send in that fool Dusswen."

The old wizard must have been waiting on the steps; arriving seconds after the Shil were gone.

"My Lord," he said, bowing deeply.

Tekt fought to contain the anger boiling through him. "That young idiot, Nitha. She was too inexperienced. She'd better pray she's dead already, if I find her I'll..."

Dusswen interrupted, "We do not know the full circum..."

"Silence! I know enough about these arrogant dragonriders. The Shil are soft-brained fools, they always have been."

Dusswen nodded obediently, his head bowed.

Tekt marched up to him. "Another dragon! When can we have another dragon?"

Dusswen shuffled back. "It takes power, my Lord. Vast energies..."

"When?" Tekt demanded.

"It is a choice, my Lord. We must rebuild the army first, and keep it supplied. We do not have the facility to do both. You know how many dragons we lost before, and with this minor gate it could be weeks or months before we are successful again, and at each attempt we lose another dragon and rider. The Shil are loyal, but they will not tolerate such waste."

Tekt advanced on Dusswen forcing him to back away. "I do not care about the Shil! They are servants of the Emperor, nothing more. They should be honoured to die for the cause. Do whatever it takes!" Tekt turned and walked away, but there was no sound of movement, no retreating footsteps. Dusswen had defied him and remained in the chamber.

Tekt drew his dagger and spun around. "What keeps you here!" he bellowed.

Dusswen dropped to one knee, his head bowed. "The dragon was a luxury, my Lord, it need not be replaced. We know Nitha left a marker stone; she will have placed it at the entrance she used. Tukkle and his band are well able to deal with any armed resistance, and Amrax is no fool, he is a master of destructive magics. The dragon was only needed to locate the entrance."

"The Library! You wizards make such hungry noises about this Library! Is it really of use to the Harrowen, or is it just some perverse curiosity that drives you to find it?"

"Truly, my Lord, it holds knowledge that has been lost from our own world and many others, powerful knowledge that will ensure the continuation of your dynasty. Never again will the Harrowen scratch in the soil like animals!"

Tekt sheathed his dagger. This was language he understood. For many years the Harrowen had stagnated, living more and more as lesser races did, through farming and commerce. It was time for the Harrowen to reclaim their warrior past, to rebuild an empire that once stretched across a score of worlds.

"Very well, Dusswen, we will not bring another dragon across. But I warn you, this had better be good advice, or you will pay with your life!"

20

"What can you see, Bort?" said Ida.

"It is very big," said Bort.

Endor stepped past Ida, thrusting his lantern into the darkness, but it had little effect. He turned to face her. "Damn it, I wish I knew how to do that trick with the light." He put down his lantern, cupped his hands and shouted, "Come on! Light up, light up now!" After the slightest pause, the room grew steadily lighter and he crossed his arms in satisfaction. "There! That was easy enough."

"Goodness gracious," said Ida, staring past him.

It was a huge circular chamber with doors leading off at regular intervals along the walls. A single broad staircase spiralled up the curving wall to a circular landing, and then went on and up to another level, and another, and on and on. Ida counted the levels to twenty-one and the distant ceiling appeared to be a dome. The floor was made from tiled marble with a small circular pool at its centre. The walls were natural rock, but finished to plaster smoothness, and there wasn't a spot of dirt or dust to be seen anywhere.

Endor stared up with his mouth open, swallowing hard before speaking. "Torven's last words were that we'd find the answer here, I'm sure he meant something that can help us fight these Harrowen." He shook his head. "Though without him, it'll be hard knowing where to look."

"The first thing we need to find," said Lineth, "is food and water."

"And somewhere to sleep," said Moleskin.

"Of course," said Endor, "no army can survive without the basics."

Ida looked around their small party. Endor had described them as an army; hardly accurate, but they were all engaged in the same struggle, she sighed, apart from one embarrassing exception.

Shoulders still sagging, Bort led them to the pool and pointed to the floor. "This is the map of the Library."

Laid out around the pool was a guide to the whole building; a series of concentric rings, each divided into segments.

Noting the doors on each level were in line with the segments, Ida counted them; there were twenty-one, and each segment contained either writing or a symbol.

"I count twenty-one segments, and they match with the doors on each level," she said, "which makes..."

"Four hundred and forty one doors," said Lineth.

"My word," said Endor, "that's a lot of doors. He peered at the segments. "Here," he pointed to one, "this one's like the eye on the door to that Palace of Visions place. Where about is that then?"

Bort stood on the segment with his back to the pool and pointed up to a distant landing near the top of the Library. "Up there."

Lineth walked around the curve of one of the rings. "It shows you exactly what's inside each room, and where it is."

"Does anyone remember which way we came in?" said Moleskin, a nervous edge to his voice.

Ida shook her head in dismay, it was a stupid question. Regardless of where it was, there was no going back by that way. "It's that one," she said, pointing. She tapped a toe on a segment next to the pool. "See, the guide has it marked as the city."

"I wonder what this is?" said Endor.

He stood over a symbol that repeated itself in every adjacent segment from the pool to the outer edge of the rings. It was a square with a triangle on top and underneath. It appeared at three points on the map, breaking up the whole circle like three huge slices of cake.

Lineth walked over to a corresponding door and opened it. "Come and see this."

Ida and the others joined her and stared inside. It was a small room just large enough for all of them to stand in. On one wall was a vertical glass tube with a green fluid at the bottom of it. A polished golden arrowhead, set with a clear gemstone, pointed to the top of the fluid. Horizontal blue bands marked the tube at regular intervals, twenty-one of them.

Ida couldn't imagine what purpose the room served. "Very strange, but I doubt there's anything in here that's going to help us." She turned away from the little room and started back towards the pool. "At least there's water, and Lineth's right, we need food and somewhere to set up base."

Endor nodded. "Practical as ever, Ida. Once that's sorted we'll need to have a look around and see if we can find anything useful." He looked up. "Mind you, just getting to the top will take a bit of effort." He suddenly became alert, pulled out his sword and pointed. "Look! Up there! There's someone here already!"

Ida saw movement on the top level; a tiny figure was waving furiously.

Bort pointed to the distant figure. "That is Moleskin up there."

Ida glanced around, Moleskin was gone. But if he was at the top of the chamber, how had he got there so fast?

When the others walked off, Moleskin lingered to examine the golden arrow. He felt sure that the clear gemstone it held was a diamond. After a furtive glance to make sure no one was watching, he quickly slid the arrow to the top of the glass tube, hoping it would lift off the end of its track.

With barely a judder, the room rose up so quickly he had no time to react. For an instant the others were visible and then they were gone. His shouts went unheeded, and he cowered in the corner of the little room gripping the walls. The pit of his stomach seemed to have been left far below and he feared he would never see his companions again. This was a deadly trap designed to capture the unwary.

He fully expected to die at any moment, but the room continued upwards, passing door after door in a mesmerising blur. It stopped when the green water in the tube was in line with the golden arrowhead, and in front of him was a door identical to the one he had first come through. Cautiously, he pushed the door open and stepped out onto one of the curving balconies. Walking forward to the handrail, he gasped in amazement.

He was at the top of the chamber, and the others were far below; tiny black dots gathered around the pool, which looked no bigger than a dewdrop. He shouted and waved. Eventually they looked up and pointed; they had seen him.

It took Moleskin barely seconds to work out how to return the little room to the ground. This time the journey seemed commonplace, and he lounged against the wall whistling cheerily.

When the room stopped moving he swaggered out, calling triumphantly, "Moleskin is back!"

They were all gone, the floor was empty. Moleskin walked to the pool, trying to decide if this was the same place he had left from.

Then he heard his name shouted from a long way off, distant and weak, "M o l e s k i n !"

Looking up he saw four tiny heads leaning from the top balcony, they were waving and pointing. He was about to return to the little room and go to join them, when he realised the stupidity of this action, they could spend the whole day missing each other.

Arriving back at the ground level, Ida sighed in dismay when Endor strode over to Moleskin and clapped his back.

"Well done," he said, "at least that's the problem of how to get around this place solved."

"Sir, it was nothing," said Moleskin, smugly.

Ida knew exactly what had happened, the little thief was fiddling with the lifting room mechanism, probably trying to steal the gem, but she said nothing, not wanting to spoil Endor's mood. In reality their investigations had done as much to solve the problem; opening one of the other lifting room doors revealed an empty chimney-like structure, but in seconds one of the little rooms had arrived to fill the space. The act of opening the door had brought the room to their level, and moving the pointer carried them between levels.

Ignoring the others, Ida returned to the Library map, quickly finding the room she knew would be there. The segment contained a simple picture of a bed and a plate with a spoon.

She raised her voice to get the other's attention. "This looks like it might be accommodation, and maybe a kitchen."

"Where's that?" said Endor.

She counted three rings out from the centre, turned to face away from the pool and pointed up. "Third level up and one door to the left of that lifting room."

"Splendid," said Endor. "How about splitting into two parties? You, Bort and Lineth make up one party, Moleskin and me the other? You lot start with that room and we'll meet back here in about an hour?"

Lineth nodded. "Good idea. Anything else you want us to look for?"

Endor stared up at the tiers of balconies. "Can't say as I've any useful suggestions to make on that count. I think we'll just have to see what there is." He pointed to a map segment containing a symbol of crossed swords. "I'd like a look in this room on the sixth level. How about it, Moleskin?"

"Of course, sir, ready when you are."

Endor waved to the others. "We'll be off then."

Ida was quite happy to have Moleskin out of her sight for a while, and at least he was doing something useful, but her skin crept when he went ahead of Endor into the lifting room, positioned himself beside the level tube, and said in the most servile of voices.

129

"Sixth level, wasn't it, sir?"

Endor nodded.

Moleskin adjusted the pointer, and as both men disappeared up the shaft the door closed by itself.

Ida shook her head in dismay; at least in Endor's eyes, Moleskin had managed to redeem himself. She turned to examine Bort, knowing he would have little enthusiasm for exploration. His drooping head was probably filled, like hers, with the terrible bloody images of Torven's death.

They rode one of the lifting rooms up to the third level, Bort trailing behind as Ida opened the door to the room she hoped would offer them food and a place to sleep.

The light came on at Lineth's request, revealing a large common room with rich wood panelling on every wall. It was filled with comfortable leather armchairs and sofas.

Ida assumed it was intended for the housing of visiting wizards and scholars. "This will do very nicely. What do you think, Bort?"

He rested his hand on one of the armchairs and barely nodded.

Ida waved him to follow. "Come on, there must be a kitchen nearby."

Lineth opened a door at the far end of the room and peered into the space beyond.

"Is that it, Lineth?" said Ida.

"No. It's a long corridor, with lots of doors off. Maybe it's dormitories. I'll take a look."

Ida opened a door on the wall opposite an ornate fireplace, finding a dining room with a large dining table that would easily seat twenty.

"Ah, yes, exactly where I would have put it," she said, trying to raise some interest from Bort.

He didn't reply, so she left him in the common room, hoping his curiosity would get the better of him. Through an open door at the far end of the dining room she saw a cooking range. She entered the kitchen and had already opened a cupboard door when Bort joined her; she made a show of inspecting shelves full of carefully stored provisions, finding many of the containers were identical to those she had seen in Torven's cottage.

"Well," she said, "we won't starve."

Bort stood by the gleaming coal-fired range, showing some interest in it.

"I wonder where the fuel is kept?" said Ida.

She turned away, busying herself with inspecting other cupboards, but kept an eye on Bort.

He opened a cupboard near the range. "The coal is in here, and plenty of kindling."

Without further bidding, he filled a bucket with both and took it to the range.

Ida relaxed, busy was better. She went across and rubbed his arm reassuringly. "Can I leave you in charge here?"

He nodded. "Bort will make some tea."

"Tea would be lovely. Lineth and I will explore some more, and we'll fetch Endor and Moleskin back here after the hour is up."

"Tea in one hour, Ida. Bort knows what to do."

Ida left to find Lineth. She felt terribly sad, but Bort needed time to grieve. She would have liked to stay with him and offer comfort, but sensed on this occasion he wanted to be alone.

Now that they didn't have to worry about their basic needs, her time would be better spent exploring the Library. Keeping herself busy wouldn't be a bad thing either.

With a good fire roaring in the grate, Bort filled a kettle with water and settled it on a hotplate. Curious, he inspected the cupboards; they were laid out much as they had been in Torven's cottage. There was everything needed to make pancakes.

With the ingredients gathered, he experimented until he had the right taste and consistency of a pancake batter. It cooked well, producing a light golden-skinned pancake. Ida would be very pleased with his efforts.

With the addition of butter, found in a cool cabinet, and pots of jam and honey, he soon had the makings of a small banquet.

By his estimation, it would be another twenty minutes before the others returned, and he busied himself wiping down the dining table and laying out cutlery, plates and cups. He also lit a fire in the dining room; it immediately warmed the room and cast a cosy glow over the rich wooden furnishings.

He was setting a fire in the common room, when he noticed a pair of worn slippers sitting to the side of the fireplace. He knew instantly they were Torven's, and tears formed in his eyes and trickled down his cheeks. His childhood memories of a kindly stranger had all but gone until he returned to his parent's home. Then they had flooded back, reminding him how close he and Torven had been, and how much warmth and love the old man had shown him. It was heartbreaking to know that he would never see him alive again.

Endor pushed open the door with the crossed swords on it, revealing a dark interior. "Well, Moleskin, I reckon we know how this works." He stepped forward, waved his arms and shouted, "Light please."

Light spread from the ceiling, illuminating a long corridor stretching into the distance.

"Seems to go on for a fair bit, sir," said Moleskin.

Endor walked to a thick book sitting on a slender stone pedestal near the door. "Here, what's this?" He flipped over the heavy cover, finding the first page contained a list of phrases in a variety of languages.

Moleskin pointed to one, it said;

If you can read this, turn to page 162.

Endor flicked the pages. When they reached the correct section there was a list of headings under the title;

The Practise of Warfare.

"This is quite extraordinary." Endor ran his finger down the list and read some chapter headings, "Tactical Treatise for Land and Naval Warfare, Defensive and Offensive Structures, Weapons of an Alchemic and Pyrotechnic Nature." He became excited. "Look at this last one, Moleskin, The Uses of Magic in Warfare. I fancy a look in there."

The door leading to the room dedicated to the Uses of Magic in Warfare had no handle, and would not move when they pushed against it.

"Ah well, likely as not it would have got us into trouble." Endor stared back along the corridor; the guide seemed a long way off. "I wonder what's in the next room?"

Moleskin went to the door and opened it. "Armour, sir."

"Perfect," said Endor. "I could do with a change. My old chainmail is getting a bit raggedy."

Ida felt a rush of pleasure when she, Lineth, Endor and Moleskin returned to their newfound sleeping quarters. Bort had prepared a tall pile of pancakes, and to go with them were jams and honey, and a large pot of tea.

"Goodness," she said, "this is wonderful."

"Tea and pancakes," said Bort, proudly. He waved them all to sit at the dining table.

Ida was glad that Bort had kept himself busy and watched carefully as he poured teas and made sure everyone was served; he seemed to be coping well enough.

The pancakes were a great success and the pile quickly began to shrink. As they ate, Endor directed their conversation to what each party had discovered.

"Ida and I went to the Vision room," said Lineth. "It's much larger than the one in the city, there's more than a dozen viewing tables. It's full of maps too, carved into the walls. I think it can view a much wider area."

"As far as Conisby?" said Endor.

"If the maps represent its viewing range, then yes."

"In that case," said Endor, "we'll have to take a look and see how the King's faring."

"We also found a room full of funerary treasures," said Lineth. "There was a beautifully carved stone casket." She smiled gently at Bort. "It looked to be something a Trollid might have made. It was empty, we thought maybe..."

"Damned good idea" said Endor. "A fitting resting place for a great man. Lineth, you and I will fetch his body and we can lay him to rest. Best we deal with that fairly soon. I don't know what his beliefs were, but I'm sure he won't be offended if we say a few words on his behalf. Ida, maybe you could say something?"

"I'd like that," said Ida. Endor might not be the most tactful of men, but his heart was in the right place.

"Was there anything else you found?" he said.

"Several book libraries," said Ida, "but I couldn't read anything. They all seemed to be in foreign languages." She suddenly remembered a find, and drew a small notebook from her skirt pocket. "I did find this on a desk though." She opened the notebook on the table, spread open the pages and watched as the others read the lines of neat handwritten text.

Bort nodded slowly. "Bort knows this." He read it out.

"The moons of Nephus; Nal and Ito, often known as the Queen and the Jester.

Little Ito runs the race,
to solemn Nal's steady pace.
Ito has no time for season,
his frantic dash seems lost to reason.

Ito races, he sprints ahead,
no care for you tucked up in bed,
or thought for beast or bird in flight,
he sweeps the skies, both day and night.

Nal serene, her beauty bold,
waits to watch the world unfold.
As month goes by she shows her grace,
with shaded scarf she guards her face.

She changes mood from coy to bold,
and tempts the seas with eyes of gold.
Adoring they rise up and fall,
blindly caught in constant thrall.

While men are born and live and die,
this odd pair will guard the sky."

Bort paused, his brow furrowed and he flicked open the front cover to read a brief note. "This was written by Torven, a long time ago."

Ida touched his arm. In part regretful that she'd unwittingly brought this reminder of Torven, in part glad that they could share this very human part of his nature.

"It's a lovely poem," she said.

Bort turned away, wiping a tear from his eye.

"Yes indeed," said Endor, "not really my thing, poetry, but it's a well written piece."

Ida sighed and closed the notebook. "What did you find, Endor?"

He looked embarrassed for a moment. "I suppose it's fairly obvious where I would go looking. We found a corridor filled with weapons and armour. Moleskin here got the measure of the guide."

"Oh yes," said Moleskin, brightly. "The weapons area has a very useful guide. And though it was written in many different languages, I quickly found it included our own."

"And what did it say?" said Lineth.

"It listed what was in each area," he said. "Different types of warfare and weapons..."

"Damn it," said Endor, "there was even a roomful of magic weapons! But we couldn't get into it. The door didn't have a handle! Probably needs some magic spell to get it open." Endor turned to Bort. "What do you say, Bort, can you get that door open?"

He shook his head. "Bort does not know any magic."

"There was one section," said Moleskin, "which was full of weapons of an Alchemic and Pyrotechnic Nature."

"And what exactly," said Lineth, "are weapons of an Alchemic and Pyrotechnic Nature?"

"Damned funny looking things they were," said Endor. "Some of them looked a bit like candles. Apparently they're supposed to blast great holes in things. But they're not just for warfare, they get used for mining and knocking down old buildings, saves a lot of hard work apparently. I'll have to do a bit of study, see if I can work out the proper way to use them."

Moleskin pulled a paper packet from his pocket. He unwrapped it and showed them a small amount of fine black powder. "This stuff is supposed to throw things a long way."

"What do you do with it?" said Lineth.

Moleskin walked to the open fire. "It's supposed to burn very fast."

Before anyone could stop him, Moleskin threw the powder onto the fire. There was a muffled whoosh, and he was instantly hidden within a cloud of pungent, grey smoke. He came staggering out of it with his hands held high, his face blackened and wisps of smoke rising from his singed hair.

"Goodness," said Ida. She quickly led him to the kitchen sink and poured cold water over his head. After establishing that his injuries were minor, she sat him down at the dining table to clean him up and dab a soothing ointment on his blistered forehead.

"I'm sure they'll grow back," she said.

"What?" said Moleskin.

"Your eyebrows, of course."

Moleskin's shoulders drooped, and he looked as miserable as Bort had earlier. However Ida felt little sympathy; his arrogant stupidity had caused the injuries.

"If that other stuff works as well," said Endor, "I'm sure we can use it to knock down that Gate at Domidia. What do you think, Lineth?"

"I've never seen anything like that before," Lineth glanced at Moleskin, "but it's obviously very dangerous stuff."

"Torven would know," said Bort.

Endor sighed. "We have to move on, Bort. I miss him as much as any, but we're on our own now."

Bort nodded.

Lineth narrowed her eyes. "If we can work out how to use it, I think the main problem is how to get close enough without getting caught."

"We'd better take a look at that viewing room, see what we're up against." Endor paused, his tone softening. "If everyone's finished eating, I think now would be a good time to fetch Torven."

While Lineth and Endor went to collect Torven's body, Ida had Bort help prepare the casket. The room it sat in was decorated throughout with rich hanging tapestries and golden statuary of strange creatures; half bird and half man. Ida couldn't help wondering if these were mythical, or representations of another real creature living on some far-off world.

The casket sat on a black marble plinth with a golden lion guarding each of the four corners, and it was lined with the softest and finest velvet Ida had ever felt. There was a moment of uncertainty when they found a small golden urn tucked into a corner. Ida quickly suggested that whoever, or whatever, the occupier of the casket was, she was sure they wouldn't mind sharing it with Torven. Luckily Bort agreed.

Draped in a fine cotton shroud, Torven's body was placed inside the casket and the ornate lid settled in place. Looking around the room, Ida thought it a splendid final resting place, and to gentle sobbing from Bort, she recited an appropriate prayer.

21

All around Tekt was a bustle of activity as the army prepared the final camp. Behind him engineers were assembling the headquarters tower, and to his front a grassy plain stretched off toward Conisby. It had been stripped of fuel and cover, and was littered with tree stumps and the charred mounds of spent fires.

Flags and pennants flew in proud defiance from every turret and spire of the city, and row upon row of archers and swordsmen in brightly coloured uniforms manned the battlements. It was a show of strength and order.

Tekt narrowed his eyes; soldiers filled the city, many more mouths to feed than its storerooms would normally need to cope with, but also many more soldiers for his forces to engage.

This outcome was unexpected; the bulk of the humans should have died at Sollas, but he grudgingly acknowledged they had shown great skill and courage in managing their retreat.

On the positive side; if he sustained the siege their food supplies would dwindle faster and the strength of the defenders would wane, while his forces were guaranteed food, either from foraging or from supplies brought from Mirt.

Dusswen approached and bowed. "My lord?"

Tekt answered without turning, "Yes."

"Scouts have located what we think may be four hidden entrances at the base of the city rock."

"Good."

"Tonight we will send up creepers to investigate."

"Excellent, the city must not be supplied from any source. But do not seal them, they may provide access for some mischief later on."

"A watch will be kept at all times."

Tekt began walking and Dusswen followed; they progressed along the edge of the camp, following a line of Clan and Family standards fluttering in the breeze. As he passed by, the common soldiers fell to the ground with his approach, only daring to rise once he had passed.

Tekt paused by one of the Death's-Wing launchers and waved the crew to their feet. They immediately resumed the task of pinning the machine to the ground with long steel spikes. He waved to another group, and they continued their work around a makeshift forge, straightening the blades of Death's-Wings recovered from previous battles. The satisfying beat of hammer on iron rang in Tekt's ears.

He spoke over the clamour, "I find myself growing impatient, Dusswen. This victory has been long in coming."

"Indeed, my Lord."

"But we will wait. There is no doubt now of the outcome."

"A victory you have assured, my Lord."

Tekt accepted this compliment with a brief nod and then walked on, finally arriving at the edge of the camp.

"It's an impressive structure, Dusswen." Tekt walked forward, away from the camp, knowing that many eyes would be upon him, their spyglasses following his every move. He stopped and planted his feet wide apart.

"It is convenient indeed," he said, crossing his arms in front of him, "that the human cattle have herded themselves into the slaughterhouse for us." He turned and smiled at Dusswen. "Such obliging creatures!"

Endor called Lineth to the viewing room for a private discussion, where he had a view of Conisby displayed on a table. As he stared at the image he felt his jaw tighten. The preparation of the enemy's camp had a slow and deliberate air to it that he recognised from similar engagements. They were settling in for a siege. The Harrowen intended to starve the occupants of Conisby into submission. By all accounts there would be no terms of surrender; the Harrowen would simply slaughter everyone in the Castle.

"I suppose," said Lineth, "that this gives us more time to prepare?"

Endor shook his head. "Not really, the longer that Gate at Domidia stays open, the stronger they get."

Lineth turned away from the table, her brow furrowed in thought. "And Conisby can only get weaker as they deplete their resources."

"Exactly. We must use those blasting sticks to destroy the Gate as soon as we can," said Endor.

The descriptions of uses for the blasting sticks, and repeated warnings regarding how dangerous they were, had convinced Endor they were perfect for the job. Both he and Lineth had spent some time in research and both felt confident they could use them.

"But if we do, then everything changes," said Lineth

There was caution in her words, instead of the expected enthusiasm.

"What're you thinking?" said Endor.

"Without supplies and reinforcements, and with winter coming, Tekt will have no reason to maintain the siege."

Caught up in the possibility of achieving such a crucial blow, Endor hadn't thought much beyond the actual act.

Endor sighed. "After all this, he's not just going to back off, is he?"

"No, and if we manage this, we'll probably force his hand; he'll need to attack, sooner rather than later."

It was a decision General Hork should be making, but there were always times when the commander in the field had to take the initiative; but for all the misery and death he could be responsible for, Endor knew there was no alternative.

"Doing nothing just strengthens his position," he said, firmly.

Lineth nodded, and turned immediately to Torven's paper map, which was laid out on an adjacent table. "It would have helped knowing what to expect."

All their attempts to operate the table showing Domidia had proven futile and Endor suspected its mechanism was damaged when Torven collapsed the city cavern.

He stared down at the map. "I've no doubt we'll be heavily outnumbered."

"It won't be a frontal attack then?"

"No, I'll have to sneak in and try to destroy enough of those Gate blocks with the blasting sticks."

"Maybe I should do it?"

"No," said Endor, quickly. "If I'm caught there's no knowing what they'll do to me. One thing being struck down in the midst of battle..." He let his sentence trail off. "Besides, I need you here to protect the Library." He pointed at the Conisby viewing table. "They might look like a rabble, but that's a well organised army, I'm sure there'll be some sort of armed support coming here, even if it's just to find out what happened to the dragon."

"Very well," said Lineth.

Chance had thrown them together, two soldiers with a common cause, and there were words that needed saying. He turned to face her. "It seems we've found a job to do here?"

"Surely, there's no getting away from it."

Endor stared into her eyes. "I'd like to think we could make a difference."

Lineth nodded, her voice taking on a cold edge, "We'll do whatever it takes, Endor."

"That we will." It was a small thing, but Endor felt better for having put those essential few words behind them. He wasn't some reckless youngster, ready to run screaming and bellowing into the midst of overwhelming odds, hopeful of a miraculous outcome. He saw a very clear line between bravery and stupidity. In Lineth too he saw this same understanding; she would confront when needed, but would not spend her life easily. But in the very end, if that was the sacrifice required, she, like him, was willing to make it.

Ida responded to Endor's call for a meeting, joining with the others in the dining room. Torven's map was already laid out on the table, the edges held down by cutlery borrowed from the kitchen.

Endor pointed to a location on the map. "You'll remember Torven said the Gate the Harrowen are using is here in Domidia." He drew a finger across the map, following a clear marked line. "This tunnel comes out of the mountain close to Domidia. Bort and I will use it to go there and try to destroy the Gate. Lineth, Moleskin and Ida will remain here and protect the Library."

"I can't let Bort go on his own," said Ida.

"I only need Bort to show me the way," said Endor. "There's no need for you to come..."

Ida interrupted. "Bort and I have a pact." She added, firmly, "It's both or none."

"Not this again, Ida, I really can't agree to it."

"It's not open for discussion," said Ida, "we both go."

Endor sighed. "This time surely, you'll trust my judgment?"

"I'm not questioning your judgment, Endor. It's very simple. Bort and I will not be separated."

"I have no choice then?"

Ida shook her head. Whatever lay ahead, and she knew it could be very unpleasant, she wanted to be with Bort. Her presence at Domidia or in the Library would matter little, but this was important to her.

Endor sighed. "Very well; Bort, Ida and I will take most of the blasting sticks and find some way of placing them next to the Gate. I know that sounds a bit vague, but we have a lot acting in our favour. I think we can get to the city without detection, they won't be expecting us and these blasting sticks will surely make short work of the Gate."

"Begging your pardon, sir," said Moleskin, "but it sounds like complete madness to me."

"Madness or not," Lineth snapped. "We have little choice in the matter."

"On the contrary, madam, I think there are many alternatives. For one, we can leave now and head north, well away from the fighting. We'll all end up dead if we stay."

"You are a pathetic little man," said Ida, fixing Moleskin with a stern glower.

Moleskin's eyes bobbed away furtively, he clearly saw little profit in challenging her, but there was something else there; it wasn't just about saving his skin.

Endor tried to lift the mood of the group. "Don't you be worrying about me, Moleskin, I'm no beginner at this lark. Besides that, you'll be perfectly safe here with Lineth."

Moleskin's eyes fell to the ground. "Very well, sir."

Ida made sure she packed sufficient food for Bort, Endor and herself for the four-day journey to and back from Domidia. Though she knew Bort was well aware of the danger ahead, she didn't want to imply that any of them might not be returning. However she also knew how crucial their mission was, and Endor's bravery and sense of duty would not allow him to turn away from the task, even if it required he make the ultimate sacrifice.

After saying their farewells, their little band set off in good humour. The tunnel had no Trollid lighting, so Ida and Endor carried lanterns and Bort managed without.

It was an easy walk, though having grown accustomed to the stronger light of the city and the Library, the gloomy tunnels soon became claustrophobic. Ignoring the deadly nature of their enterprise, Ida would be glad for even a glimpse of the outside world again.

With Endor, Bort and Ida gone, Moleskin finally found an opportunity to search the area of the Library that interested him most; the door marked on the guide by an unmistakable pile of coins. It was another long corridor, with about thirty doors off to either side.

With nervous excitement, he swung the first door open and called for light. As the room brightened, his knees went weak and he began to tremble. In the centre of the room was a stack of solid gold ingots.

His palms began to itch and he knew that the best possible balm would be to press them against the cool metal. He walked towards the stack, arms outstretched in anticipation.

"Moleskin!" Lineth's shout came from some distance.

He cursed quietly, she had almost spoiled the moment. He paused, considering whether to respond, but the gleaming stack beckoned. His fingers were almost on the polished metal when Lineth shouted again, her voice nearer this time.

"Where are you, Moleskin?"

The last thing he wanted was to draw her attention to his true interests. Reluctantly, he turned and left the room. Pausing in the corridor, he glanced wistfully at the other doors. There were so many treasure rooms to explore, but they would need to wait for another time.

Reaching the balcony in the main hall, he leant out and shouted, "I'm here!"

Lineth's voice came from the level just above. "There you are. Meet me in the Vision room."

"What for?"

"We've got trouble."

Her words sent a surge of fear through Moleskin and he was still struggling to control his breathing when he arrived in the Vision room. Lineth waved him over to one of the viewing tables and his heart beat even faster as he examined a line of figures pressing through the snow.

"It's more Harrowen," he said, a tremor in his voice.

Lineth rested her hand on the table and the lead figure, taller and wearing a black cloak, distorted around her fingers.

"They're on their way here."

"Will they find a way in?"

She nodded. "If the dragon did, I think we can assume they'll manage it too. You've seen the maps; this mountain is full of passages, once inside, they'll find a way here eventually."

"What will we do? They'll kill us easily."

She adjusted the viewer to look closer at the Harrowen, and then ran her finger carefully along the column, counting their numbers. "Thirty-one in total."

Moleskin was horrified. "You can't fight that many!"

"I'm not so sure about that." Lineth smiled wickedly. "After all, we do have a wonderful storehouse of fancy weapons to hand."

The word *storehouse* conjured up a different mental image for Moleskin. To his complete surprise he felt a rush of anger; he now had a vast wealth to protect.

"Very well," he said, firmly, "how do we do this?"

Squad leader Tukkle crossed his arms and looked around; he and his men stood knee-deep in snow at the foot of a sheer rock face. The late afternoon sun was barely warming them, and their breath fogged in the icy air. They would need to find shelter for the night, and soon.

"Come, Wizard Amrax," he said, "you take too long to find this door."

Amrax closed his eyes. "Patience, we are near."

"As near as we were a thousand paces ago?"

After turning scornful eyes on Tukkle, Amrax pointed his staff at a large snowdrift that had gathered against the vertical wall of grey rock. "It is there."

Tukkle clucked his disbelief and shook his head, no door was visible.

Amrax pushed his way forward until he was waist deep in snow.

Tukkle stayed where he was. "Well," he called, "show us this Trollid door, Wizard Amrax."

Amrax sneered. "You could dig, but I have a better way."

Tukkle had seen wizardry before. Often it involved a lot of shouting and staff waving, but Amrax must have been feeling the cold; he missed out the shouting bit and jumped straight to the staff waving, making the tip circle around and around over a small spot of snow.

A tiny whirlwind formed beneath the tip, and like a puppeteer, Amrax nurtured and caressed the small wavering form, and gradually it grew larger, hissing constantly as it spun and writhed. The hiss became a roar, and soon the whirling column was taller than the wizard.

Tukkle pulled up the edge of his cloak, shielding his face as the whirlwind gathered more and more snow into itself. He had to admit, this was good wizardry. With the snow stinging his exposed skin, he peered through a slit in his fingers and watched the snowdrift shrink away to reveal the Trollid door.

With a final flourish, Amrax let out a roar and threw his hands in the air. The whirlwind blew apart, scattering its powdery cargo in all directions.

Tukkle should have known the shouting bit would come at some point. When the air cleared he was covered head to foot in snow.

He brushed snow from his head. "Maybe next time, you'll give us a little warning to get clear, before using your fancy magic."

Amrax laughed, but Tukkle was not amused; everyone was covered in snow, with one notable exception, Amrax. There was not one speck of it on him.

"The way is open," said Amrax, with a dismissive wave.

Biting back an angry reply, Tukkle turned to his men and barked, "Move it!"

They progressed down the tunnel for about ten minutes before arriving at a jumble of rock that filled the passage from floor to ceiling.

Amrax seemed to sniff the air before announcing, "The direct way is blocked, but there is a side passage a few paces from here." He pointed to one side of the tunnel.

Tukkle folded his arms again and stared at the rock, wondering if the wizard would manage a repeat of his earlier skills.

"I could help you with this," said Amrax, "but I must conserve my powers. You can dig a way through."

Noting the use of the word *you* rather than *we*, Tukkle snorted disdainfully. "Very well," he said. "Let's get this done!"

22

The afternoon had come and gone in the unchanging gloom of the tunnel, and night approached in the world outside. Aware they were nearing the end of their trek, Ida felt a rising tension. Endor's manner too had altered; not quite as jovial and positive, but she sensed his growing determination and resolve.

They entered a section of tunnel where the wall was fractured and hollowed with dark recesses, and from one of these wafted a most unpleasant rotten egg smell.

Ida pinched her nose and covered her mouth. "Oh my, what an awful stench!"

Endor nodded in sympathy, but Bort seemed oblivious to it.

Bort held up their map. "Soon be there."

Ida peered at the map, using her lantern to illuminate its detail.

Bort tapped the paper with his finger. "Soon we come to the Firewall."

"The Firewall?" said Endor. "What's that then?"

"Bort does not know, the map just says Firewall."

Endor fanned a hand across his face. "Lead on then. The sooner we get away from this place, the better."

Bort folded the map carefully, returned it to his bag and then set off at a good pace.

Ida stepped smartly to keep up, noting with some relief that the offensive odour faded quickly. After about fifty paces they turned a sharp corner, entering a deep chasm, and an orange glow appeared ahead.

The path had been hewn into one of the chasm wall; it was almost as if they were still in a tunnel, but with one of the walls missing. It was wide enough that they could still walk three abreast, and the builders had sensibly left some of the rock on the missing wall intact, forming a stout parapet to protect the edge.

The orange glow grew brighter and the air around them warmer as they approached the light's source, a huge waterfall-like feature with molten rock flowing gracefully into the chasm.

"That is astonishing," said Ida.

"I can see why they called it the Firewall," said Endor.

"This is not the Firewall." Bort pointed to a black passage branching off from their path. "The Firewall is through there."

Ida exchanged a puzzled look with Endor. "Well," she said. "Let's see what this Firewall looks like."

Bort led off and the glow receded behind them, then gradually it began to brighten ahead. They emerged into a large natural chamber and Bort pointed.

"That is the Firewall."

Ida had never seen a structure like it before. It was a tall dam of translucent crystal blocks, sitting on one side of the chamber, and it held back a reservoir of molten rock, which moved in a constant slow swirling pattern. The heat from it should have been unbearable, but some property of the crystal prevented the full strength of it from reaching them.

Ida wet her finger and cautiously touched the crystal surface; it was hot but not enough to burn. At the foot of the dam was a wide walkway, but beyond that the ground sloped away, gradually narrowing to become a deep "U" shaped channel. Scoured and shaped by ancient lava flows, it looked like a dried-up riverbed.

"My goodness," she said. "This is incredible! What is it for?"

Endor rubbed his forehead and leaned back to stare up the vertical face of the dam. "Torven mentioned something about the Trollid using this stuff for heat and light. Is this where they get the light from, Bort?"

Bort shrugged.

Science or magic, it was beyond their understanding, and they had to remain focused; Ida peered down into the deepening gloom of the channel. "One slip, and who knows where we'd stop."

"Quite," said Endor. "Which way now, Bort?"

"Over there." He pointed to a path clinging to the wall above the channel.

Endor glanced nervously at the Firewall. "Well, let's get on then."

They had barely taken three steps when a distant moan, like the deepest pipe of a church organ, echoed up from the depths of the channel.

"What in Loftin's ghost is that!" said Endor.

Ida had never heard anything like it. Even the air around her was vibrating, and her scalp and ears began to itch. "Goodness, it goes right through you."

"What's causing it, Bort?" said Endor.

Bort rubbed his ears and shrugged, "Bort does not know."

Endor urged them on. "Let's not hang about!"

The bed of the channel was soon lost from sight in the deep shadows far below, and now a cooler draught swirled around them, more noticeable in contrast to the comforting warmth of the Firewall.

At irregular intervals the distant moan trumpeted like one of death's messengers, and Ida was glad when the path finally led into another tunnel, leaving the strange, unsettling sound behind.

About a hundred paces on they came to a rock door; the smooth stone coated with a fine layer of frost. They stopped to dress for the night and for the cold, pulling on heavy jackets and cloaks. After shuttering their lanterns, Bort grasped a metal lever at the side of the tunnel and threw it over. There was a brief shudder, the door swung towards them and immediately a howl of bitterly cold wind scoured the tunnel, sweeping away the last remnants of warm air that had persisted from the Firewall. From ahead shone pale moonlight.

Endor went first, shuffling forward into the mouth of a cave, the wind snatching at his coat.

Ida stepped up beside him and stared out into the night; they were halfway up a vertical rock face, and just visible through a swirling, manic dance of snowflakes, the Queen's moon, Nal, was overhead in quarter phase.

Shielding her eyes, Ida looked down; the jumbled remains of a large snow-carpeted city lay beneath her, its farther edges submerged beneath landslides of scree and earth. Near its centre, and almost directly below, was the Harrowen camp, marked by a horseshoe of guttering fires that sat to one side of a freestanding stone arch, the World Gate. Just below her was the start of a steep path, which zigzagged its way down through the dark shadows clinging to the rock face. For a second she felt dizzy, but she took a deep breath and calmed herself.

Endor leant in close. "You can stay here, if you'd like, Ida."

"No, I'll be fine." She glanced down the path. "You'd never manage all the blasting sticks by yourself."

Endor hesitated before answering, but eventually nodded. "Once we get down, I'll manage them on the flat. You'll come straight back up here, understood?"

Ida nodded and swallowed back a lump in her throat, realising it wasn't just her promise to Bort that made her want to go on. She wasn't ready to say goodbye to Endor.

"Best we get these packs sorted," she said.

They retreated into the shelter of the tunnel to remove unnecessary weight from their packs, setting aside spare clothes, sleeping mats and the food for the return journey.

They had just finished splitting the blasting sticks between the two packs Endor and Bort would carry, when Ida noticed a stronger blue light flickering on the roof of the cave.

Without exchanging a word, they all crept forward and stared down into the Harrowen camp. The light came from beneath the arch of the World Gate, and was bright enough to illuminate the area around the camp.

Ida's heart leapt as a pair of running figures emerged from beneath the arch; each carried a large backpack and were both pulling a heavily laden handcart.

"More damned Harrowen," whispered Endor. "Keep a count if you can."

Every three or four seconds Harrowen came running through, two abreast with the handcarts, and then dispersing quickly to gather away from the Gate. This continued for almost two minutes until the blue light pulsed and guttered. The gathered soldiers became animated, their attention centred on the Gate, shouting and gesturing as the last two Harrowen appeared.

There was a moan of disappointment as they emerged, icy and still as statues. One was run down and crushed to powder by the cart they pulled; the other tumbled to the ground, shattering like glass on impact. Then the light flickered out completely.

"The poor devils," said Endor.

Endor's sympathies confused Ida, but it was likely some connection common only to soldiers, even those on opposing sides.

His compassion was short-lived, and his tone hardened, "How many did you count, Ida?"

"Sixty-four, not counting the last two."

Endor nodded. "I can't see them setting off in this weather. Likely they'll bed down for the night."

Confirming his words, the new arrivals dispersed around the fires and began settling in.

"That's not so bad," said Endor, "and this Gate can only open once every twenty hours. To be honest I'd expected more to come through."

Ida sighed. "But given enough time, even a drip can fill a bathtub."

Endor nodded grimly. "Still, they must have lost thousands at Sollas. There's not been enough time to recover anything like those losses. At this rate it'll take weeks to rebuild their strength."

"True enough," said Ida.

Endor peered down the path. "I'll use the dark and this foul weather to get closer, hide among some of the nearby ruins. Shouldn't be too hard, and you'll remember Torven said their wizards won't sense me because of the Gate. I imagine most of this lot will move off tomorrow in daylight, so I'll wait until it gets dark again before attacking the Gate."

They gathered up their packs, and with Bort leading the way, they struggled slowly down the icy path.

Mindful of her promise to Bort, Ida continued for as long as she could, but eventually her fingers grew numb, and a pressing chill began to gather across her back and chest, as the harsh wind penetrated her clothing.

It was Endor who stopped her, leaning close to speak, "This is madness, Ida. You can't keep on." He waved Bort close and the two men crowded around her, their bodies providing some shelter from the wind. "Ida's in a sorry state here, Bort, she'll have to go back."

"I'm sorry," she said. "I'm just being a nuisance."

Bort pointed down the track. "There is a cave ahead, good shelter."

Before Ida could object, Endor lifted her onto Bort's back and she clung tight against him with her eyes shut to avoid seeing the sheer drop. When the wind noise died and its fierce fingers stopped tearing at her clothes, she opened them again.

They were inside the cave, but it was almost completely black, with only a glimmer of moonlight at the entrance. When Bort set her down he immediately wrapped his coat around her. The heat trapped in it was a welcome luxury.

Endor lit a lantern and carefully shone it around, revealing the cave's walls; they were strangely ribbed, and the cave stretched well back into the mountain. Then he knelt and wrapped his warm, calloused hands around hers.

"Not a good night for you, eh, Ida?"

"I'm sorry," she said, her teeth chattering. "I'll have to go back."

Endor nodded. "Best thing, best thing." He grinned. "I'm not such a fool that I can lose my way now, and the last bit doesn't look half as bad. I doubt I'll need to, but even if I have to make two trips, I can manage the blasting sticks on my own now. You and Bort go and warm yourselves back at the Firewall. Keep the door open for when I return." He stood. "Hear that, Bort, you and Ida are heading back."

Bort nodded, but wore a troubled expression.

Endor clapped his arm reassuringly. "Don't worry, lad, you've done your share. You look after Ida now. And you keep a good watch on this path. The slightest sign of trouble, you shut that door and leave it shut. And if I don't return before midnight next again night, I'm not coming back. Do you understand?"

Bort nodded again.

Ida knew that this moment would come, but she hadn't expected it so soon. She struggled to her feet, Bort's heavy coat cocooning her and stretching to the ground. She took a deep breath and steadied herself, there was so much she wanted to say, but this was neither the time, nor the place.

She took hold of Endor's strong, calloused hands, gripping them firmly. "Goodbye, Endor, and good luck. We'll be waiting."

Endor smiled, returning the pressure. "That's the way, Ida. I've a grand job to do here, one I'm proud to be doing."

Endor shook hands briefly with Bort, pulled his collar up, shouldered the two packs and headed to the front of the cave. As he stood in the cave mouth to turn and wave goodbye, the irregular moaning of wind died completely, and then he was gone.

Ida took deep breaths, fighting the anxious pain growing in her chest and blinking back the tears that threatened. This was probably the last time she would see Endor, and it felt awful.

A sudden fierce gust of wind surged and moaned in the cave mouth, and for a few disconcerting seconds Ida's ears itched. It was a revelation.

"Bort," she shouted. "Go quickly and fetch Endor."

When the men returned their clothes were plastered in snow.

"What is it, Ida?" said Endor, gently.

She smiled. "I think there might be an easier way to do this. One that keeps us all well away from the Harrowen."

"What're you thinking on then, Ida?"

"All we need to do is destroy the Firewall."

Endor frowned. "I'm not with you? I can't see what good that would do."

"Without the dam to hold back the molten rock, I think it will pour down that big channel and out through this cave."

Endor tilted his head up, examining the cave. "Is that right Bort, is this the end of that bit up top there?"

"It is the same rock," Bort's face split in a huge grin, "and the same channel."

Endor strode to the entrance and stared out. He returned wearing the same grin as Bort. "Damned obvious, when you start using your head! That Gate is right below us here. Well done, Ida! How'd you work it out?"

"It was that strange noise up at the Firewall. Something had to be causing it. It's the wind blowing across the cave entrance; it's acting like a giant flute."

Endor grinned. "What a treasure you are, Ida."

Ida felt her cheeks warm. Not just pleased that her solution would destroy the World Gate, it also meant that Endor avoided almost certain death in the Harrowen camp.

It was a simple plan; Endor placed the blasting sticks in a small hollow at the base of the Firewall and attached a long fuse, and then Bort covered them with as many boulders and heavy rocks as he could find to help concentrate the blast.

After lighting the fuse, Ida trailed the others as they quickly returned to the howling winds of the cave mouth to watch their plan unfold.

The fuse seemed to take longer than expected, and then, from deep within the mountain, there came a dull thump. They felt the ground tremble, and loose dust and debris rained from the tunnel roof.

"I know it don't sound like much," said Endor, "but I'm sure it did the job."

Ida worried at her bottom lip. "I hope so." If it hadn't, they had just wasted a significant resource.

Endor leant close, putting a hand to his ear. "Can't you hear it?"

Ida listened. It wasn't a noise exactly, more of a deep vibration, and it was growing. Shielding her eyes from the cold winds, she stepped to the edge of the cave mouth and peered down.

Like steam from the spout of a boiling kettle, dense black smoke was already billowing from the opening below them. She reeled in surprise when a spume of fiery rock spurted out like water, but barely had time to watch it arc towards the unsuspecting Harrowen, before a wash of heat flowed up the rock face, instantly turning all the snow in its path to steam.

Cowering back from the blistering air rolling into the cave mouth, she sought refuge with the others further back in the tunnel.

Then an unearthly screeching and wailing filled the air, which Ida knew had nothing to do with the Harrowen troops below. Flickers of red light swept by the cave entrance, and then a brighter light approached and she cowered as a horrible, ghostly face entered the tunnel and swept towards her. The apparition was a Harrowen, no more than a boy, his features twisted and his mouth stretching open to swallow her. With a tormented scream the spectre swept through her and for a moment she felt such a terrible, sorrowful loneliness, she found she was sobbing; mourning the loss of a creature she had never met or known, and somehow knowing it had been trapped within the Gate and was now released.

But before she could even contemplate what this meant, she felt her throat constrict. Was this ghostly Harrowen now wreaking its revenge? Struggling for breath she sank to her knees. No, it was the smoke and fumes billowing out from the depths of the mountain. They were trapped, caught between the heat outside and these awful fumes.

Ida's eyes began to blur and she felt faint; the fumes weren't just depriving her of air, they were poisoning her. She hadn't thought the idea through; they were trapped and about to die. She wanted desperately to shout an apology, but the best she could manage were short, painful breaths.

Looming close, Endor gripped her hand briefly before his eyes fluttered shut and he collapsed. She had one last consoling thought before she too succumbed to the darkness; they had succeeded. The Gate and the newly emerged Harrowen were now covered in a layer of molten rock.

Bort's first concern was for Ida. He rushed to cradle her in his arms.

"Ida! Ida. Wake up!"

When she didn't respond he tried to rouse Endor, but he too was unconscious. The fumes were troubling them more than him; only he could rescue them. But how would he manage it? They were trapped in the tunnel with no way forward and no way back.

He crept to the front of the cave, shielded his eyes from the heat and peered over the edge. Molten rock still flowed from the opening below; the bright tongue of fire arcing down through the windblown snow and disappearing into a roiling mass of misty steam that was spreading over the valley floor. The heat was too great to go that way.

He headed back down the tunnel with the slim hope of finding a side passage that he hadn't noticed before. The further he went, the hotter it became and the thicker the irritating, smoky gasses were. He searched the walls as he moved along until eventually he was forced to stop. The way ahead was blocked by a creeping carpet of molten rock; the air above it shimmering with the intense heat. He staggered back towards the exit, gasping for breath. Halfway there he fell to his knees, tears flowing from his eyes. With the promise to watch over Ida ringing in his ears, he turned to the nearest wall and hammered his hands against the rough stone.

In despair he let out a growl of anguish, but there was another sound, high and thin, that seemed to flow around him, clawing at his scalp. Then it changed, becoming like the ringing of a hundred tiny bells.

He heard Torven's voice in his head; *little by little*, he said, *little by little*.

Concentrating hard, and fighting the sharp pain growing behind his eyes, Bort spread his fingers and inspected the rock. Instantly he knew there was a cavern on the other side of the wall; he could almost feel the cool air in it. He also knew that the rock was cracked and laced with voids. If he pushed hard enough he could force his way through.

Preparing himself for an immense effort, he braced his feet firmly on the ground and pressed against the rock, but nothing happened. He took another deep breath, preparing for an even bigger effort, but before he could push any harder, the wall crumbled. He fell into the other chamber and a chill breeze of clean, fresh air flowed over him. Scrambling to his feet he ran quickly to fetch Ida and Endor.

The first thing Ida felt was the cooling touch of a damp cloth on her forehead. Then she felt the stony ground pressing uncomfortably into her back; thankfully her head was pillowed. Opening her eyes, she blinked away grimy tears to find Endor leaning over her. She took a breath to clear away the foul smell in her nostrils, but a spasm of coughing wracked her body. A thick sulphurous mucous filled her mouth and she turned her head to spit it into a rag that Endor quickly pressed to her cheek.

Bort held out a flask of water. "Ida must drink."

Ida sat up and accepted the flask; her hand shaking as she pressed it to her lips and took a mouthful. She swilled it around her mouth and ignoring good manners, spat it onto the ground.

Endor offered the rag again. "Best way, Ida, best way. Get it all out; you'll feel the better for it."

"What happened?" she croaked, her throat dry and sore.

Endor grinned and nodded towards Bort. "Bort here found a side passage and carried us to safety."

"Thank you, Bort."

"How is Ida?" he asked.

"A bit weak I'm afraid."

"Silly of us not to realise what would happen," said Endor. "Bort's quick thinking got us out of a sticky situation there."

"I thought we were all going to die." Ida coughed again to clear her throat. "And it was all my fault."

"Nonsense," said Endor. "Utter nonsense! Your idea worked a treat, there's nothing left of the Gate. All the Harrowen down there are gone."

Ida found it difficult to share Endor's enthusiasm, but she nodded and smiled weakly. She took another sip of water, adding quietly, "Did anyone else see those ghosts?"

Both Bort and Endor nodded solemnly.

"Something to do with the Gate," said Endor.

Ida nodded. "I sensed that too."

"And not something I'd ever like to experience again." Endor quickly changed the topic of conversation. "We've upset their plans something terrible, Ida. I'd love to see that Tekt's face when he finds out what's happened."

"I'm sure he'll be very surprised."

"Surprised! He'll be as angry as hell! I only wish there was a way to let King Malcor know what's happened. It would help to keep everyone's morale up!"

"I'm sure it would," said Ida. "Now, how are we going to get back to the Library?"

"Don't you worry about that. Bort here has already worked it out. We'll have to make a bit of a detour, but there are passages all over this mountain, we'll manage back just fine."

Ida found Endor's enthusiasm infectious, particularly noting that he didn't revel in the deaths of the Harrowen.

Woken as if in the throes of a hideous nightmare, the deaths of the twenty wizards at the Gate at Domidia struck Dusswen like a hammer blow to the head. Though nauseous, reeling and unsteady, he knew that

Tekt would need to be told immediately. Fearing for the life of a lesser messenger, Dusswen took it upon himself to relay the bad news.

After confirming that Tekt was awake, a guard waved Dusswen up the steps of the command tower. It had always been this way, Tekt often slept in daylight, seeming to prefer the solitude of night for his thoughts and planning. Entering the audience chamber, Dusswen saw Tekt's dark outline on one of the tower's balconies.

Dusswen cleared his throat noisily as he approached, announcing his presence. Tekt lifted an arm to wave him forward, but kept his back to Dusswen.

There was no easy way to start. "I bring terrible news, my Lord."

The sinews in Tekt's wrists tightened as he gripped the handrail. "Speak it, Dusswen." His voice was devoid of emotion.

"The World Gate at Domidia was destroyed, my Lord. It is lost."

An awful silence hung over the audience chamber and Tekt remained on the balcony, staring out into the night.

Suddenly he spun around and roared with maniacal laughter. "Destroyed, Dusswen! Destroyed! Is there no worse piece of news you can bring me?" His voice became menacingly hollow. "How can the Gate be destroyed?"

Flashes of dying memories flooded Dusswen's mind. "It was immersed in molten rock, my Lord!"

Tekt's face went through a series of painful contortions before he spoke again, this time in a whisper, "Immersed in molten rock. What misfortune is this?" He shook his head and laughed quietly. Finally he waved a hand in dismissal. "Leave me. Wait outside!"

Dusswen bowed and left, glad still to be alive. Twenty minutes later he was recalled. He entered the audience chamber and found Tekt still on the balcony, leaning against the banister and staring through the darkness towards Conisby.

"Come," said Tekt.

Dusswen walked cautiously to the balcony. "My Lord, you would speak with me?"

"Had you not the foresight to bring a second set of Gate stones, Dusswen, I would be talking to your replacement. We must have the Conisby Gate as soon as possible. A prolonged siege is no longer an option; the balance of circumstances has changed. Now it is us who are under siege, cut off from our supplies and surrounded by all the hostile forces this world can muster, but we have no walls to protect us, and those within can outlast us."

"This is all true, my Lord," said Dusswen, carefully. He felt a spark of hope; Tekt had risen to power because he was quick witted and, unusual among Harrowen, flexible enough to adapt quickly to new situations. These traits had always served him well before.

Tekt banged a clenched fist against the banister rail. "First we must breach the wall." He turned to Dusswen, his eyes piercing and calculating. "Can your remaining wizards do this for me?"

"It can be achieved, my Lord, but it will leave us weakened. I would not recommend starting an attack until we have time to recover."

Tekt's jaw tightened.

"A day later, two at the most," Dusswen added quickly.

"If it must be, then we can wait," said Tekt.

"That is wise, my Lord." Dusswen felt relief, a lesser Harrowen Lord would have lashed out, might even have destroyed his own best resources in a fit of anger. He stared in admiration as Tekt turned again to the dark outline of Conisby.

"It will be a mighty battle, Dusswen, a mighty battle indeed; one that will live forever in the proud history of the Harrowen."

"It will, my Lord, and we, your servant wizards, will do our part."

"I know, Dusswen, and I also know that from the start this was never to be any easy enterprise. Tekt looked him up and down. "Go and rest. Come daylight you have work to do."

"Yes, my Lord."

Wearily Dusswen returned to his bed, his mind filled with thoughts of revenge, and of his champion Amrax. Fearing defeat, the old wizard Torven must have acted ahead of their encounter; Amrax was a true master of destructive magics and Torven would be as a child against him, the outcome of their confrontation was certain. Amrax would crush Torven, and any humans he had in his company, like insects under foot.

23

Moleskin had never worn armour before, but Lineth had insisted, warning that even if he never got close to a Harrowen soldier, he was still vulnerable from arrow and spear. They found him pieces made from Trollid metal, which, thankfully, was much lighter than Endor's old armour. However, with the Harrowen so close, Moleskin began to doubt if even the wealth contained in the Library was worth fighting for. Unfortunately, it was all a bit late for that conclusion.

Six levels up from the Library floor, he crouched with Lineth behind a thin wooden barrier placed against the balcony's railings. Prepared earlier, it was painted to match the colour of the walls behind them. He watched through a narrow slit, anticipating the arrival of the Harrowen, flinching when Lineth touched his arm.

She whispered, "They're here."

At ground level, a door swung open and three Harrowen sprang noiselessly into the Library.

The painful drumbeat of Moleskin's heart increased instantly to a higher tempo as the Harrowen formed a loose semicircle, their heads snapping from side to side to inspect the chamber.

Moleskin's hands shook so much, he pressed them behind his knees, and when the Harrowen looked up he drew back involuntarily, though he knew there was little chance they would see him.

One of the Harrowen signalled and more darkly-clad figures trotted into the room, expanding the semicircle.

Moleskin counted all thirty of them, before the last figure emerged; different from the others, he wore a flowing black cloak and held a long staff in his hands.

Immediately his eyes came up, staring directly at their hide. Shouting something, he pointed to their position with his staff, and all the Harrowen turned to stare.

"This doesn't look good," Lineth whispered.

Moleskin was too frightened to answer.

Some of the Harrowen started up the steps, but the wizard barked an order and they stopped. The wizard walked clear of the group, held his staff in both hands and presented it square towards Lineth and Moleskin. Even from this distance, his eyes seemed to burn red with malice.

Small fiery streamers began trickling backwards and forwards along the length of the staff, and Moleskin held his breath wondering what would happen next. Then he felt a pain in his head and became aware of a strange metallic taste in his mouth. His nose started running, as if he had a bad cold, and he wiped the drip away with the back of his hand; staring in horror at the bright red smear of blood coating it.

"Quickly," Lineth whispered, "we've got to get away from here."

Moleskin was shocked to see two thin trickles of blood spilling from her nostrils and her helmet glowed a weak blue.

She grabbed his shoulder and both recoiled; it was as if a wasp had stung him, but they had both felt it.

Ignoring the painful sparks passing between them, she tugged him to his feet. "Move," she growled.

Thrust into motion, Moleskin ran around the curve of the landing, but from the corner of his eye he saw a crackle of lightning pursue him along the banister. It suddenly leapt out to lash him like a fiery whip and he was barely able to control his legs; running with a jerky, spasmodic motion.

Suddenly the awful fluttering tension in his muscles stopped and he sank to his knees, a deep ache lingering throughout his body. Then he heard it, deep and horrible, the Harrowen below were laughing.

Lineth collapsed against the wall next to him.

"What will we do?" he pleaded.

"Run if you can," she managed through painful sobs.

The Harrowen laughter faded, replaced by cheering and the constant clatter of steel on leather.

Moleskin crept to the edge of the landing and looked down. Like some grand stage performer, the wizard was turning in a slow circle in front of the soldiers, his arms high, and with his free hand waving an invitation for their raucous applause. Moleskin felt sick.

Lineth joined him, just as the wizard finished his turn. He stared up and pointed his staff straight at them; his eyes narrowing and his mouth spreading into a grin. The tip of his staff burned white and with a loud crack, a ball of fire erupted from it.

Lineth dragged Moleskin away from the banister and pulled him to the floor. He stared at the underside of the level above, whimpering in fear as the stone grew brighter, lit by the approaching fireball. There was a flicker of intense heat and then the light was gone, the furnace roar of the fireball receding as it rose higher and higher. He let out a spasm of nervous laughter as the relief surged through him; the wizard had missed!

Slowing all the time, the fireball rose to the domed ceiling, where it performed a smooth loop, and then started down again.

"Gods no," he croaked, "it's coming back for us."

Just then, a loud, clear voice boomed through the air. It said, "The use of destructive magics is not permitted in the great hall."

Lineth gripped Moleskin's sleeve and pointed. "Look!"

The fireball gathered speed; heading not for them, but straight back towards the ground.

Moleskin crawled to the edge of the balcony to watch.

"By the gods," said Lineth. "It's going to hit the wizard."

Every eye was on the fireball; some of the Harrowen closest to the wizard had the presence of mind to leap away, but many remained fixed to the spot.

The fireball struck, and a tall column of flame erupted around the wizard, burning a bright rainbow of colours; reds and blues, with flashes of green, purple and yellow. Within the flame the wizard screamed and writhed as the flesh burned from his bones. He shrank ever smaller, and the flame too, until finally all that remained was a smoking column of carbon and ash.

Moleskin was barely able to breathe; that would have been their fate had the wizard's fireball reached them.

After a long pause, the Harrowen who had survived the blast lurched and staggered to their feet. Then one of them bellowed a command, which had the immediate effect of sending the survivors roaring and shouting up the first flight of steps.

Lineth slapped Moleskin's back. "That's taken care of a good few of them. Off you go then. Stick to the plan and we've got a good chance of surviving this."

Strangely, Moleskin's confidence was rising, partly a reaction to the fortuitous outcome of the wizard's fireball, and partly due to shock.

"I'll get to it," he said, mustering a purposeful voice.

"Good man!" Lineth saluted him. "The very best of luck to you."

Moleskin managed a sincere, "Good luck!" in response, then turned and trotted painfully towards the nearest lifting room.

Tukkle stared at the charred figure caught within the column of flaking carbon and the edge of his mouth began twitching. He fought to control it, but eventually gave in and allowed a lopsided grin to form on his face. A single mocking word erupted from his mouth, "Wizards!"

Amrax's earlier revelation that there were no human wizards present in the Library had been surprising, but also liberating. With no wizards to fear, Tukkle could now rely on the more conventional tools of combat; razor sharp steel, a quick eye and hardened muscle. Where Amrax had failed in his vanity, he would not.

Tukkle had already sent the survivors up the steps. Of those still on the ground, a few were still alive though horribly wounded. He went to each man and ran him through; better that than leave them to suffer. This honourable task complete, he set off in pursuit of his men. He had lost eight in the first encounter.

As he caught up with some wounded on the steps, they picked up their pace, but he passed them easily. Still standing was the rule; any who failed this simple test were afforded a quick death.

Looking up, Tukkle saw that one of the humans had gone. The other, a woman, stood her ground. He immediately increased his efforts, sprinting up the steps; wanting to be the first to reach her and enjoy the pleasure of cutting her down.

He quickly gained on the leaders, until there was only one flight of steps between them and him. Four of his best were still in front, but as they leapt onto the steps just below the woman, there was a ferocious bang.

Tukkle was thrown backwards, caught by a fierce blast of scorching hot wind. He saw two of his men tumble over the banister; the high-pitched whine in his ears almost drowning their screams as they plummeted towards the ground. When the smoke cleared, pieces of the other two were scattered all around. A sword lay on the ground by Tukkle's head, a clenched hand still holding the grip. Amrax had promised there were no wizards in the Library, so what had caused this carnage?

With an angry shout he jumped to his feet and raced up the flight of steps, quickly reaching the next level. Impossibly, the woman had gone. He scanned the landing and the next flight of steps. Then, through the persistent whine in his ears, he heard a distant jeering shout. He clung to the banister and looked up. She was above him, another six flights of steps away.

Two more bangs came from beneath him. He looked down to find the wounded stragglers now strewn about the lower steps, obviously dead. The other human was scuttling down the steps behind them.

"Get him!" Tukkle screamed.

Tukkle was appalled, only eight faces looked up. They had all paused, torn between the original order to go up, and the new one to go down.

Tukkle pointed to a soldier. "Akor, take those last four and go down. You other three, follow me!"

Akor began the pursuit, just as the human ran across the chamber floor and disappeared through one of the doors. Satisfied the situation was handled, Tukkle turned and ran towards the next flight of steps, but stopped dead at the first step.

The woman now stood at the top of this flight. He shook his head in disbelief. How had she managed to come down so quickly?

She held something in her hand. It looked like a candle, but it burned too fiercely. She lobbed it down the steps, turned and ran off.

As it tumbled towards him, some basic instinct took hold of Tukkle; he ducked past the steps and threw himself under them. There was a loud bang and loose pieces of stone and dust trickled onto his head. He emerged from cover to find three more of his force dead; two crumpled against the wall, the third draped across the banister.

The woman was gone and Tukkle leant over the banister to scan the levels above; she was four levels up, leaning over the banister and looking down on him. Their eyes met, and Tukkle saw both fear and determination in her face. No wizard surely, but a wielder of some outlandish alchemic craft. These burning firesticks were fearsome, but they needed to be thrown from close to, and this put the thrower at risk; he could work with that. He glanced down; at ground level, Akor and his band crowded around a single door. Their inaction told him they had lost the other human.

"Work it out," he bellowed. "There must be a quicker way to get between levels."

Lineth's sword came up in readiness as the nearest lifting room door swung open. Moleskin stepped out, his face smeared with his own blood and his eyes wide with fear, but she was proud of him; he'd overcome that fear and done his part.

"How m-many are left?" he stammered.

"I count seven," she said.

"Why aren't they chasing us?"

Lineth pointed. "They're trying to work out how we get up and down so fast."

"What do we do now?"

Lineth took the last two blasting sticks from a pouch at her waist and handed one to Moleskin. "We must make these count."

Moleskin stared at the stick for a few seconds and then turned and opened the door to the lifting room. "Lineth!"

"What?"

"It's gone!"

"Go up now!" She pushed Moleskin towards the steps and backed away from the door, making her way around the curving balcony. Pausing at the next lifting room she listened at the door, but there was no sound of movement.

Just then the first lifting room door slammed open and five Harrowen emerged. She kept moving until she stood opposite them. After a brief discussion they split into two groups and approached slowly, three from one side, two from the other.

Moleskin appeared opposite her, one landing up. The Harrowen hadn't seen him. He lit his blasting stick and threw it towards the group of three. It spun lazily through the air, end over end, leaving an undulating trail of smoke, but her heart sank as it fell beneath the landing.

The blast did no damage, other than to shake the Harrowen.

Then the powerfully-built leader of the group emerged from the third lifting room. His deep voice barked a guttural command at the pair closest to him and they scuttled off up the stairs in pursuit of Moleskin.

Lineth watched helplessly as Moleskin made a dash for a lifting room on that level. There was nothing she could do for him, so she brought her attention back to her own situation. The Harrowen were advancing, three from one side and their leader from the other direction.

Shielding her actions Lineth lit the last blasting stick, if she could get to the lifting room the bigger group had used she could put some distance between her and any survivors. Drawing her sword, she charged towards them. When the fuse was almost burnt down, she skidded to a halt and threw the blasting stick, immediately pressing herself into the nearest doorway.

As soon as the stick went off, Lineth sprang from the doorway and ran on through the grey, choking smoke. A figure loomed, and she brought her sword up in a desperate sweeping stroke. To her complete surprise the Trollid sword clove the Harrowen in two, cutting through armour, tissue and bone, but she had little time to reflect on the quality of the weapon, the Harrowen leader was almost on her. Still retreating, she turned to face him, her sword held ready.

He sneered, forming words in an uncomfortable parody of her language. "Enough running," he grunted. "Are you not brave enough to fight Tukkle?"

Lineth examined the creature Tukkle's powerful muscles and athletic build. If she ran he would catch her easily and cut her down from behind. She brought her sword up and saluted him. "I will fight you."

A deep gurgle of approval came from Tukkle's throat. He returned the salute before examining the two she had struck down with the last blasting stick. With a slow, deliberate motion he ran one of them through. The creature kicked once and was still.

Tukkle stalked forward, stepping carefully over the blood pooling around the remains of the Harrowen Lineth had sliced in two.

Lineth braced herself for Tukkle's first powerful lunge, and when it came she responded automatically, her sword deflecting the blow and cutting a thin groove across his chestplate. She didn't know who was more surprised, her or him. Her time in practice with Endor had not been wasted.

Tukkle retreated a few steps and eyed her carefully before sinking into a low stance and creeping cautiously forward again, his sword poised and ready.

Sparks flew as their weapons cut a deadly pattern between their bodies. More than once Lineth felt the breathy glide of sharpened steel close to her body, but she managed to deflect or avoid each stroke before it found flesh.

The fighting came in swift, furious clashes followed by moments of resting and appraisal. At some point Lineth forgot that she held a sword in her hand. It became a part of her, an extension of her will to survive; but she was tiring and a burning pain was growing in the muscles of her arms and shoulders. Would she finally collapse to her knees, her arms leaden, unable to raise her sword in defence?

Tukkle fell back, his deep chest rising and falling. "You fight well, human." A broad grin split his face. "Almost as well as a Harrowen."

Lineth did not answer, instead filling her lungs with deep, slow breaths. She took the opportunity to brush drips of sweat from her eyes with her forearm, and stretched and flexed her fingers on the grip of the sword.

With a flourish, Tukkle held up his sword and made a show of testing its edge with his free hand. "I promise it will be a sweet death."

This gloating was too much for Lineth, she danced forward, her sword a polished blur in the air between them, and it was over in an instant.

Sagging to her knees Lineth's eyes fixed on Tukkle. He towered over her for an instant and then toppled onto his back; a pool of blood gathering around his head and shoulders, pouring from a deep wound to his neck.

Exhausted, she settled with her back to the wall. In her present condition she was no match for the two remaining Harrowen and she listened anxiously for any sound of movement, but the Library was silent.

She could only imagine that Moleskin lay dead at the end of some long corridor, and felt a wave of sadness. He was no warrior, but he had found the courage to fight alongside her. She promised his death would not be in vain; the longer the Harrowen took to return, the better her chances against them.

Dusswen was torn from a troubled sleep by another bright, fearful moment of death. At first he was confused and thought his senses were reliving the loss of the wizards at the Gate, but clarity came quickly. The burning fire that consumed this particular wizard was quite different. Amrax was lost, and again it fell to Dusswen to inform Tekt.

In the grey of dawn the army was rousing from sleep and Dusswen hobbled past a few soldiers that had already risen to rekindle fires and start preparing the day's first meal. All bowed respectfully; though fearless warriors, they still valued the help the wizards gave them in battle.

The headquarters tower loomed dark against the dawn, and there, silhouetted on the balcony, stood Tekt, almost exactly where Dusswen had left him some hours before. Tekt's head turned, and he watched Dusswen's approach without any acknowledgment.

Almost resigned to the possibility he was about to die, Dusswen laboured up the timber staircase to the audience chamber. He raised his hand to knock on the doorframe, but Tekt spoke first.

"Come, Dusswen, I sense you have more bad news for me."

Dusswen entered the chamber and joined Tekt at the balcony. He kneeled. "I am sorry, my Lord. I have just felt Wizard Amrax's death. Likely it is connected to the loss of the Gate."

"No doubt Tukkle is dead as well."

"There's no way of knowing, my Lord."

"But likely." Tekt's clawed fingers drummed on the banister rail. "This must be the work of Torven, the feeble old wizard."

"It would seem so," said Dusswen.

"Then it is also likely that he will bring aid to the humans. We must act quickly. Can you and your wizards best this Torven?"

"Yes, he is one, we are many."

"Are you sure? This wizard has already laid waste to our Gate, and bested your champion Amrax. What other destructive magics can he muster?"

"Wizardry," Dusswen risked a harder edge to his voice, "is like anything else, it has limits. We will best him, my Lord!"

Tekt raised an eyebrow. "Very well. And when we have secured the Conisby Gate, you can explore the mysteries of this Library to your heart's content." Tekt laughed, and his voice took on a darkly sarcastic tone, "Though I would advise caution. It seems a very unhealthy place to visit."

Dusswen remained silent as Tekt openly scrutinised him from head to toe.

"If your brother wizards are as weak as you, I sense little will be achieved today."

Dusswen bowed. "It is true my Lord, the attack on the wall would best be delayed another day."

Tekt turned his back on Dusswen, his eyes for the army and the camp. "The timing is better that way, there are still many preparations to make. Rest well, Dusswen, I doubt I can tolerate further disappointment."

Dusswen backed away quietly, too weary even to be glad to have survived the meeting.

24

By Endor's estimation, it was mid-morning when he entered the Library. A strong smell, the same deathly odour the Harrowen had brought to the battlefield at Sollas, had already warned him that all was not well, and he'd cautioned Bort and Ida to remain in the tunnel while he investigated.

Dead Harrowen lay strewn about the floor and a mound, like the remains of a bonfire, sat close to the pool. Endor crept forward, alert to the sound of any movement.

There were Harrowen dead on the steps and their outlines were visible on higher levels; he counted close to twenty corpses, adding another to that number after inspecting the blackened mound. A clawed arm projected from within it, the charred flesh barely clinging to the bone.

A rattle came from one of the lifting room doors and Endor brought up his sword, tiptoed to the door and pressed his ear to it.

"It's me, sir," Moleskin whispered, from the other side. "Are there any Harrowen out there?"

"Just dead ones that I can see." Endor heard a noise behind him and spun around. It was Lineth, emerging from one of the other lifting rooms.

She scurried across, calling quietly, "Careful, Endor, there's two more Harrowen still alive. Is someone in there?"

"It's Moleskin," Endor whispered.

Her face lit up. "I thought he was dead." She leant close to the door and whispered through it. "Well done, Moleskin."

He returned a feeble, "Thanks."

She whispered again. "The two Harrowen chasing you, where did they go?"

"No idea," was his muffled reply.

Endor tried the door handle, but it wouldn't turn. "You can come on out now, Moleskin, you'll be safe with us."

"I can't," he said. "The door won't open."

"Nonsense." Endor tried the handle again, giving the door a firm tug, but it wouldn't open. "It does seem to be jammed. Here, you push, I'll pull."

Endor heaved on the door handle, but the door wouldn't budge. "Are you sure you're pushing?" he said, impatiently.

"Why doesn't he just move to another level?" said Lineth.

Endor pressed close to the door. "Why don't you move to another level?"

"I can't do that either," said Moleskin. "The room won't move."

"Maybe Bort will manage it?" suggested Lineth.

Endor nodded. "I'll fetch him and Ida."

When Ida entered the Library, her mouth fell open and she shook her head. "Goodness, what a mess."

Endor put a finger to his lips. "Careful, Ida, there's still a couple of them on the loose."

She shuddered and stepped closer to Bort, her eyes scanning the levels above.

After a quick explanation, Lineth and Endor kept watch while Bort grappled with the door. Finally it flew open, banging hard against the wall; the noise echoing from the distant ceiling.

"Damn," said Lineth, "that's bound to get their attention."

"The Harrowen are here," said Bort.

Endor turned and chuckled. "So they are."

Ida felt quite uncomfortable, the lifting room had settled at an uneven angle on the remains of two crushed Harrowen.

"What happened?" said Endor.

Moleskin jumped out, his face ashen. "They must be the ones that were chasing me. I managed to get into the lifting room just before them. First I went up, and then I remembered that the door from the Trollid city had a lock, so I came down. I knew if I could get to it I'd be safe. They must have fallen down the shaft just after I moved the lifting room."

Lineth laughed. "If the fall didn't kill them, the room did. You've flattened them."

"Wonderful," said Endor. "Then we've had two fine victories."

"You were successful?" said Lineth.

"Successful," roared Endor, "we were magnificent!

Ida frowned, but had to agree Endor was right.

But this," Endor waved his arm around the hall, "how was this marvel achieved?"

"It's an incredible story." Lineth gazed wistfully at the high domed ceiling. "We thought we were dead at the start, but the Library saved us."

"That sounds a bit mysterious," said Endor, "what happened?"

"You'd hardly believe it..." began Lineth.

Ida couldn't stand to be among the corpses for any longer than was necessary, she interrupted, "Maybe we should tidy up a bit first?"

Lineth nodded. "Yes, the story will keep." She held her hand out to Moleskin. "For a civilian, you fought well."

Lineth's voice held such sincerity, Ida felt a surprising glow of warmth for Moleskin. It seemed the man had finally redeemed himself.

Endor clapped Moleskin's shoulder. "Well done, that man! Well done!"

Ida prepared lunch while the others removed the Harrowen dead; Moleskin and Lineth clearing the mess of pungent blood and other remains as best they could, while Bort and Endor tumbled the Harrowen corpses into the chasm at the end of the passage leading to the city. By the time their gruesome tasks were finished, and they returned to sit at the dining table, none of them felt much like eating.

Endor had also taken time to visit the viewing room, and shared his findings. Having searched the landscape around the mountain, there were no signs of more Harrowen on their way to the Library, and as before, the Harrowen camp at Conisby was busy, but they were not massing for battle.

After clearing the meal Ida laid out a decanter of strong spirits and a glass for each of them. She poured a small measure for herself, and bigger ones for the rest. Then, in front of a warm fire, they exchanged tales.

As Lineth's story emerged, Ida was astonished, what she and Moleskin had achieved against such odds, even with the Library's assistance, was incredible. Though she still had her doubts, she would try to treat Moleskin with greater respect in future.

Their own tale brought similar reactions and much to Ida's embarrassment, Endor took great pleasure in pointing out her and Bort's part in its success. He failed to mention his initial plan, though Ida had no doubt Lineth was well aware of his intentions. Then, tales told, dangers shared, Ida knew it was time to move on. But if all their party were as tired as she was, they would gain little by denying themselves rest.

Endor agreed. "I think we can allow ourselves the remainder of the day off, but when those reinforcements fail to turn up, Tekt will know something is wrong. We might have a couple of days while he sends someone to investigate, but eventually he's going to know that the Gate is gone. First thing in the morning, we'll start a proper search of this Library. I doubt there's more Harrowen on their way here, but we'll keep a watch going to be sure. Lineth, maybe you can work out a rota for that?"

Lineth nodded.

"Now, if nobody minds, I can hardly keep my eyes open another minute. I'm off to lie down and rest."

Lineth assigned herself the first watch in the viewing room, and insisted everyone else turn in.

Ida was happy to comply; the prospect of a warm, comfortable bed was very enticing. Tomorrow would come soon enough, and with it, she had little doubt, some new challenge. By denying the Harrowen the means to reinforce their army, and, for the time being, free access to the Library, they must already have made a difference to the conflict. But she knew Endor and Lineth would not sit by and watch their fellows suffer; if they found nothing else in the Library to help defeat the Harrowen, they would still want to return to Conisby. It worried her that Torven's dying words might only have been about destroying the World Gate. She hoped for all their sakes there was more.

25

Endor had finished his breakfast, and was leaning on a bannister in the main hall outside their quarters, when Lineth appeared a few levels up and on the opposite side of the hall.

She wore a grim expression. "Endor, come quickly. I think they're about to start an attack on Conisby!"

This was troubling; the news of the loss of the Gate at Domidia had travelled impossibly fast, likely the result of magical means, which was worrying. He quickly found the nearest lifting room and joined her.

She had the image centred on the open plain to the east of Conisby, and Tekt's forces were massing in deep ranks at the front of their camp.

"It's much sooner than we expected," she said.

Endor nodded and took hold of the table's controls. He searched through the massed army, but found none of the expected siege engines, towers or ladders. He had counted on a week at least while these devices were built. "He can't be about to attack, they've no way to scale the walls."

Just then the Harrowen soldiers moved aside, forming a wide path through which about fifty black-cloaked figures walked.

"Harrowen wizards," said Lineth, a slight tremor in her voice.

Having heard the misery one wizard had inflicted on her and Moleskin, and remembering the strange fiery energy Torven had flung against the dragon, Endor realised this was not to be a typical attack. He wondered what vile magic would be unleashed on the defenders at Conisby; this was warfare beyond anything he had imagined possible.

The wizards walked onto the bare plain and spread out to stand in a circle, each about five paces apart; the noiseless nature of the viewing machine adding a strange unreality to what was already a very odd spectacle.

The wizards turned inwards to face each other, each holding a staff, which they pointed into the centre of the circle.

An indistinct blur formed over the wizards and Endor wondered if the viewing table had lost focus. But the blur began to glow and take shape, becoming a huge spinning disc of light that flashed and sparked, spinning faster and faster. Endor held his breath as the disc contracted into an intense burning ball, and then leapt towards the city, striking the outer wall with a bright cascade of smoke and flame.

When the view cleared the wall still stood.

"Magic!" said Endor, with contempt. "Nothing will take those walls down."

But even as the words left his lips, a huge block of stone tumbled from the battlements and a visible crack opened in the wall as loose masonry began falling away. After about twenty seconds the movement ceased; a large section along the top of the wall had collapsed, and the crack had spread to almost its full height.

"It's still standing," said Lineth.

"But for how long?" said Endor.

Doubt nagged at his conscience; had he just made things worse? But then he thought of what might have been; Tekt's army vastly larger, their own forces weakened and starving, and the same wizard's attack. At least this way the defenders had a chance. He stared at the table, expecting the wizards to create another light ball, but the cloaked figures seemed smaller and many hung to their staffs for balance.

Endor breathed a sigh of relief as the wizards turned to make a slow retreat through the ranks of the Harrowen. The effort had drained them, but how long would they take to recover?

"That wall won't take another battering like that," said Lineth.

Endor stood for a second, pondering the wizard's attack. "We need a weapon we can use at a distance, something that will cause immense damage, and we need it quickly."

"If we had something like that flying star-scythe thing," Lineth suggested. "I'm sure I saw a something like it in one of the weapon rooms."

"Surely, it was a fearsome weapon, but at Sollas it was neither very accurate nor particularly destructive." Endor nodded towards the table. "What we need is something that can cause as much damage as that wizardry did. Something with the same power as those blasting sticks. Gather everyone together and meet me in the weapons corridor."

Dusswen hobbled into the audience chamber. The magic they had just used was unusual and seldom practised. It had drained them much more than expected, but he knew that all Tekt would see was their failure.

"My Lord, I can only beg forgiveness..."

Tekt raised a cautionary hand and turned away from the balcony. "Were I to manifest my frustration, Dusswen, there would not be one wizard left standing. But I am not a fool; I knew there was little chance of breaching the wall at the first attempt."

Dusswen nodded wearily.

"Come, sit." Tekt beckoned Dusswen towards his throne chair.

Dusswen hesitated, it was a seat reserved exclusively for Tekt's use.

"Sit," Tekt commanded.

"Of course, my Lord."

After Dusswen was seated, Tekt paced in front of the chair. "You said a day, maybe two?"

"Yes, my Lord, but..."

"Do not strain my patience," said Tekt, displeasure clear in his voice.

"It cannot be done sooner, my Lord. It would be foolish, a waste of effort..."

Tekt silenced Dusswen with a scowl. "Two days it is then." He turned his back on Dusswen and walked to the balcony. "Go and rest. Rest well. In two days you will take down the outer wall."

"Very well, my Lord." With difficulty, Dusswen rose from the throne chair and shuffled from the audience chamber. Two days was the bare minimum his brother wizards needed to recover. For some of the older ones the coming effort would damage them sorely, might even kill them, but like all Harrowen, it was a sacrifice they were willing to make.

Though resolved to help with the exploration of the weapons area, it troubled Ida that their goal was to find the most destructive weapon they could, one that would take the most lives in the quickest way possible. It didn't help that she had already summarised their needs in this way, but she saw no other way to describe it. The equally grim reality was that if they failed to find such a weapon, the Harrowen would win and many, many more innocents would die. It was the nature of the Harrowen to spare none, soldier or civilian.

When they arrived at the weapons corridor, Ida crowded around the guide book with the others, and after a brief discussion it was decided to examine the sections on; **Weapons of Siege and Machines of War**.

Their search then narrowed down to a group of weapons cross-referenced in both sections as; **Projectile Weapons**.

"I think you should read this." Lineth pointed to an entry.

Endor read it aloud, "For reasons of safety, only a small quantity of the blasting powder is kept in the Library. This can be found in the section; Weapons of an Alchemic and Pyrotechnic Nature."

"How much was there?" said Lineth.

"Barely a cupful," said Endor. "Damn it! That surely won't be enough."

Ida sensed Endor's desperation, and how close he was to panic.

"Blasting powder!" she said, firmly. "Only a few days ago none of us had heard of blasting powder, or those blasting sticks. Clearly what we need to find is something that doesn't use blasting powder."

"Yes, of course." Endor slapped the open book. "Bort, we'll take this with us. Let's head along and have a proper look at these things."

The guide led them to the very last door in the corridor, where the largest weapons were kept. Endor threw the door open and marched inside.

As the light came up an incredible and terrifying sight greeted Ida. The room was by far the biggest chamber she had seen anywhere in the Library, and was filled wall to wall with a baffling array of engines of war, some so large they almost touched the ceiling.

They inspected the machines, constantly referencing the book, only to dismiss them one after the other. Some excluded themselves immediately by being too big, and though some operated on familiar principals, catapults and crossbows, Endor or Lineth would quickly dismiss them as requiring too much effort from the operators for the limited amount of damage they could cause.

Inevitably they concentrated on the weapons operated by alchemic means, the destructive potential of these being described as much greater than the more familiar weapons. Most had a cylindrical chamber into which a heavy ball was inserted, but they all had the same problem, they used the blasting powder to throw the ball from the cylinder.

Ida hung back as Endor continued his search. One weapon in particular had caught her interest; it stood amongst a group they hadn't inspected yet. It attracted her not because of any destructive potential it might have, more because of its elegance and fine decoration.

Made from polished brass and copper it sat on top of a large circular platform, which in turn sat on a sturdy carriage frame, with four wheels, each as tall as her.

At the front of the carriage was a complex pulling harness, neatly arranged over three pairs of horses, which were modelled in timber and thick wire. Four leather and brass buckets hung from the rear, and on a neat rack above these was a plunger, not dissimilar to the one she used to churn butter. Anything not polished to a mirror finish had been painted in black lacquer and intricately detailed with fine gold lining.

Narrow metal steps mounted near the rear of the carriage gave access to the platform. Intrigued, Ida climbed up onto the machine, barely rocking the carriage's deep elliptical springs.

The barrel of the weapon was twice her height in length, and hung between two cast metal supports. What appeared to be a potbellied stove enclosed one end of it, though it had no hotplate or oven. The tall copper chimney projecting from the stove was capped with an elegant filigree crown, which would not have looked out of place on the head of a King.

On one side of the central supports was a complex arrangement of thick metal gears and winding handles. A pair of short brass telescopes were embedded in this assembly; their single shaped eyepiece level with Ida's shoulder. She bent down and peered through it, and the back of Endor's head sprang into view, though distorted and out of focus.

She straightened and called out, "This is... ah... lovely."

Endor shouted back over his shoulder. "I hardly think *lovely* is a word I would use to describe a weapon, Ida." He turned to see what had caught her interest. "Oh! Indeed, Ida, I have to admit it's a fine looking piece."

Ida wound one of the handles and the barrel of the weapon smoothly and slowly changed its angle, pointing more towards the ceiling. She wound another handle and let out a surprised, "Goodness!" as the platform rotated majestically like a merry-go-round.

Endor strode towards the machine, waving Bort to follow. "Bring that book over here and let's see what it's supposed to do."

Bort laid the book on the edge of the circular platform and Ida knelt beside it.

Endor flicked through the pages until he found a matching illustration. "It's called a *Steam Bombard*. The damn thing is made from copper mostly, and throws a blasting bomb two thousand paces." He stood back and examined the machine, his eyes calculating and alert. "Two thousand paces, eh!"

Ida read on. "A fire heats the first third of the barrel. When it is sufficiently heated, a charge of water is released into the heated part, where it instantly transforms to steam. The steam pushes the bomb from its end..."

"Let me see that," Lineth pushed forward to examine the same piece of text. "But that's wonderful! It doesn't use the blasting powder."

"What about those bombs?" said Endor, cautiously.

Lineth flicked to another section of the catalogue. "There are thirty of them in storage. Seems they're perfectly safe until primed. If they're anything like the blasting sticks, they'll cause a lot of damage."

"By the gods, Ida!" said Endor. "It looks like you've found exactly what we were looking for." He slapped the edge of a metal shod wheel. "Damned fine looking it is too."

"How is it aimed?" said Ida.

Lineth pointed to a footnote. "There's a manual explaining how to use it."

"Excellent!" Endor stepped away from the machine and examined it from end to end. "Now all we have to do is work out how to get it to the battle field."

"There must be some way of getting all these exhibits in here," said Ida.

Lineth pointed. "Over there."

Ida had never seen a pair of doors so large. They were at least four times the height needed for the bombard, and curved to a point at the top to follow the shape of the chamber's vaulted ceiling.

Bort slid a well-greased bolt aside, and Endor and Lineth lifted a pair of drop pins, one for each door. It then took the combined efforts of Endor and Bort heaving on a large iron handle to get the first door moving, and once there was space, Lineth and Moleskin stepped to the other side to add their shoulders to the effort. Almost noiselessly the door swung inward on a pair of massive ornate hinges, the hinge pins easily as thick as Bort's forearm.

Ida's curiosity took hold, and while the others struggled with the second door, she stepped into the darkness of the tunnel beyond. It had the same smooth floor as the Library, but the walls were rougher hewn. The weapons corridor was well above the Library's ground level, and Ida assumed access would involve a long sloping ramp. She could not have been more surprised when the smooth floor stopped abruptly at a wide metal gate that guarded a sheer drop.

"Come and see this!" she shouted back.

Ida peered up and down the immense shadowy chimney. In the centre, and well beyond reach, hung eight thick wire ropes. She noticed a lever set on a post near to the wall and pushed it down against firm pressure, but as soon as she released it, it rose back to its original position. She pulled it up, and this time it remained in that position.

From far below, came a noise like a millwheel in motion and the wire ropes trembled and began moving, some going up and some down.

Creaking and clattering, a massive metal cage rose from out of the darkness below, four enormous pulley wheels on top of it turning slowly and hypnotically as the wire rope coiled around them.

Ida's mouth fell open as the cage drew closer; her cottage would almost fit within it. She became aware of Endor, Lineth, Moleskin and Bort standing around her, all equally silent.

"Well done again, Ida," Endor whispered.

The cage slowed to a halt, there was a clatter behind her and when she turned to look she found the lever had returned to its rest position.

Lineth unlatched the gate and swung it back. "It's the same as the lifting rooms." Cautiously she stepped onto the thickly-planked floor of the cage. It didn't move a hairsbreadth. "Is anyone coming?"

"It would help if we had some light," said Ida.

An array of stone balls fixed to the roof of the cage came to life, spreading a warm yellow glow over the floor.

"Maybe one of us should stay here?" Endor suggested.

"I'll stay," said Moleskin, quickly.

"Good man. Don't go wandering off," said Endor.

"I won't be doing that, sir."

Ida could have predicted Moleskin's offer, but she detected a disconcerting hint of deception in his voice. As she joined Lineth, Bort and Endor in the cage, she examined Moleskin's face carefully, as he made a pantomime display of closing and securing the gate. When he gave Endor a friendly parting wave, her stomach churned. Endor couldn't see what was now obvious to her; Moleskin had no intention of helping with the fight. It didn't bother her particularly, he was more likely to hinder their efforts than aid them, but she felt sorry for Endor and the inevitable disappointment that was coming.

She operated a lever in the cage, and from below came another swish of water. Slowly the cage began to descend and she felt a strange almost naughty excitement; they were exploring behind the facade of the Library, beyond the public spaces, like the audience at a theatre exploring back of stage where normally only the actors, stage hands and musicians were allowed.

Staring up at the huge wheels turning above her head, she realised the small lifting rooms probably operated on the same principle, though the mechanism powering them was invisible, almost magical, which of course it wasn't. But here on this huge skeleton of a lifting room, the mechanics of this wonderful machine were on full display.

She knew that great weights could be lifted using a block and tackle, and here someone had taken the idea one step further and on the grandest of scales. She wondered at the kinds of minds that could contemplate and design such a complex device.

Finally, the cage came to rest facing another smooth-floored but roughly-hewn tunnel and Endor stepped forward confidently, calling for light. When the tunnel grew brighter, Ida was drawn to a window set in one of the walls. Cupping her hands around her eyes, she pressed against the glass and peered through it.

The shadowy room was filled with a complex web of metal levers, rods and cranks; the whole mechanism polished and greased. At the opposite side of the room was another larger window, and through it she saw an immense paddlewheel partly submerged in a dark pool of water. Constant drips seeped from a sluice sitting above the wheel.

Endor joined her. "It's like a water mill," he mused, "how ingenious."

It struck Ida that this mechanism was almost within the grasp of the scientists and engineers in Carolin. But then she had another humbling thought, it had already existed here in the Library for many hundreds of years. The same was true for all the exhibits.

What had happened on the worlds that gave birth to these ideas? What scientific wonders did they now boast, or had their growth been stunted or stopped by events similar to those unfolding on Nephus? Even if she had been able to ask Torven about this, she suspected his answers would have been enigmatic and evasive.

Leaving the waterwheel behind, Ida followed the others along the tunnel. It opened onto a cavern littered with massive hoisting and lifting devices, and huge trolleys and barrows. She hadn't felt out of place in the Trollid city; the scale of the buildings fitting the scale of the cavern, and the streets, though wide, only gave it a sense of grandeur, but here Ida felt like a small child creeping through an adult's world.

There were chambers to either side containing all manner of craftworking machinery for wood and metal, and smaller booths had been set aside for more intricate crafts; bookbinding, upholstery and jewellery making being among the more obvious. All had the air of having been abandoned for a long time.

Ida was drawn to a booth containing a machine that she was amazed to find was for sewing. She lifted and inspected the edge of a dusty panel of cloth that still sat in the machine. It had been stitched together using the most regular and even of stitches she had ever seen. She sat at the machine and stretched her toes to reach a treadle footplate beneath it. She'd seen a wood turner using a similar device made from rope and bent wood to spin his wood, so she had a good idea what to do next.

After a few attempts, she set the machine in motion, and a stout needle just above the cloth darted up and down at an incredible speed. The cloth caught under the needle advanced in quick regular jumps, and in seconds she had completed a line of stitching that would have taken even the most nimble fingered seamstress about ten minutes. It was nothing short of miraculous.

Endor was busily inspecting another nearby booth and admiring neat rows of woodturning tools.

"This must be where they prepared everything before putting it on display," he said.

Ida joined him. "It's all a bit humbling."

Endor nodded. "Can't help feeling a bit ignorant when I see all this around me."

Bort called them to a huge wooden door at the far end of the cavern, pulling it open to reveal a semicircular chamber with three tunnels fanning out from it. These had no lighting, but from the light spilling into them further branches and side tunnels could be seen.

"Looks like a bit of a maze," said Endor. "Any idea where they all go, Bort?"

Bort stared into the darkness. "The tunnels go a long way, but Bort does not know where."

"There's bound to be a map," said Ida.

An office was soon located; a musty place filled with rolled up drawings, loose papers and file wallets, all stacked neatly on high shelves. In the centre of the room was an immense desk, littered with all manner of drawings, sketches and notes.

Ida leant over it and inspected a sketch. The paper was aged and brown but the drawing was still clear, with cryptic notes and arrows pointing here and there on it. Down one side was a numbered list, with a series of ticks against each item. She felt sad and also strangely warmed.

"I think I would like to have met the person who worked here," she said.

A map showing the tunnel complex covered one wall of the room.

Endor pointed to one line. "This," he said to Bort, "what's this?"

Bort stared at the map and nodded. "A tunnel, a big tunnel."

Endor grinned at Ida. "If this map is right, this tunnel gives us a way to get the bombard to Conisby without ever going outside. We'll travel right by the Harrowen and they'll never know we're there!"

Ida felt the mood of enchantment drain from her, for the briefest of times she had forgotten the purpose of their explorations. With this discovery, the reality of their purpose came flooding back. Thinking back to the size of the bombard, it seemed an impossible task, but their small party would attempt to drag it from this mountain all the way to Conisby. She wanted to smile back at Endor, offer at very least her moral support, but all she felt was a desperate, hopeless emptiness.

26

When Endor arrived back at the weapons room, he was annoyed to find Moleskin was gone. With growing anger, he called for him in the main hall, but there was no answer. Sending the others to explore more obvious locations; their quarters and the viewing room, he went to the Library guide to find a door he knew would exist, but had seen no need to visit. Lineth joined him just before he opened it.

"No sign of him?" he asked her.

She sighed and shook her head. "None."

It wasn't the answer he wanted, but he had to admit it was the one he expected. He entered the corridor, opened the door to the first treasure room and stared in; it was piled high with gold ingots.

"By the gods," he finally managed, "there's a fortune here."

"A hundred thousand fortunes at least," said Lineth.

Her thoughts probably echoed his; they would both have shared in bounty confiscated from robbers, when the owners could not be found, but he knew that during battle, nothing weighed a man down more than gold, and the desire to protect it.

"I'll admit it could make life very comfortable," he said.

"Surely," said Lineth.

She drew Endor's attention to a small sack tucked behind the door. Lifting it, she turned it upside down and gave it a shake. A single gold coin dropped out and rolled across the floor.

Endor trapped it with his foot, and then picked it up and felt its weight. "Confound the fellow!"

"I'm afraid," said Lineth, "that Moleskin's greed is stronger than his sense of honour."

Throwing the coin aside in disgust, Endor spun on his heel and made for the door. "He can rot in a pit for all I care! Come on, we've a job to do."

Ida found it hard not to feel a little smug at this revelation about Moleskin, and shook her head in disgust. "I knew that pathetic little man was not to be trusted."

Bort offered no opinion on Moleskin's disappearance, and Endor was strangely quiet too.

"Do you think he's still hiding somewhere in the Library?" said Lineth.

Ida smirked. "Not him, he's long gone." She spoke to Endor. "You should have thrown him out long ago. The man's an out-and-out scoundrel."

Endor sighed. "Mostly he was good at his job."

Ida snorted her contempt. "He cheated you, all the time he was cheating you."

She could see how much Endor was smarting from the betrayal, and then had a sudden insight. He must have known about Moleskin's dishonesty all along, and chosen to ignore it. Had Endor been so lonely he would accept companionship at any cost?

Ida felt terrible remorse; in Silvermeadow she had never made any special effort to socialise with Endor, quite the opposite in fact. She wanted to change that, but looking ahead it seemed unlikely that either of them would survive to realise that desire. Suddenly overcome by emotion she quickly excused herself, seeking refuge in the privacy of her room.

She sat on her bed, struggling to contain the tears brimming at the edge of her eyes. As soldiers Lineth and Endor had already accepted the possibility of death. Obviously Moleskin had worked it out too, which was why he had run away. Could she really blame him? Bort had promised to help, but had he considered where their journey might take them? She felt a melancholy rush of pride, of course he had. She might wish it were different, but her future was just as uncertain.

She stood and took a deep breath, there was no time to waste on self-pity; with the situation so dire at Conisby, her duty was as simple and clear as it was for Endor and Lineth.

Laden with a large treasure-filled pack, Moleskin strode purposefully along a Trollid tunnel. With the discovery of the steam bombard, it looked like the others were set on returning to the fight, and there could be only one outcome to such a foolhardy act; they would all end up dead.

He had considered hiding in the Library, but with the strong possibility that the Harrowen would come again, it wouldn't be safe for long. And now immensely wealthy, he saw no reason to live in misery on the edges of some frozen sea to the north. He would skirt around the conflict and head south to find a new life in a warmer climate.

To that end, he had chosen this tunnel carefully; it led to a long shallow valley that would bring him back to the village the dragon had ravaged. He shuddered, remembering the awful scene there, but Torven had not mentioned another dragon, so he felt safe on that count.

Eventually he came to the exit, a stone door with a metal lever beside it. The mechanism was in good order and operated with the minimum of effort; the door swinging noiselessly aside to admit a glare of sunshine that stung his eyes. Beyond the door, a smooth plain of undisturbed snow stretched off into a flat-bottomed valley. The village was only half a day's walk away, plenty of time to find shelter before nightfall.

He stepped from the tunnel and the door swept shut behind him. When he turned to look, he couldn't see its outline and there was no obvious handle to reopen it. Not that it mattered, he wasn't going back.

Taking a step, he sank up to his knee in snow. The next step took him up to his thigh and the next to his waist. This was worrying; the walk to the village would take longer if the snow remained as deep, and his preparations had not included the possibility of staying out overnight. There was also the problem of food; he had packed very little, so that he could carry more precious metals and gems.

The situation worsened steadily; the sky clouded over and tiny wet flakes of snow began drifting lazily down, clinging to his clothing and catching on his eyebrows. His clothing became sodden and his legs were soon chilled through. Then a thick fog descended, allowing him to see little more than a few steps ahead of him, and it wasn't long before he lost all sense of direction. He tried not to lose heart, but a nagging panic lurked at the edge of his thoughts. If he couldn't find shelter, he would be dead before morning.

27

Tears dried and face washed, Ida presented herself in the dining room, and during a hasty lunch, Endor organised the expedition. She got the job of gathering provisions while Bort, Lineth and Endor would move the Bombard to the head of the tunnel.

She collected a hand cart from the workshops and began moving the provisions. Unsure of another route, she repeatedly passed through the weapons room, before taking her tiny cargo onto the lifting cage and down to the tunnel mouth. Each time she passed the others, the bombard was further along. Though heavy, its carriage was well maintained and rolled easily on the smooth floors of the Library and the workshops. A team of horses would have made the task much easier, but once Bort applied his muscle power, it was clear that the task was far from impossible.

Endor had also assigned Ida another duty, one that troubled her, but which she accepted stoically. She was to familiarise herself with the manual for operating the bombard, in order to be its captain and aimer.

By mid-afternoon they were ready to leave, and rather than waste another night in the Library, it was decided to move on and spend that night in the tunnel.

Ida was the last to leave their quarters; pausing in the doorway to give the lounge one final inspection. The fireplace was raked clean, and all the fireside tools were neatly stacked on their rack. The coal scuttle was brimming with coal and a little pile of kindling sat in a neat basket beside it. Everything was as they had found it, which was as it should be.

Walking alone through the vast emptiness of the main hall, Ida took time to take in every detail. Probably most notable was the lack of any bloodstains or marks left by the Harrowen corpses; the Library had cleaned itself. She was glad of this, if at some future time someone returned to it, or, she supposed, discovered it, they would find it in the same pristine state they had. She had little doubt that this was the last time she would see it.

Pausing in the doorway to the long weapons corridor, she stared up at the domed ceiling and wondered if there was some way to turn off the light. Though, looking back to their arrival, no doubt the Library would eventually note their absence and do this on its own.

Again she contemplated Torven's words about the purpose of the Library. She could not easily accept his reasons for its existence, but considering the effort and ingenuity that had gone into creating it, there were many who did. Regardless of what she thought, without it they would not be alive, and they would not have this chance to defeat the Harrowen. With one last nod of approval to the Library's creators, she closed the door and turned to walk the length of the long weapons corridor.

The last journey down in the lifting cage felt terribly lonely, and Ida was glad to find Bort waiting at the bottom of the shaft. He immediately offered to carry her bag. It was no great weight, but she sensed he took pleasure from the act. He had changed so much from the timid creature she had first discovered in the woods, but the parts of him she treasured most endured.

They walked silently through the workshops to the Bombard, finding Endor and Lineth had already lit a row of lanterns set high on the front of the carriage, and a pool of light spread down the tunnel.

Bort placed Ida's bag on the carriage.

"Are we ready for the off?" said Endor.

Ida fought to contain her emotions and keep a positive mood. "Just one last thing." Turning to the carriage she opened one of the packs and produced a bottle of wine. "I think a small drink to mark the start of this venture might be in order."

"Splendid idea, Ida." Endor accepted the bottle and took a mouthful. "I say, where did you find this? It's rather good."

"I found it tucked away in one of the kitchen cupboards."

Endor handed the bottle on to Bort, who inspected the label.

He sighed. "Trollid wine."

"Oh, I'm sorry," said Ida.

"Oh no," Bort raised a smile, "the wine is very good." He took a deep swallow and passed the bottle on to Lineth.

"To success," said Lineth, and then she took a mouthful.

The bottle ended back with Ida who took a small drink before forcing the cork back in.

"Is there any more of that?" said Endor.

Ida scowled, but said with an indulgent smile, "There might be."

"Have no fear, Ida," said Endor. "I'll leave the dispensing of provisions in your capable hands."

"I think that arrangement will work best for all of us." Ida replaced the bottle in its pack and then gathered up her skirt, tying it in a large knot at her back. "Let us clear a decent stretch before you set out."

Endor clapped Bort's shoulder and announced in a jovial tone. "This is the life, eh, Bort? Looks like we get to rest before we've even started."

Ida smiled at Endor; he'd given himself the job of maintaining morale, and no doubt they would need all the help they could get with that before this job was over. An earlier exploration of the tunnel had revealed it was littered with pebbles and rocks. These would cause no end of trouble with the steering and progress of the Bombard, so Endor had decided that she and Lineth would go ahead to clear the way, leaving him and Bort to pull the carriage.

Bort and Endor prepared themselves, easing their shoulders into a pair of harnesses, and Ida handed gloves and a broom to Lineth. She drew on her own gloves and, without another word, began sweeping the rocks and pebbles to the side of the tunnel. It seemed such a simple job, but she knew it was important. The more diligent she and Lineth were, the easier the task for Bort and Endor.

They worked until they were almost at the edge of the lamplight, stopping as there was little point in going further until they could see more.

Ida turned and waved to Endor and Bort, who appeared as shadowy outlines in the weak light.

"Come ahead now!"

Endor called back. "Right you are, Ida."

A second later Ida heard the harness straining and with a creak the carriage began rolling. To the steady metallic rumble of its wheels, she returned to her work.

Some areas were easy to clear, some more littered with stones and occasionally there were larger lumps of rock that needed lifting by both of them. She and Lineth worked as fast as they could, but gradually the carriage caught them. As it drew nearer the sounds of the wheels striking any stones they had missed became more obvious; from a simple crunch as a stone was crushed to powder, to a teeth-jarring screech as the a wheel skidded to a stop, which was usually accompanied by a muffled curse from Endor. Without the weight and power of horses to maintain the momentum, the carriage was too easily diverted, or worse, stopped entirely. But even with these setbacks, they still managed to catch up.

"Ease up there, Bort," Endor panted.

The carriage rolled to a halt, barely three paces from where Ida and Lineth struggled with a larger boulder.

"Best we stop for a spell," said Endor.

Wearily Ida abandoned the boulder.

"I'm sorry," said Lineth. "We just can't keep up with you."

"Endor will move rocks," said Bort. "Bort will pull the carriage."

Ida began to protest; it seemed too much for one man, even one as strong as Bort, but Endor interrupted.

"I hate to admit this, Ida, but the lad here has the better of me most of the time. I can hardly keep my side taut. Half the time I'm probably making it harder by letting the steering turn to my side. If we can keep things clear for the wheels, it's going to make things a lot easier." Endor slid the harness from his shoulders, unbuckled the draw lines and secured them to Bort's harness. "We'll stick to the same system, Bort. Wait until we get to the edge of the light, and then bring the carriage forward."

Bort nodded and sat down, with the harness still about his shoulders.

Endor placed his harness on the carriage and then moved around the group dispensing water, finally sitting beside Ida, who had settled at the side of the tunnel with her back against the wall.

"How're you doing, Ida?" he said.

She grimaced. "Reminds me of when I was a girl, and we used to pick the potato harvest."

"That's right," said Endor, "I remember the potato picking. Don't know why we had to do that."

"We would have felt pretty silly with just the two of us sitting in the classroom, while all the rest were out on the fields. Besides, according to my father, it was character building."

Endor laughed. "My father used exactly the same line with me. I don't suppose it was that bad." He smiled. "Who was that awful boy with the big teeth that was always late in the morning?"

"Kenneth Tucker it was."

"Whatever happened to him?"

Ida was surprised Endor didn't know this. "He's a clockmaker now. He married Lizzie Watford and set up home in Cadford. They've got four lads."

"Clockmaker, that was probably the only way for him to be on time for anything."

Ida smiled. It was odd what Endor did remember, and he was right, Kenneth was always a terrible timekeeper.

"And four lads," said Endor, wistfully.

Ida nodded. "The oldest apprenticed with his father, he works in Silvermeadow now, you'll have met him."

"Of course. Nathanial the clockmaker, a fine young man."

Ida nodded. "The next one apprenticed with a cabinetmaker, the other two are still in school."

"You've kept in touch?"

"I was visiting them every other week."

"You never wanted to start a family of your own," he said, carefully.

"Me? No, I've always been far too busy for that." Which was true, but might have been different if the right man had come along.

Endor stared at his boots. "I lost touch with everyone when I went away."

"But you've been back for a while now." Ida felt bold enough for some home truths. "You hide away in that manor house when you should be getting out and about more. Everyone would be happy to see you."

"Would they?"

"Of course they would."

"I suppose I could make more of an effort."

"There's the winter fair, for a start."

Though he wore a troubled frown, Endor smiled and gripped the back of her hand. "Well, Ida, maybe I'll do that."

All too aware of the warm pressure of Endor's hand on hers, Ida looked up into his eyes. "Endor, I never expected to be in a position to make such a difference to so many people. What we've done already, it's extraordinary."

He sighed. "It is that, Ida. But I'm still sorry I brought you along in the first place. You didn't sign up for any of this."

"Maybe I didn't, Endor, but I'm here anyway. And I'm glad you're here too. And... it's me that should be apologising to you."

"I can't think what you mean, Ida."

"I've never stopped thinking of you as that boy who used to vex me so much at school." She shook her head. "Oh, and your drinking..."

"Ah well," Endor shrugged and smiled, "a few little pleasures, is that too much to ask for?"

"But I can see beyond that now." Ida paused. "What I'm trying to say is, you've truly gained my admiration and respect. I had no idea about the life you led, how dangerous it was, and how honourably you've always acted."

"Ida, I…" Endor stammered, "I hardly know what to say."

"You don't have to say anything." Ida slid her hand free and rose to her feet. "Now, we'd better get on."

Endor stood. "Of course, yes."

Ida walked to where Bort sat. "Are you sure about this?"

"Bort is sure."

"Very well, rest a bit longer, and wait until we get ahead before you set off."

He nodded slowly. "Bort will wait."

28

Late in the day Moleskin's luck changed; the fog lifted and the low sun allowed him to gauge his direction of travel. He set off with renewed optimism, but this did not last. As the sun sank towards the horizon the air temperature dropped, and with it his mood.

With his collar pulled up tight he trudged on, his only encouragement the constant reminder of how much wealth he carried; in time this dreadful journey would be a distant memory, and he would sit in his grand manor house, warming himself by a log fire and drinking the finest brandy, thinking back on these troubled times. It would all be worth it in the end, but only if he kept going.

It wasn't long before he was shivering constantly and his fingers and toes were starting to ache. It was so cold, tiny frosty droplets of ice were forming on his hair and eyelashes.

When a small stand of trees appeared ahead, he breathed a sigh of relief. As he plodded wearily towards them, he congratulated himself; the worst of his troubles were over, he could light a fire and build a shelter, he was saved.

Approaching the edge of the trees, he saw the flickering yellow light of a campfire illuminating the undersides of a ring of high branches. If it looked safe, there was a chance he could befriend this other traveller or travellers, and save himself the bother of preparing his own fire.

A steep ridge separated him from the campfire. Teeth chattering, he cautiously picked his way up the slope and then bellied forward until he could see better.

Below him large, indistinct figures clustered around the fire, at least twenty of them, the flickering firelight glistening on their armour and chainmail.

To add to the cold shivers wracking his body, a spasm of fear went through Moleskin. These weren't Harrowen, but might they be robbers? He slid back and crawled across to a small hollow beneath a tree. Slipping his pack into the hollow, he carefully noted its position and then covered the pack with snow. This precaution taken, he crept forward again.

Drawing closer to the campfire, the tempting scene served only to emphasise how cold and uncomfortable he was.

The men crowded around the flames; all red-cheeked, hearty and delighting in its warmth. The carcass of a deer hung from a spit by the fire and a light breeze treated Moleskin to wafts of the mouth-watering smell of its cooking flesh. They didn't look like robbers, and he wondered if this rowdy band would share their hospitality with a fellow traveller?

The answer came quicker than he expected when a coarse hand fell on his neck.

"What have we here?" said a strong voice.

Moleskin found himself suspended from the arm of a large ruffian.

"What're you doing lurking up here?" the man growled.

The constriction caused by the man's powerful grip on Moleskin's collar prevented him from answering. He flailed his feet and croaked an unintelligible reply.

The man set off towards the fire, still holding Moleskin by his collar. As he entered the circle of warmth he gave Moleskin a shake, presenting him like a newly-caught piece of game.

"See what I found creeping about in the snow over there!"

Dropped to the ground, Moleskin landed on all fours.

"What have you got there, Rodney?" said one of the men.

"It's not one of them is it?" said another.

"Too skinny," said a woman's voice.

Still crouched, Moleskin searched the group for the last speaker, but none had a form that suggested femininity. This close, the heat from the fire was almost unbearable, and the deer was close too, with droplets of glistening fat dripping onto the stones by the fire, and sparking and flaming on the glowing embers.

An immense man dressed in chainmail and studded leather stood from his log seat and came over to Moleskin.

His hand shot out. "Gregor's the name, I'm the leader of this band!"

Moleskin stood uncertainly and extended his hand, watching in amazement as it disappeared into the other man's grip.

"Moleskin," he said, through clenched teeth.

"Moleskin is it? You look like you could be doing with a good meal, m'lad!"

Moleskin wasn't too sure if he approved of being addressed as *m'lad*, but he wasn't about to argue the point.

The others found it amusing though, they guffawed and laughed outrageously.

"You'll join us for a bite to eat." Gregor made a show of winking at his companions. "I doubt you'll be eating enough to leave us starving!"

This brought another loud roar of laughter.

A hand clasped Moleskin's arm and pulled him back to sit on a makeshift log bench. He found himself between two men whose shoulders came level with the top of his head. One of them used a dagger to saw a piece of meat from a large chunk he held, and handed it over. The other passed him a hard leather mug full of wine.

Moleskin sat for a moment holding his newfound bounty in front of him. For an instant he couldn't decide whether to bite into the meat or pour the wine down his throat. The meat won the race and he gnawed into it fiercely. He looked up as he chewed; they were all watching him. He nodded appreciatively and waved the wine and meat in the air.

There was a good-natured cheer, followed quickly by laughter as his salute was returned.

Moleskin smiled, he had landed squarely on his feet. The heat from the fire pressed into his body, the meat tasted wonderful, and the wine was strong, sweet and spicy. Whoever they were, their hospitality was beyond reproach.

Later, Gregor came over and sat by Moleskin.

"It's a coarse bit of country to be wandering about on your own," he said.

"I was running from the Harrowen."

"Harrowen!" Gregor exclaimed, and for the benefit of the others he shouted, "Hear that! This lad thinks that lot are Harrowen!"

A fresh peel of laughter ran through the group.

"Harrowen, lad. That's old wives tales. Where did you get an idea like that?"

"They are Harrowen," Moleskin insisted, the wine giving him fresh courage. "Up close they look just like Harrowen. Their eyes are blood red, and they have pointed teeth and leathery skin."

"He's got a point," said a voice from the circle.

This comment brought a flurry of discussion as the band exchanged views on Moleskin's claims.

Gregor silenced the group with a loud shout and a gesture. "Even if they are Harrowen, how would you know?" He pulled Moleskin to his feet and made a show of examining him, feeling the muscles on his arms and turning him around to look him up and down, obviously assessing his doubtful abilities as a warrior.

The band watched in quiet amusement.

Finally Gregor let out a loud dismissive grunt, and said, "You'll never have been close, or you'd be dead like the rest of them."

"I've fought them!" said Moleskin, indignantly, and was about to recount his feats of valour in the Library, but thought better of it. No point in giving away the location of such a vast source of wealth. He settled for an easier tale. "I fought with the King's army at Sollas."

Gregor squinted at Moleskin in disbelief. "You're never a King's soldier!"

"Archer in the Silvermeadow Militia," said Moleskin proudly.

Leaning back, Gregor folded his thick, sunburnt arms. He took a few seconds to consider his reply. "Militia man, eh?"

Moleskin felt a moment's panic, if Gregor handed him a bow he had little chance of drawing the string, let alone hitting a target.

Gregor nodded slowly and the humour faded from his voice. "You make me ashamed, lad. A skinny thing like you volunteering for the militia." His eyes went around the group. "We're all mercenaries, paid fighters." He picked up his mug, raised it high and called to the others, "A toast to the militia man here!"

There was a moment's silence as the assembly of seasoned warriors toasted Moleskin's character.

"We're moving on," said Gregor. "It's not a fight for us. Looks like King Malcor's set for a long siege. Maybe he'll see it out too." Gregor's eyes rose to the night sky. "It's a harsh winter coming. Those Harrowen of yours might not last it through. Anyways, we're not staying around to find out."

"I was thinking of making my way to Conisby," Moleskin boasted.

"You'd be a fool to do that!" Gregor stared down into his mug, and then dashed the wine into the fire. "Either that or a damned brave man!" He peered across the campfire searching out a particular member of the band. "Duff," he roared, "you were in King Malcor's army once?"

A clean-shaven man with long brown hair lifted his head. "That's true, what of it?"

"You know of any way of getting this lad back with his fellows?"

"Into Conisby?"

Gregor stared down at Moleskin, mistaking the look of wide-eyed panic for one of anticipation. "That would do him fine."

"I'm to risk my life for that?"

Rodney, the man who had found Moleskin, spoke up, "It's the least we can do for him."

"I'll make it worth your while," said Gregor. "I've not much honour myself, but I respect it in other men!"

"Come on, Duff," said Rodney, "can't you see how keen he is."

"How much?" said Duff.

Gregor rubbed his chin. "Ten crowns."

"Thirty," Duff countered.

"Fifteen."

"Twenty five!"

"Fifteen, and not a crown more! That's all you'll take from me, Ethan Duff."

"I'll give you another five," said Rodney, "that makes twenty."

Duff spat in his hand and strode over. "Twenty it is, Gregor, Rodney."

Rodney shook coins from a suede pouch and handed them over. "Here's my share."

"Five now and ten when you get back," said Gregor.

Duff shook his head. "Very well, Gregor. I know how hard it is for you to part with your money all at once."

Gregor spat in his hand and held it out. "You'll look after him, now?"

Duff shook hands with Gregor. "Don't you worry. I'll see him safe into Conisby."

Rodney clapped Duff's back. "Safest moving at night, best you be off now. We'll be waiting for you when you return!"

"Oh, don't worry," said Duff, "I'll find you."

Gregor turned to Moleskin and smiled. "That's it then, lad. We'll have you back among your comrades sooner than you think. What do you say to that?"

Moleskin was speechless.

Rodney waited until Moleskin and Duff had disappeared into the gloom before backtracking to where he had first observed Moleskin. He came back and called for attention before shaking the contents of a damp backpack onto the ground, silencing the whole party in an instant.

Gregor leant forward, scooped up some gold coins and a huge grin spread across his face. "Yes, it's the little ones you have to watch out for."

The roaring laughter of the mercenaries echoed into the treetops above them. It hadn't been a wasted trip after all.

29

Bort stared constantly at the ground ahead of his feet, carefully avoiding any missed pebbles or ruts that could cause him to slip and stumble. As he trudged he recited Torven's poem, finding it helped him to ignore the growing pain in his legs and shoulders.

Little Ito runs the race,
to solemn Nal's steady pace.
Ito has no time for season,
his frantic dash seems lost to reason.

Ito spins and sprints ahead,
no care for you tucked up in bed,
or thought for beast or bird in flight,
he sweeps the skies, both day and night...

Bort wished he was little Ito; the running sounded good, though a nice warm bed sounded even better. They had already slept two nights in the tunnel, and each night he had stepped from the harness sore and exhausted.

Sleeping was not a problem, and he was even used to the pain now, and knew he could keep going, but the work was relentless and demanding.

"Hold up there, Bort," said Endor. "You've caught us up again."

Bort barely looked up. He relaxed his straining muscles and sank to his knees; chest heaving with his exertions, he leant forward on all fours, waiting to recover his breath.

Ida came and gently brushed the top of his head. "Here, Bort, drink some water."

He took the bottle and nodded. "Water, thank you, Ida."

She knelt in front of him. "How are you managing?"

"Tired." He eased the harness from his shoulders, and then sat back cross-legged.

Ida touched one of his shoulders and he flinched. He looked down; a dark stain of blood marked his shirt where the straps had been.

"I'm sorry," said Ida. "I should never have brought you along."

Ida sounded very unhappy and Bort tried to reassure her. He lifted his head and smiled. "Bort is not sorry. Bort is just tired."

Endor knelt beside Ida. "What's that you're saying, Bort? Tired, is it. Maybe you'll let me share the load then?"

"No, Endor must be strong for the fighting. Bort does not like fighting, Bort will pull."

"Does anyone know how much further it is?" said Lineth.

"I've lost track a bit," said Endor. "Can't be forever though."

"Not forever," Bort agreed. Normally he was good at judging distance, but he'd let his mind wander too much.

"Maybe there's something I can do with these straps." Ida left, returning with several bandage rolls.

Lineth took one shoulder strap and Ida the other, winding the bandages around them.

Bort nodded his thanks, the extra padding would help.

"How about we stop for an early lunch?" said Endor.

"Good idea," said Ida.

"I'll get it." Endor went to the back of the carriage where their food was kept.

"Will you manage, Bort?" said Lineth.

Bort hoped that he was returning a reassuring smile. "Bort will manage. Eat lunch and then go."

Ida patted the back of his hand. "I'm very proud of you."

Ida's words were comforting, but what really drove Bort on was the memory of what the Harrowen had done to his people. He didn't like to think of this as revenge, though the Harrowen deserved no consideration or leniency, but if he, the last of the Trollid, could help stop the Harrowen doing on this world what they had done on the Trollid homeworld, it would be a worthy way to honour the memory of his race, and if he died in the process, what better end for the Trollid.

After lunch they continued on through the rest of the afternoon; Ida aware that Bort was taking longer to catch up with them, and that each time he did, the padded shoulder straps were more stained with his blood.

Bort ended their day, sinking to his knees and collapsing. The carriage rolled on, coming to rest with him underneath and the harness stretched tight in the wrong direction.

"Get him out," Ida yelled.

Endor crawled beneath the carriage to grapple the harness clear of Bort's shoulders. Then he and Lineth grabbed an arm each and pulled him clear.

Ida placed a folded pad under Bort's head and then listened at his chest; his heart was beating furiously. She felt a huge hand gently touch her head and looked up.

"Ida is not to worry," said Bort.

She sat up and took his hand in hers. "How do you feel?"

"Tired and thirsty," he said.

"Just you lie still." Ida snapped a finger at Endor. "Water, now! Lineth, my medicine bag." She turned to Bort. "First thing, I want that shirt off before the blood dries."

After allowing Bort a little water, Ida unbuttoned his shirt and slid it off. She gently washed the worn and raw skin around each of his shoulders, applied a salve and then put on light bandages. She helped him slide on a clean shirt and then made him move to a comfortable seat she made from a folded bedroll, making him sit against the tunnel wall.

"Now," she said, firmly, "you will sit there and do nothing while we prepare tea." She placed a water bottle in his hands. "Small sips only, but keep drinking until you finish that. Understood?"

He grinned. "Yes, Ida."

As soon as Bort had finished eating, Ida placed a blanket over him and turned the lanterns away to leave him in darkness. He fell asleep almost immediately. She sat with Endor and Lineth and whispered to them. "He can't keep on like that."

"You'd be surprised," said Endor, "at what can be achieved with a little determination."

"I won't let him do it," said Ida, "he's killing himself. This has to stop!" She took deep breaths, struggling to contain her tears.

"Nonsense," said Endor, "he'll be fine."

Ida thumped him in the chest. "You stupid man, he's not fine!"

Endor took a deep breath. "I might seem like an idiot at times, Ida, but I know men, and I know what they're capable of."

Endor's words seemed too brutal to contemplate. Tears welled into her eyes, and she buried her head in her hands. "I don't want to hear this."

Lineth touched her shoulder. "Come, Ida, walk with me."

Ida sniffed, rubbed her eyes dry with the hem of her skirt and then stood. "I don't know what to do!"

"Come with me." Lineth put her arm around Ida and led her down the tunnel. With the light fading behind them, Lineth stopped and said, "Endor is right. But more than that, and you must know this, Bort has made his own choice. It doesn't help him if you cast doubt on that decision."

Ida shook her head. She could follow Lineth's logic, but when she looked back towards the light, and to where Bort slept, she just wanted it all to stop. "I feel so responsible, Lineth. Bort wouldn't be here if it weren't for me."

"And none of us," said Lineth, firmly, "would be here if those Harrowen had stayed where they belong."

Ida took a deep breath and sighed. "Then I pray we're near."

30

Duff was an efficient, if sullen, workman. By stealth and cunning he brought Moleskin across country and to the edge of the barren perimeter surrounding Conisby. When nightfall came he told Moleskin to remain quiet and to follow three simple instructions, two hand signals, wait and come, and the third instruction, if he started running, Moleskin was to stay on his heels at all cost.

Without another word, they crept between the campfires of the Harrowen pickets and then out onto the open ground. The broken, grassy plain was slippery and wet from an earlier fall of icy rain, and thin trails of pungent woodsmoke drifted over the ground like mist. Apart from the crackle of fires and the occasional distant exchange of Harrowen voices, the only sound was the soft rhythmic brush of their bodies over the thick grasses as they crawled ever nearer to Conisby.

Moleskin became so engrossed in this constant slithering movement, he didn't notice the signal to wait, and it was only when his nose was pressed against Duff's boot that he realised the man had stopped.

Duff glared at him, but said nothing. Conisby now loomed over them, a huge dark mass that partly obscured what little starlight was in the sky. Duff pointed ahead, and then pointed to his ears.

Moleskin listened; somewhere ahead of them, two Harrowen were conversing in low tones. Duff gave the wait signal, and then slid off into the darkness.

No nightmare could have been worse; Moleskin was in the middle of open ground, effectively surrounded on all sides by the Harrowen army, but without the advantage of Conisby for protection.

The Harrowen conversation stopped abruptly with a dull thud and a noise like someone clearing their throat. A little later Duff crept out of the darkness.

He brought his mouth close to Moleskin's ear and whispered, "They were out here watching your entrance. Lucky for us they were more concerned about people trying to get out than in. Now pay attention, and stay close."

Duff led off again and the city grew ever larger, blacking out more and more of the sky. Only when they were in the deepest shadow next to the vertical rock at the base of the city walls, did Duff indicate they could crouch.

He quickly located a narrow slit in the rock. "Follow it in," he whispered, "and you'll soon be back with your comrades." He held out a hand. "Good luck to you."

Moleskin managed a thank you, and then Duff was gone, lost immediately from sight.

He stared out at the ring of picket fires and the darkness between, considering whether to follow Duff; but the arguments against this piled up. What if he encountered more Harrowen hidden on the plain? Could he sneak past the picket line? Even then, could he escape the Harrowen patrols further out? Also, was Duff sitting quietly in the dark, just out of sight, waiting to make sure he entered the city?

Ito glided into view, its pale light barely illuminating the ground around him and Moleskin stared up; the jester moon, how appropriate. Resigned that he had no other choice, he turned and stepped into the narrow cave, shuffling forward into the blackness with his arms outstretched.

The cave continued for about fifty paces, and then he felt the surfaces to either side of him change; the rock becoming smoother. Another fifty paces on and a sudden rattle came from behind. He quickened his pace, fearing some Harrowen had followed him, but immediately blundered into a wooden door and fell back nursing a sore nose.

He lay still, listening carefully. There were no sounds of pursuit, in fact no sounds of any kind. What should he do next? Then he remembered his reserve of gold coins, a small pouch kept close to his skin. Carrying this much money might be considered suspicious.

Standing, he turned and felt his way back along the tunnel. After about fifteen paces he came to a wooden barrier. The earlier noise had been made by it sliding into place. He placed his pouch into a hollow by the wall, and then sat a smooth, round stone on top of it.

A rattle at the far end of the corridor caused him to jump and a weak, flickering light appeared.

"Right you!" said a sharp voice. "Move this way. And if there's any funny business, we'll leave you there to rot."

"I'll be no problem to you," Moleskin called. "Glad I made it in safely."

Three soldiers met him, their swords drawn. They peered at him suspiciously.

"Who are you then?" said the one with the sharp voice.

"The name's Moleskin. I'm with the Silvermeadow militia under Baron Endor Caffri, King's chosen."

"Never heard of them," said the sharp voiced man. He exchanged a look with the other men, but they just shook their heads in agreement. "Standing orders," he said, "we put you in a cell until an officer can come and question you."

"Surely that's not necessary?" said Moleskin. "We are on the same side."

"I don't know nothing. You could be a spy for all I know, or sent to poison our water. You don't look like any kind of soldier I met before." He waved his sword towards a narrow corridor with a set of steps at the end of it. "Now up the stairs with you."

After a search, Moleskin was bundled into a small cell. The jailer turned the key and then called through a hatch in the door, "Just you wait there. Officer's busy just now; he'll have a word with you in the morning."

A straw mattress in the corner of the room proved surprisingly comfortable, and having no other choice, Moleskin settled to sleep out the remainder of the night.

Moleskin was startled awake by the echoing sounds of troops running to position, their armour clanking and rattling, and spurred on by urgent, shouted commands.

Daylight filtered through a narrow slit set high on the cell wall. It was past sunrise, but neither the jailer, nor any officer interested enough to come and interrogate him, had come by. They must have forgotten about him.

Suddenly the ground shook and loose mortar fell from the ceiling as a deep rumble echoed through the jail corridors. He barely kept his feet. Moments later, another echoing sound reached him, a far-off roar of voices similar to that at the battle at Sollas.

A tremor of fear passed through Moleskin; the Harrowen had breached the walls and were about to fight their way into the city. They would find him trapped in this cell, and kill him. To have any chance of escaping he had to get out, and now was not the time to be greedy. He took off his left boot and from beneath the insole produced a single gold coin; more than enough, surely, to gain the jailer's interest.

He leapt to the hatch in the door, gripped the bars and shouted at the top of his voice, "Guard! Guard!" As he shouted his mind worked furiously, preparing a story that might just gain his release.

Lord Tekt paced the balcony of the command tower, seething with frustration. The second attack of the wizards had proven a complete success, the damaged section of the outer wall crumbling away and carrying with it a good number of the defenders. As an added bonus there was now sufficient rubble piled against the base of the city rock to provide a steep ramp into the breach. Not an easy route, but still a way to gain access.

The city's occupants would be demoralised now, unsettled and in chaos. It was the perfect time for a full assault, but without the wizards' magic to deflect arrow shot, losses would be unacceptable. Also, the morning's work had been marred by many of the wizards collapsing after the attack. It was something that neither his troops nor the city's defenders should have witnessed.

Tekt turned as Dusswen entered the audience chamber. "Fetch a chair for the wizard," he barked at an aide.

The aide rushed off, returning moments later with a high backed chair.

"Come, Dusswen." Tekt had the chair placed to allow a view of the city. "Come and see what you have achieved."

Dusswen slumped into the chair. "I hope Lord Tekt is pleased with our efforts?"

Tekt bit back the response he wanted to give; putting aside their very public display of weakness, Dusswen's wizards had delivered their promise. "You have done well." Tekt leant over a small table and poured a goblet of wine. "Something for your thirst." He pressed the goblet into Dusswen's hand.

"Thank you, my Lord."

Tekt waited until Dusswen had taken a drink. "When will you be ready to assist with the main assault?"

Dusswen stared out, his brow deeply furrowed.

"I need an honest answer," said Tekt.

"We lost four," said Dusswen. "Melingor, Russtas, Mirtor and Krat, they killed themselves for the greater glory of the Harrowen Empire."

"A worthy death, then," said Tekt. "Their memory will be honoured along with all that have fallen, and will fall. When can you give me the arrow cloak?"

"If the assault is kept narrow," said Dusswen, "and concentrates solely on the breach and nothing more. We can offer it in a days' time, daybreak tomorrow."

"Are you sure?"

"Of that, yes, my Lord, but we can offer little more."

Tekt knew that Dusswen would not dare to lie to him. It was a better offer than he had expected. "Very well, at daybreak tomorrow we will begin the attack. I thought of sending creepers among them tonight. To cut a few throats and lower their morale."

"A good tactic, my Lord."

Tekt turned to Dusswen. "Can you give me a fog, enough to cover this part of the field?"

"It can be done, my Lord. A simple matter, but it will not last."

"That will serve best. While it lasts, I will move the army forward behind shields of woven timber. When the fog clears they will be in position. Then I will shower the breach with arrows and Death's-Wings. On a given signal, the creepers and other hidden ones will spring out and confuse the enemy as the main assault force makes their charge."

"Indeed, it is a good plan." Dusswen paused. "Will you honour the humans first, my Lord?"

Tekt rubbed his chin. "The Song of the Dead?"

"Yes, my Lord."

Tekt pondered; other than recognising the humans as a worthy foe, there was another more useful aspect to the ceremony. "Yes, Dusswen. We will honour them. It will serve to bring fire to the hearts of our army."

"It should be properly done, my Lord."

"I am in your hands then. It has been a long time since the Harrowen have honoured an enemy."

"I will make the necessary preparations."

"And my part, Dusswen?"

"I will explain it, my Lord."

It took a day of persistence before Moleskin's jailer finally showed some interest.

After biting the coin to test its worth, he said, "If you're a spy, he'll catch on quick. Maybe you'd be best sitting it out in there?"

"No," said Moleskin, "I need to see him. I have information vital to the conflict that he needs to hear."

"You could just tell me, I'll pass it on."

Moleskin mustered all his reserves and drew himself as tall as he could manage. "That would not be acceptable."

"Well," said the jailer, touching a mocking hand to his forehead, "since you puts it like that, I'll get it sorted for you."

He laughed as he walked away, and Moleskin feared he was being ignored, but twenty minutes later the man was back.

"Come on then, officer's agreed to see you. But don't you be wasting his time now!"

Prodded from behind, Moleskin was led up some stairs, and then out through a door onto a steep cobbled street in bright daylight. Squinting and shielding his eyes, he looked around. This part of the town consisted of long staggered terraces of houses to either side of the street. Most were whitewashed and had neat painted shutters folded open from their windows. Lined up three to four deep on both sides of the street were militiamen and soldiers, all waiting the call to the front.

As he was marched up the hill, grim, silent faces observed him with piercing indifference. Feeling uncomfortable under their gaze, he tried to walk confidently, but he knew they would be wondering what crime he had committed to be under guard at such an important time.

He searched ahead, hoping to see the familiar green and yellow uniforms of the Silvermeadow militia, so that they could vouch for him, but none were visible.

There was a clatter from behind and the jailer pulled him roughly out of the way to avoid a horse, its hooves sparking on the cobbles as it fought the incline.

"King's messenger," said the jailer.

"What's happening out there?" said Moleskin.

"Best you don't be asking questions." The jailer shoved Moleskin's shoulder. "Just get on up there."

A tight bunch of soldiers parted to allow them into a building, which looked no different from any other on the street, and Moleskin was taken to a room with a single tall window. An officer with a neat moustache and short brown hair sat behind a table. He leant back and crossed his arms as two soldiers, already in the room, took up position either side of Moleskin. Curious soldiers on the street peered in through the window.

Moleskin panicked when he saw the bag of coins he had hidden sitting in the centre of the table. They would want to know where the gold had come from.

The jailer stepped up to the table. "This is him, sir."

"Come on then," said the officer, "let's hear this *vital* information." He sat back with a pessimistic glint in his eye as Moleskin recounted another carefully edited story.

He mentioned the defeat of the dragon, the Harrowen and World Gates, the immersion of the World Gate in lava, the fight in the Library, the discovery of the bombard and the efforts of his party to bring it to the battle. The gold, he said, was proof of the existence of the Library.

"And enlighten me," said the officer, "what was the purpose of your coming here?"

"I was sent ahead to secure assistance."

The officer nodded slowly and then turned the bag over, emptying the coins onto the table top. He picked one of them up and examined it in the light from the window. "These are very old."

Moleskin waited expectantly. His best hope was to join with a party of men to go and assist with the bombard. Once out of the city, he could surely manage to sneak away from them. At the very least he would be freed from the cell, and that way there was still some chance of escape.

The officer burst into derisive laughter. "Absolute nonsense! You spin a fine tale, and you tell it well, but I spoke to your Master Sergeant, Peter Stamp. He said you were an absolute scoundrel. I'll tell you what really happened. You stole this from your master, or worse robbed it from a grave. You're a thief. Anyone with a bit of sense can see that!"

"No!" Moleskin protested.

"Dragons, magic, Harrowen and, what did you call it, a steam bombard! You must take us for simpletons?"

"It's all true," Moleskin insisted, but his voice had lost its conviction.

The jailer and two other soldiers in the room took their cue from the officer, all laughing and shaking their heads.

Moleskin looked around the mocking faces. "Please, why won't you believe me?"

The officer stood and stepped around the table, towering over Moleskin. His voice became menacing and cold, "We're facing death here. If these Harrowen of yours don't kill you by the end of the day, I'll be back to do the job myself." The officer waved to the guards. "Take this fool back to the cells. I've no more time to waste here."

Still protesting, Moleskin was dragged from the room by the two soldiers. With the jailer leading, they marched him back down the road. Some of the soldiers on the streets jeered, some just turned away and many spat on the ground as he passed.

Dishevelled and morose, he was thrown back into his cell. The door slammed shut and the key turned in the lock with a loud clack. The jailer had no parting words, he just sneered through the hatch before marching off. His footsteps faded down the corridor and Moleskin was alone again.

He slept fitfully that night, woken by a strange deep resonant sound, like the voice of a giant chanting. It seemed to go on and on without pause. When a slow, distant drumbeat began, the hairs on the back of Moleskin's neck stood on end, and one of his eyelids began to flutter.

31

Ida waited to offer Bort water. He had halted, doubled over with his hands resting on his knees, and struggling to catch his breath. When he finally drew himself erect, his eyes grew wide, focusing over her shoulder.

He pointed. "The door! The door is there!"

She turned and stared into the gloom ahead, all she saw was blackness. "How far, Bort? How far is it?"

"It is near," he said. "Soon be there."

For a moment there was complete silence in the tunnel, and then Ida whispered, "Thank the gods."

Endor rested his hand on her shoulder. "Truly, Ida, thank the gods." He patted Bort's arm gently, "Well done, lad, well done."

Had Endor insisted they move on straight away, Ida would have protested, but instead he smiled gently at Bort. "Whenever you're ready, lad, but take a moment first."

Bort handed Ida the water skin. "Bort is ready."

When she considered the weight of the bombard and the distance he had covered, she knew no normal man could have managed the feat. A longer rest would not be amiss. "Are you sure?"

"Bort is sure."

Endor was waiting for her consent; she sighed and nodded.

"Then let's get this done!" he said.

They all gathered around the carriage, and when Bort began pulling, Ida added to the effort as best she could.

It didn't take long, and when they arrived at the door Endor instructed Bort and Ida to unload any unnecessary weight from the carriage. He and Lineth would dress for battle.

As quickly as she could, Ida removed their remaining food boxes and sleeping rolls, stacking them to the side of the tunnel. By the time she and Bort were finished, Endor and Lineth were ready. Both wore armour selected from the finest and lightest on display in the Library, and Endor had added his faded blue tabard.

With a flourish he swept his sword from the scabbard. "Are we ready?"

Ida nodded and stood to the side, her hands gripping a large metal lever. "I'm ready here."

Endor and Lineth stepped up to the door; ready to deal with any Harrowen patrol that might be close by.

Endor glanced over to Ida. "Open it up," he said.

With a thin squeal of rusted metal, she forced the lever over. The rock grated, a flurry of loose stones fell from the ceiling and the door jerked away from the floor.

A thin line of daylight appeared, painfully bright after the dark of the tunnel, but then the door shuddered to a halt with only a narrow opening at its foot. Immediately, Endor snapped his sword into its sheath and sprang forward. Bending his knees, he grasped the bottom of the rock and with a grunt put all his strength into lifting it. Nothing happened.

"Some help here," he roared.

Ida abandoned the lever, and in seconds, she, Bort and Lineth were crouched alongside Endor.

"Ready, on three!" said Endor. "One, two, three!"

Ida gritted her teeth and strained, hoping that what small strength she could add would be enough to make a difference.

There was a tremor, a shower of small stones rained down on her and the door started rising smoothly.

Endor sprang back, snatching out his sword in readiness, but the excitement Ida saw in his face disappeared the instant the door rose past his eye line.

She turned to look; a huge boulder blocked their path. She could barely see over it. Beyond it, daylight streamed past a thick jumble of bushes and long grasses. She looked up; a deep V of daylight broke the uneven curve at the edge of the tunnel entrance. The boulder had broken loose from there.

"Lineth, go and have a look outside," said Endor.

Lineth moved forward, crouching as she pressed through the foliage, returning almost immediately. "We're safe, there's no Harrowen nearby." She paused by the boulder, a furrow creasing her brow. "What are we going to do about this?"

Endor paced around it. "We'll try and push it aside," he said, but his voice betrayed his doubt.

They applied their shoulders to the boulder but even Bort's huge strength could not move it.

When Endor sank to his knees, Ida placed a hand on his shoulder. We tried," she said gently. "At least we tried."

Endor scooped up a handful of pebbles and damp earth, clenching them in his fist before casting them aside. "We need a lever of some sort!"

"You know that won't work," said Ida. "It's too firmly stuck in the ground."

"I can't accept that," Endor roared. "We can lever it aside, the four of us together, surely..." His voice faltered and faded. He looked desperately around and then pointed back down the tunnel. "The bombard! We can blast it aside."

"Not this close," said Ida. "It's in the instructions, a warning, the closest target it can be steamed on needs to be four hundred paces away at least." She knelt beside Endor and took his hands in hers. "I wish there were something I could do to help."

"Dear lady," he said, quietly, "there is nothing anyone can do now."

It pained Ida terribly, but she knew he was right.

Except for a loincloth, Lord Tekt stood naked before his army. A small ornate blanket lay on the ground in front of him and placed on it were a dagger and a goblet.

He bent to pick them up and then held them aloft, turning full circle to show them first to his army and then to the city.

Time seemed to slow; his was the glory, and this was his day, the name of Tekt would echo forever in the Great Hall of Heroes. Songs would be sung about this very moment, and his exploits would bring fire to the hearts and minds of young Harrowen until the end of time.

With a slow precise movement he cut the palm of his hand, barely feeling the sharp pain as the flesh parted. Dropping the dagger, he held the goblet under the wound and gathered the blood.

This was the signal for the great Staxgoe horn to begin its song and from the mouth of an immense beaten copper instrument, came a deep vibrating note. Drummers joined it, beating out a slow, steady rhythm.

As one, the army sang the Song of the Dead, a dirge that grew louder as it moved towards its climax. They thumped their fists against their chests in time to the drumbeat, gently at first, and then firmer until the combined sound was so loud it echoed against the city walls and into the nearby mountains.

The song ended abruptly and after the last echo had passed there was complete silence.

Tekt held the goblet aloft and turned full circle again. He presented it towards the city and shouted, "The blood we spill today shall nourish us forever. From death comes new life, and life is but the journey to death." He brought the goblet to his lips, paused and drank it down. Finally he stretched his arm back and threw the empty goblet towards the city.

The army erupted in a loud cheer; fighting against an honoured foe bestowed immeasurable status on a Harrowen warrior and his descendants.

Tekt turned and with a wave signalled for Dusswen and his wizards to begin their magic.

At first the fog appeared more like a heat haze, but then it thickened into wraith-like spirals of grey that spread and merged until the city faded from view.

Woven timber panels, which had lain flat and hidden, were lifted upright and arranged into a line. The army then pressed forward behind them, a cluster of black-cloaked wizards at their core.

Tekt stepped out onto the balcony of his command tower just as the fog cleared. It was as he and Dusswen discussed; a fortified wall seemed to have sprung from the ground itself.

The first Death's-Wings were launched, cutting the air with a loud, rhythmic whirr, and as each huge metal blade leapt from its engine, elation coursed through Tekt.

He raised his spyglass to follow their deadly progress. The blades sparked and flashed as they struck rubble and stonework on their way into the city, and then severed limbs, bodies and buckled armour flew into the air, marking their lethal passage. Tekt smiled as one Death's-Wing bounced vertically into the air; its energy almost spent, its bloody blades barely turning. It hung for an instant before falling back into the ranks of the defenders, surely causing further death and destruction.

Tekt centred his spyglass on the troops defending the barricade on the collapsed wall. Volleys of arrow shot rained down on them and the defenders cowered behind hastily raised shields, many collapsing as the arrows found their mark.

Dusswen broke Tekt's concentration. "Does all go well, my Lord?"

Tekt spoke, his eyes still on the battle, "Very well, Dusswen. The fog was everything I could have wanted."

"Thank you, my Lord."

Lowering his spyglass, Tekt waved Dusswen forward. "Come, watch the battle unfold."

Dusswen joined Tekt at the railing.

"Now!" said Tekt, sensing the moment was right for the attack. An aide in the tower waved a flag, and the field commander signalled for the Harrowen hidden among the rubble to emerge.

"Yes!" Tekt hissed. "Death be among you!"

Several sections of the timber panels slid aside and large groups of Harrowen spilled through the gaps. Immediately they were on their way the panels slid back.

The defender's arrows rained down on these groups, but fell short or glided over their heads, deflected by the invisible shield created by Dusswen's brother wizards. Tekt laughed derisively.

The greater bulk of the Harrowen forces still waited safely behind the shield. Once the assault groups had cleared the way, the main force would go forward to enter the city proper. Then, with this foothold secure, they would advance through the streets, scouring them of all human life; man, woman and child.

32

Bort rested a hand on the boulder and without conscious effort began examining the structure of the stone; looking for a weakness, maybe some way to split it and make it easier to move. Torven would have known what to do; and as he thought this, he heard Torven's voice again; *little by little* it said, *little by little*. It made Bort think again of his rescue of Endor and Ida at Domidia. Suddenly, it was as if Ida had struck his head with one of her mixing spoons; a veil lifted and he knew exactly what to do next.

"Bort will move the rock," he said.

Ida rushed to stand between him and the rock. "No, Bort! You can't, it's too big."

"Ida must trust Bort," he said, gently. "Move aside."

She moved slowly away, her brow furrowed with concern.

Bort turned to the boulder, took a deep breath and placed his hands on its rough surface. He tried to remember the moment in the tunnel at Domidia, and the feeling in his head, and especially the way the wall had crumbled.

At first nothing happened, and he felt panic and doubt, but then he saw Ida's face; fighting tears, but bright and full of pride. Then he felt a strange tickling sensation in his hands, and almost immediately a fine, sparkling powder slipped from beneath his palms to trickle down the face of the rock. He shut his eyes and concentrated; the tickling sensation strengthened and soon his hands felt like they were immersed in a stream. Curious, he opened an eye; finding the trickle was now a flow. Then something shifted, as if suddenly the top of his head were open to the skies, and the flow became a cascade. Excitement filled him; this is what it was to be Trollid.

The rock disintegrated, and as it shrank a ring of dust formed around it, building to a sloping mound that covered Bort's feet and crept towards his knees.

By the time he stopped, the dust mound had grown so large it was halfway up his thighs. He stood erect, took several deep breaths and then leant forward and picked up what remained of the boulder. Turning, he flexed his bulging muscles and threw it aside. It landed with a deep thump that shook the ground; rolling over once before striking the wall with a loud crack and splitting in two.

Revelling in the moment, and the wide-eyed stares of his companions, he marched backwards and forwards through the pile of rock dust, kicking it aside and flattening it out. Then he walked back to the carriage, picked up the harness and dropped it over his head. "Bort is ready to go now!"

Endor stared at Bort open-mouthed. "By Loftin's ghost!" he roared. "Now we've a job to do!"

He turned, scowling at the barrier of bushes and saplings still blocking the mouth of the cave. "Now this is something I can manage." He unsheathed his sword and strode forward, hacking the foliage aside to create a path.

Ida and Lineth came behind, dragging the cut branches clear. Finally Bort pulled on the harness and applied his great strength to the carriage. They all ran back to help, and together they heaved the bombard out of the tunnel.

Endor signalled for them to stop when the bombard sat in the centre of a small grassy plateau, and after applying the brakes, he strode to the plateau's edge. From careful study of the images in the viewing room, he already had a good idea where the tunnel would emerge. It was exactly as he had hoped; they were high on the hillside in a position that overlooked and flanked the Harrowen army. What he hadn't anticipated was the mist obscuring the Harrowen; it would make aiming difficult, and he could only hope that the weak sunshine would soon burn it off.

The main battleground in front of the damaged wall was almost at the limit of their range. This distance and elevation offered them some protection; it would take time for a Harrowen force to climb to them and, unless they were unlucky, their presence would go undetected until they actually steamed. Beyond the plateau, the ground fell away sharply, mostly loose stone and scree, but with scattered clumps of gorse and elder dotting the slope. Barely discernible, an overgrown track curved off around the contour of the hill and down towards Conisby.

Lineth joined him and he watched her face, sharp with concentration as she took in the details of the landscape. Native to the city, and more familiar with the surrounding countryside than him, her council would serve them well.

"What will we do now?" she said.

Endor frowned. "The best we can. I'd hoped we would find a way to bring a party out to protect the bombard, but that's not looking likely."

As Endor watched, the mist suddenly dissolved away to reveal the Harrowen attackers, and Endor allowed a moment's grudging respect for Tekt, the mist had been a magical device to hide their movements.

The Harrowen were massed behind a long wooden barricade close to the huge crack in the city wall. The damage was much worse than before, but the city's defenders had built a crude barrier along the top of the rubble and deployed forces on it.

Glittering in the sunlight, star-scythes arced across the battlefield, flying over the heads of the Harrowen and into the city. A volley of arrow shot followed, showering the defenders.

"We're too late," said Lineth.

"We'll have none of that," Endor growled. "Bort didn't pull this ruddy great thing all the way here for nothing." He waved Lineth back to the bombard. "One to a wheel, let's get this thing lowered."

He paused for a few seconds more; the Harrowen had sent an assault force against the defenders at the breach. It was a fierce engagement, but the defenders were holding their positions. Reluctantly, he turned his back on the scene and joined the others. Working together, they wound cranked handles that lifted the carriage wheels, allowing the bombard's rotating platform to settle onto the ground.

Endor barked out his next commands, "Bort, get the fire started. Lineth, fetch more water. Ida, ready the bombard."

Though Ida had memorised the loading and steaming sequence, she still took a few seconds to check a small list she'd prepared before surveying the busy scene around her. Endor was laying out the blasting bombs and short, tightly-bound rolls of canvas packing on the ground close to the bombard's barrel. Lineth had dashed off, carrying the empty buckets to a nearby stream, and Bort was busy at the firebox. All was progressing as it should.

Bort soon had the fire roaring; pumping furiously at a set of bellows to force air through the fuel, and having finished his task, Endor joined him, dropping more and more coals into the firebox until it was almost full with a fiercely glowing mass.

Lineth was almost back from the stream, running at an awkward trot, and with water slopping from two overfull buckets. They had some water left from the trip, but it might prove difficult to collect more later.

Taking a deep breath, Ida took up position alongside the weapon's controls. In preparation for the next stage, she wound the handle that dipped the barrel, stopping when it was at a shallow angle and with the end in reach from the ground.

Seeing that they were almost ready, she shouted, "Endor, I need Bort to load the bombs."

Endor nodded and took over at the bellows. "Is that it ready, Ida?"

She glanced at the heat gauge; the wavering pointer was just short of reaching the steaming temperature.

She nodded. "Almost there."

"Very well, Ida," he said, "it's time to prepare your weapon for steaming."

Taking a deep breath, she shouted to Bort, "Insert the wadding."

Ida watched carefully as he placed a canvas roll into the end of the barrel, pressing it in with a wooden plunger.

"Wadding in," said Bort.

She called out, "Arm and load the bomb."

Bort pushed a square key into a hole on top of one of the bombs and rotated it through half a turn to arm it. He then lifted the bomb and slid it tail first into the end of the barrel.

"Bomb in," he said.

"Secure the load," said Ida.

Bort used the wooden plunger to push both items down the barrel. "Load secure," he said.

Ida turned and caught Endor's eye. "Where do you want to place our first bomb?"

Endor barely paused his efforts, panting, "What do you think, Lineth?"

She spat the words out, "Start with those wizards!"

"Are you sure?" said Ida. The wizards were standing in a group apart from the main force. She was no tactician, but it was a small target compared to other concentrations of Harrowen.

Lineth's voice took on a venomous tone. "I promise you, the wizards are the better target. You'd know that if you'd been with me in the Library."

Endor nodded, accepting Lineth's counsel. "Very well. Ida, aim for the wizards!"

Ida knelt, pressed her eyes against the sight and the distant sounds of battle became powerfully real; in terrifying detail, she saw the fierce fighting raging along the top of the tumbled down wall.

Winding a brass handle, her view shifted; the weapon's sight tracking across the rubble and open ground until it filled with the Harrowen behind the tall wooden shield. There, at the centre of the shield, the wizards stood in an isolated circle. She could only guess at what magic they were practising, but it must be giving the Harrowen some unusual advantage. A final few adjustments to the winding handles drew a pair of horizontal lines in the sight together; joining them with a single vertical line to make a cross, which centred on the wizards.

Suddenly it was all very real; Ida Fairweather, who had never injured a single soul in all her life, was about to become a killer. She shuddered and swallowed; it didn't take much to remind herself of all the misery that had gone before, and all that would surely follow if the Harrowen were not stopped.

She glanced at the heat gauge; the needle was hovering in the centre of the firing range. "We're ready," she said.

Endor met her eyes with a firm gaze. "Very well, let's see what this thing can do."

Ida checked the water indicator; it required a full charge. Using a small brass vessel, she scooped water from one of the buckets and poured it into a chamber mounted at the rear of the barrel.

She put down the measure, turned to Endor and immediately an anxious pain filled her chest. Up until this moment everyone had blithely assumed the bombard would work, but it had to be hundreds of years old. Would it still function, or would it blow apart, killing her and everyone nearby?

She waved to Endor and the others. "Stand well away!"

Endor's brow furrowed.

"Normal procedure," Ida lied.

Endor nodded and stepped away, ushering the others back.

"On your command, Endor," she said.

Very well, Ida," he said, "steam the damned thing!"

Ida said a small silent prayer, took a deep breath, closed her eyes and pulled the lever. With barely a gurgle, the water dropped into the heated chamber. Her ears rang with a loud chuff, the turntable shook beneath her feet and a shroud of hot, steamy vapour enveloped her.

Endor appeared through the haze of steam, a look of alarm on his face. "Are you well, my dear?" he said.

She patted her cheeks, they felt hot and damp. "I... I think so," she said, adding after a brief pause, "Did it work?"

They both turned to stare across at the battlefield. There appeared to be no change and Ida's heart sank. The weapon had failed.

Suddenly a huge ball of flame and smoke erupted amongst the wizards and she stared in horror as scorched and burnt figures flew in all directions. She'd never seen anything so awful before.

"By all that's holy!" Endor bellowed, triumphantly.

Seconds later, the deep rumble of the explosion rolled by, echoing in the mountains behind them like distant thunder.

Endor grabbed her hands and danced on the spot, roaring with glee until she pulled away from him, scowling.

"Now we've something to fight back with!" He bowed to her. "Madam, if you'll ready your weapon again, I'd like to put another bomb among them at the front there."

33

"What was that!" roared Tekt. The words were no sooner from his lips than a giant invisible hand rocked the command tower, forcing him to cling to the guardrail.

Dusswen had collapsed into a ball, his arms wrapped around his head. "They're all gone, all gone," he managed through clenched teeth.

Tekt pulled Dusswen to his feet. "What are you talking about?"

Dusswen staggered and gripped the guardrail. "My brother wizards, they are all dead."

Tekt quickly assessed the new situation. The arrow shield allowed greater freedom of movement and also disheartened an enemy, but casualties from arrow shot could be minimised with tactical formations. He felt sure they could manage without the wizards and their shield, but if this new weapon could not be stopped it would spell disaster.

"Mourn later," he snapped. "I need your counsel now. What caused this?"

Dusswen concentrated and then pointed to a small patch of rapidly fading smoke on the side of a hill to the north. "There, my Lord, there."

Tekt swung up his spyglass. "It's a war machine of some sort."

"It must be from the Library of Banna, my Lord."

"The wizard Torven, no doubt!" Tekt growled. The machine and Torven would need to be dealt with quickly. "Dusswen, you will go with an armed troop and put an end to this."

"Torven is not among them, my Lord. I would sense his presence."

"Very well, in that case you can serve me better here." Tekt used the spyglass again, and laughed. "The fools have no support, it will be easy to capture." Turning to an aide, he barked, "A message for the field commander."

The aide snapped to attention. "Your order, my Lord?"

"Dispatch a party to capture that machine."

"By your will, my Lord." The aide saluted and dashed from the chamber. Emerging from the foot of the tower he ran to the field commander and after an exchange of words the commander turned to face Tekt's position. He saluted, and then relayed the order to a junior officer. This officer quickly gathered up a band of thirty or so soldiers and set off at a fast trot towards the hillside.

"It has not shot again," said Tekt.

"No, my Lord." Dusswen closed his eyes, and then laughed. "Steam, my Lord, it uses steam! And I sense it takes time to rearm."

"Not a perfect weapon then," said Tekt, "but still a marvellous machine."

"It will make a fine addition to your army," said Dusswen.

"It will, and it seems this Library of yours is worth a visit after all?"

Dusswen lowered his head in deference.

Tekt looked out over the battlefield. His forces had quickly regrouped and closed the shield to protect themselves from arrow shot from the city. This new weapon was the only thing standing in the way of their victory. He swallowed back a sudden surge of anger. If they had brought across another dragon before the Gate was lost, they could have silenced it in minutes, but it served little to dwell on matters that could not be changed.

"We can still win this battle, Dusswen."

"Yes, my Lord, there is little doubt of that."

"When we do, we will open the Master Gate and march victorious back to Mirt."

Dusswen bowed. "Indeed, my Lord. You will be first among the Harrowen Lords. Your place at the Emperor's right hand is assured."

Tekt slammed the handrail with his fist. "Never again will I bow before another!"

"Never again, my Lord. Never again."

Watching from the edge of the plateau, it came as no surprise to Endor when a group of soldiers broke away from the Harrowen army to head in their direction. But the speed of their approach troubled him; the weapon was taking far too long to heat up again. At this rate, they would be lucky to steam two more times before having to abandon it and retreat into the tunnel. Then he had an awful thought; if they left the bombard outside, there was nothing to prevent the Harrowen from turning the weapon on Conisby.

"Is it ready yet?" he shouted.

"Very soon," Ida called back.

Just as the Harrowen began the climb towards them, Ida shouted, "Steaming." Her words were instantly lost in the weapon's roar.

Endor trotted back to the bombard, considering the quickest way to remove the bombs. He could only manage one at a time, and without stopping to explain, he picked one up and carried it back towards the tunnel. He was halfway there when he looked up and stopped in his tracks.

Torven had emerged from the tunnel mouth. The old wizard leant heavily on a wooden staff and limped along slowly.

"Loftin's grandfather," Endor bellowed, "you're dead!" He lowered the bomb and ran to offer assistance.

Torven took Endor's arm. "My dear Endor, I feared the same of you and the others." He looked around. "Where is that scoundrel Moleskin, has he not survived?"

"The little worm ran off."

Torven shook his head and indicated that they should walk towards the plateau's edge. "Not a surprise, surely?"

"I suppose not, but you, we put you in a casket!"

"As is the way with my kind, my body stilled until it recovered. And thank you, it was a lovely casket. I'm sure King Tultepo's ghost did not object to sharing it with me for a while. I must admit it felt a bit strange, waking to find myself an exhibit in the very Library I was supposed to be caretaking." He nodded at the steam bombard as they walked by. "You've chosen a fine weapon for the job. Very fine indeed."

Torven waved a greeting to Ida, who stood with her mouth wide open, and another to Bort, who wore the grin of grins.

Lineth joined them and shook Torven's hand. "It's good to see you, sir."

"And me you, my dear. Now tell me, what's happening down there?"

Endor pointed down the slope. "That raiding party will be here soon."

Torven shook his head. "I'm sorry, but I am too weak to be of any help with that particular problem. But it's a good steep incline, so we've a little time to work." His eyes quickly took in the battlefield. "There is something you can do that will have a profound influence on the outcome of this battle." He used his staff as a pointer and called out, "Ida, do you see that black tower at the far end of the plain?"

"I see it," she called back.

"Lay your sights on that and we'll give them a bit of a surprise."

Endor helped Torven back to the bombard, and they waited expectantly as Ida adjusted her aim.

"There's a problem," she said.

"What's that?" said Endor.

"We can't reach the tower, it's too far away. According to this gauge we'd need to increase the water charge by a quarter." She glanced at the water vessel and her brow furrowed. "But that's impossible; it can't be more than full."

Torven carefully produced a small glass bottle from a fold in his cloak. "Oh, not entirely true, my dear, there was a later modification to the operating procedure. A quarter more you say?"

Ida nodded.

"I can't seem to think straight." Torven tapped his forehead. "How many drops to make one be equal to one and a quarter, when eight drops makes one equal to two? We'd have to add, ehm?"

Endor stood for a moment trying to think it through, but his brain seemed as sluggish as Torven's.

"Two drops," said Ida.

"Goodness, yes," said Torven. "That's right. Two drops exactly." He smiled up at Ida. "Kindly prepare your weapon." He released Endor's arm, adding, "I'll thank you to help me up there."

Endor assisted Torven to climb onto the bombard, and then looked to Lineth, who was keeping an eye on the approaching Harrowen. She made a quick hand gesture; a familiar signal indicating the enemy was still a safe distance away.

Endor pointed back to the bomb he had dropped. "I thought to remove those in case the Harrowen capture the bombard and use it against Conisby."

Torven lifted his little bottle. "If it comes to that, there's enough energy in here to overcharge the bombard and blow it to bits."

Endor had already noted the careful and gentle way Torven handled the little bottle. If that was the final solution, he hoped it could be achieved without one of them remaining on the bombard to operate the trigger.

Under Ida's instruction they worked quickly, priming and loading the bomb. After Ida filled the water cylinder, Endor held his breath as Torven very carefully added two drops of his fluid with a small glass eye dropper.

Ida brought the weapon onto target, and then waved the others clear of the bombard.

"Stay back," she said, her mouth a thin determined line.

After ensuring that everyone was safe, Endor raised an arm in salute and shouted. "Steam when ready, Ida. Steam when ready!"

The bombard belched mightily and a loud metallic ringing reverberated across the hillside.

Endor was relieved when Ida stepped clear of the haze of steam, straining to see her target. He turned to watch as well, and tense seconds went by in which nothing happened. This time he knew there would be a result, but would it be on target?

The tower erupted in a magnificent display of multicoloured flame and smoke. Large pieces were thrown high into the air, leaving long spiralling trails of smoke in their wake. Endor was thrilled and impressed, and imagined this must be something like the volcanic eruptions he and Torven had discussed in Garn.

Just after, a thunderous clap rolled by, and in its wake a distant moan of despair from the Harrowen army.

"Well aimed, Ida!" Torven beamed. "I think you'll find that makes a big difference all round."

Though satisfied with the first three steamings, Endor wasn't so sure about Torven's assessment. In reality they had done little to reduce the mass of the Harrowen army. Logically they should all retire into the tunnel, but even one more steaming might be critical.

"Try and get another steaming," he shouted. "And if Lineth and I can't hold them, you must retire to safety, understood?"

Endor looked to Ida, and she nodded. Reassured that she and the others would be safe, he joined Lineth and peered down the slope. The officer in charge of the approaching Harrowen had rallied his men, and they were approaching as fast as they could manage. The incline had spread the force, which would make their job easier, but examining the size of the party, Endor had little doubt about the eventual outcome of the encounter.

A quick glance across at Lineth told him she understood the situation. He wanted to say something profound, but nothing came to mind. In essence he was a simple man, gifted in physical skills, and now was the time when all his training and years of service were to be tested. It was a soldier's decision; this sacrifice could save the lives of many.

Lineth saluted him. "Time to make mother proud."

"You already have," said Endor, returning the salute. "You already have."

Shoulder to shoulder they waited.

Horribly, Ida knew what both Lineth and Endor intended. Struggling against the pain welling in her chest, she examined the heat indicator. The previous steaming hadn't cooled the bombard as much as the first;

almost definitely due to the fluid Torven had added. If she worked quickly, maybe there was a chance to get them all to safety.

"Bort," she shouted. "Reload!"

While Bort busied himself with the reloading, Ida worked the bellows as best she could. Torven tried to assist, but he was very weak. Her spirits lifted when Bort finished the loading and took over at the bellows; it was all happening faster than before.

Ida had just filled the water cylinder when the sharp clatter of sword on sword startled her. Endor and Lineth had engaged the first of the Harrowen.

Spinning the aiming wheels furiously, she targeted a dense cluster of Harrowen massing for an assault. She rested her hand on the steaming lever and checked the temperature. It wasn't quite hot enough, and she prayed her target wouldn't move before she had a chance to steam.

Torven gripped her shoulder. "Patience, Ida, don't waste the steam."

Ida worried at her lip as the clash of swords drew closer and the Harrowen raiders forced Lineth and Endor steadily back towards the bombard. She gasped in panic when three Harrowen slipped by them, and immediately glanced at the heat gauge. It still wasn't hot enough.

"Ida will work the bellows," Bort shouted.

He leapt from the turntable and snatched up the ramming rod. His first blow swept a Harrowen from its feet, sending the brutally deformed creature spinning off through the air. The other two Harrowen tried to run around him, but he chased them down, smashing them to the ground with blows to left and right.

Ida cursed herself silently. Concentrating so hard on Bort, she had ignored his instructions to work the bellows. When she turned, she found Torven labouring them up and down.

"The gauge," he gasped.

She stared. It was ready. Bort, Lineth and Endor were backing steadily towards the bombard, fighting off another surge of Harrowen, and though Endor had told her to run to safety, she knew there was little chance of that now. She threw herself onto the lever and the bombard steamed.

Lost from sight in the cloud of steam, the clash and clatter of swordplay stung her ears, and she knew that in seconds they would all be dead. Torven staggered over and put an arm around her; holding up the small bottle, poised and ready to dash it to the platform.

Ida looked up to catch one last vision of the rolling green hills and clear blue sky above, wanting it to be the last thing she saw; but through the clearing steam she saw another more wonderful sight. Loping down the hill and across the plateau were a mass of soldiers in the green and yellow uniforms of the Silvermeadow and Cadford militias.

Shouting and roaring, the militias streamed past the bombard and crashed into the Harrowen, just as the echoing blast from the battlefield arrived.

The sudden surge of familiar uniformed bodies around Endor came as a very welcome surprise.

After the initial contact, which swept the plateau clear, Peter Stamp quickly ordered the bombard's defence, presenting a closed rank of shields, bristling with pikes.

"Where in Loftin's name did you lot spring from?" said Endor.

Stamp saluted. "It was Moleskin, sir. He said you'd come, and he knew of a way out of Conisby. We circled to avoid contact, and here we are."

"Damn that Moleskin! He'd climb from a pile of manure smelling of roses."

"Your orders, sir?"

"Carry on, Mr Stamp, you're doing a fine job!"

The last of the Harrowen reached the plateau, formed up and advanced. Stamp engaged, and then ordered his flanks to press forward to encircle them. It was a short, bloody encounter, resulting in the obliteration of the raiding party.

Afterwards, Endor found Lineth sitting with her back against one of the bombard's wheels. She was covered head to toe in dark coppery blood, and he probably looked no different.

"Are you hurt?" he said.

Her voice was flat, unemotional. "No."

He sat alongside her, suddenly wishing he had a flask of wine or spirit to toast their success.

"I didn't see that coming," he said.

She nodded slowly. "We live to fight another day."

It didn't take a special skill to see Lineth was deeply troubled. "What ails you, lass?"

"I'm weary," she said, "weary of it all." She gave Endor a weak smile. "Of course, I'm glad we're still alive, but it's all been a bit much."

In his years of service Endor had witnessed many different reactions to warfare. Lineth was a good soldier, but not so hardened to the realities of the task that they didn't trouble her. He could see her choosing another path in the future.

He pressed his shoulder in against her, offering what comfort he could without drawing attention to her moment of weakness.

He spoke softly, "There's nothing easy about what we do, lass. But today you did a hero's work. It might not sit right just now, but when you see the faces of the innocents and those that can't stand as we do, those that would have died had we not stepped up, then you'll find it all makes a lot more sense. And from this day on, we're bound, you and I. Neither would have survived without the other, and if you ever have need of anything, you call on that bond and I'll honour it."

They sat in silence for a while, and then Lineth smiled and rested her hand on his. "You're a good man, Endor Caffri." She glanced up towards Ida and smiled. "It surprises me that some equally fine woman hasn't seen that yet."

Endor returned the smile; if he and Ida survived the day, he planned to do something about that situation. "Best we see what's happening, eh?" he said.

Lineth stood first and stretched out a hand, helping Endor to his feet. An act of kindness, as his whole body was wracked with fatigue and starting to stiffen.

Ida and Bort were already preparing the bombard, with several of the militia offering help where they could.

Endor called up, "Everything in hand, Ida?"

"To be honest," she said, "I'd feel better if someone else took over the aiming."

Endor nodded. Lineth wasn't the only one wearying of the conflict. If he thought about it, warfare must be the most alien thing imaginable to a gentle creature like Ida.

"Mr Stamp," Endor shouted. "A word with you." Stamp was well known for his aptitude with machines and mechanisms.

The task was explained to him, and he took over as the bombard's aimer. Endor indicated the target for the next steaming and Stamp wore a fierce smile as he threw the lever.

When the steam cleared and the bomb found its target, he nodded in satisfaction. "This will do nicely, sir."

"Load it up again, Mr Stamp," said Endor.

While waiting for the heat to rise again, Endor looked around the plateau. Ida had recovered her healer's bag from the tunnel and was tending to the militia wounded, keeping busy, as she always did. He smiled when he saw that Lineth had gone to sit with the militias on the edge of the plateau; better to stand with your comrades and take strength from them, than sit alone. Unasked, Bort had gone to collect the bomb Endor had moved, lifting and handling it with deceptive ease. He could not have picked a finer group; every one of them extraordinary in their own way.

The bombard was winning the battle and Endor judged that the balance had swung in their favour. His only fear was that the Harrowen might attempt to assault their position again, but nobody had made that decision yet. Possibly the remaining leadership had decided that gaining a foothold in the city offered the best protection from the bombard. Whatever their reasoning, the bombard was not a target, a mistake that would cost them dearly.

Each new blow to the Harrowen forces drew a loud cheer from the militias. Then, as the supply of bombs dwindled, Endor found it harder to find sufficient concentrations of Harrowen to justify each steaming. Some last rallying charges provided targets for the remaining few bombs, until finally there were none left. Their work done, Endor shook hands with the crew who had manned the bombard and then joined the militias at the edge of the plateau.

A thin pall of brown smoke hung over the battlefield, and deep craters pockmarked the ground. For a short time a strange unnatural silence lingered, then, to a fanfare of trumpets, a rousing beat of drums and a loud roar of voices, the defenders spilled from the city. Men on foot advanced over the uneven rubble of the broken wall, and a long line of cavalry rode down the ramp from the city gate.

"Should we join them, sir?" said Stamp.

Endor examined the remains of the combined militias and a deep pain filled his chest. They were barely fifty strong. Stamp had mentioned a handful more, some injured and some too weak to leave the city, Otric among them. The communities of Silvermeadow and Cadford had a lot of grieving ahead, and no doubt this was also true for towns and villages all over Carolin, but Endor saw no shame in preserving the lives of these brave men and women who had risked all in a dash across open countryside to aid them.

"We've done our share," he said. "Rest your troop, Mr Stamp. Tend their wounds."

Torven caught Endor's attention and took him aside. "I've a little information that might interest you."

"What's that then?" said Endor.

Torven checked to make sure that nobody could hear them. "The girl Lineth, you don't seem to know that she's your daughter."

Endor felt himself choking up. "Is she! Gods, her mother said the father was someone else."

Torven smiled. "Her mother may well think that, but this is the truth. Do with it as you will. She's a fine young woman and any would be proud to have her in their family. I know you'll do what's best." Torven was distracted by something over Endor's shoulder. "Now if you'll excuse me, Endor, I've another matter I need to attend to."

Endor stared wistfully across at Lineth. He'd never been a father to her in the past, and wondered if it made any sense revealing the truth now. She had her own life in Conisby, and with her mother; this new information could be unwelcome. He hoped he would find the right thing to do, but at present he had no idea what that was.

After tending the wounded, Ida turned away from the brutal scene. Though the tide of battle had turned in favour of the King's army, she sensed that the remaining Harrowen would fight on until every last one of them was dead. It wasn't something she cared to watch. She searched out Moleskin, finding him sitting alone on the hillside behind the bombard. He stood as she approached, but kept his eyes cast sheepishly down. Seething with anger, she waited for him to speak.

"Miss Fairweather," he said, "I'm sorry I ran off. It was foolish of me. I was frightened. I, ah... took the treasure so that I could start again, but then I felt terribly guilty. I knew you'd need help so I came here and told them what you were planning. They didn't believe me at first, but when you steamed the bombard they had to."

Ida shook her head. "Mr Moleskin, beyond any measure of doubt, I know that is not the whole truth."

Moleskin shrugged. "I suppose it's my nature, Miss Fairweather. I always like to present myself in the best possible light, whenever I can."

Ida stared for a few seconds, then, against all her better judgement and reason, she found herself warming to Moleskin. Strangely she understood why Endor tolerated the man. And, in the final reckoning, here he was, risking his life like the rest of them.

"It was very brave of you to come out with the militias," she said. "Now, I don't think you should be sitting on your own back here, go and join the others."

Ida watched Moleskin walk away, only to be intercepted by Torven. It seemed an affable exchange, Torven's arm around Moleskin's shoulder, and Moleskin nodding to Torven's words. Advice no doubt on how to live a better life in future, though Ida felt sure the words would fall on deaf ears. Still, she had to admire Torven for trying.

With the battle over, the King's soldiers standing among the scattered Harrowen dead on the battlefield turned as one towards the group on the hillside and began cheering.

Ida raised her eyes to the sky and said a silent and sincere prayer of thanks, and barely a few heartbeats later, the bells of Conisby started pealing.

Torven took advantage of the distraction and asked Ida to gather Endor, Lineth and Bort together at the tunnel mouth.

"I'm returning now," he said. "I'll have to leave the bombard. But without the bombs it is no more than your own alchemists and engineers might have created in a few years' time. Though I hope you never have need of it again."

Endor held out his hand. "I thought we'd never get a chance to thank you for saving us from the dragon."

"In the end you did as much as I," said Torven. They shook hands.

Lineth said her thanks and then Ida added hers. Torven had proven himself everything he claimed to be, and a good and loyal friend.

Torven gripped Bort's hand firmly. "Young man, you have an important choice to make. You can stay here with these good people, or you could return with me to the Library."

Torven produced a handful of stone dust from his pocket, and Ida recognised it from the huge rock Bort had dissolved.

Torven let the dust trickle through his fingers. "Your Trollid talents will be invaluable to me, and I can help you to understand and hone them. The Library does not maintain itself completely. For a start," he smiled, "there's the Firewall to rebuild. It appears that some thoughtless wretches have knocked it down!"

Bort stared uneasily at Ida, his forehead deeply furrowed. "Ida and Bort have a pact."

Ida knew it was time to let go. "You will always have a home in Silvermeadow, Bort, but it's time to change our pact. You should go with Torven. He cares for you as much as I do, and he can offer you a chance of the future you deserve." She placed a hand over her heart. "And while you are away, you'll be with me here."

227

Bort sighed. "It was a good pact."

"A very good pact," said Ida, fighting back her tears.

"Then Bort will go with Torven," he said.

Pulling Bort down, Ida stretched on tiptoe and kissed his cheek. "I'll miss you terribly."

"Bort will miss Ida too."

Ida still held his hand. "You'll come and visit when you get a chance?"

Bort nodded.

Endor presented his hand to Bort. "It's been an honour. I'd be proud if you'd count me as a friend."

Bort hesitated, and then shook Endor's hand.

Lineth saluted Bort. "We couldn't have done this without you. It's been a real privilege."

Bort returned an awkward salute. "Thank you," he said, his face reddening with embarrassment.

"There is one final matter." Torven drew the group together. "The existence and location of the Library must remain a secret. The knowledge it contains would be too great a source of danger and conflict for this world and its peoples. Might I suggest the weapon came from the Trollid City, which of course is now collapsed? And that confusion within the tunnel has left you uncertain of the city's location?"

Ida glanced around the group. "I think you can rely on us to remain quiet."

"A solemn oath," Torven suggested.

"I'll agree to that," said Endor.

"What about Moleskin?" said Ida.

Torven rubbed his hands together and smiled. "Oh, I have already discussed the matter with Moleskin."

Ida suddenly knew what Torven had been doing earlier. "You didn't harm him," she said, surprising herself.

"No, good lady, but his memory of events is no longer as accurate as your own."

This was probably a kindness to Moleskin; he could waste years of his life, and get into a lot of trouble, trying to locate the Library.

Ida smiled. "When Bort visits, you'd be very welcome too."

"A kind invitation, Ida. I will accept, though I cannot say exactly when that will be. Bort and I do have a lot of work ahead of us."

"Of course," Endor added, enthusiastically, "that invitation is also true for me. You're very welcome to come by any time."

Torven smiled around the group. "I look forward to meeting with you all again. Now, I do think it is time for us to go."

Ida's last sight of Bort was when he and Torven stopped in the tunnel mouth, ready to close the door. Bort wore a gentle, calm smile, and in that moment she felt intense pride and great sorrow. He waved as the rock panel slid closed.

Endor rested a hand gently on her shoulder. "A cook, eh, Ida?"

"What?" she said, confused.

"Oh, I was just thinking back to when you first came by and asked me to give him a job. I had my doubts, and here, I was right all along."

Ida appreciated Endor's attempt at humour, but nothing he said could take away the great emptiness she felt. But this was right for Bort; he fitted better in Torven's world, and if he could master some of the skills evident in the Trollid city, then his future was bright.

"Now," said Endor, "we should go and join the rest of them down there."

Ida was hesitant; the battlefield was surely covered in the Harrowen dead, but now was not the time to be squeamish.

Endor directed Peter Stamp to line up the militias, and then invited Ida to join him, Lineth and Moleskin at their head. Together they marched down the track towards Conisby.

The King's army had massed as a loud and jubilant mob at the foot of the city's cobbled entrance ramp, but as they approached, it fell silent; those closest shuffling aside to allow them passage. Ida felt uncomfortable being the focus of so much attention, and determined not to look foolish, threw back her shoulders, lifted her chin and walked with as much poise as she could muster.

King Malcor and General Hork rode down the ramp to meet them, with an honour guard of ten King's Chosen flanking them.

Endor put the militias at attention, and when the King and Hork dismounted, he knelt on one knee and bowed his head. "Sire, your humble servant, Endor Caffri, Baron of Silvermeadow."

"Rise, Endor," said the King.

The King stepped forward and embraced Endor firmly and Ida could barely hide her surprise. Without bidding, a loud cheer rose from the ranks of the soldiers around them and from all those still manning Conisby's battlements.

The King raised a hand to quiet the commotion. "Endor, I'd like you to introduce me to your companions."

Endor smiled proudly at Ida. "This charming lady," he said, "is Miss Ida Fairweather. It was due to her splendid management and aiming of the bombard that it proved so effective."

The King took Ida's hand and she curtsied. "My very sincere thanks, Miss Fairweather."

Ida smiled weakly. "Thank you, Sire."

Endor then waved Lineth forward. "Without the quick wits and martial skills of this fine soldier, our enterprise would have faltered on many occasions. Sire, may I present one of your own Guard, Lieutenant Lineth Tobias."

Lineth snapped a salute.

The King returned it. "You've done a grand job, Lieutenant. What you did here today will not be forgotten." He paused, his brow furrowing. "I am also very sorry to be the bearer of sad news. Your mother, Colour Sergeant Tobias, suffered terrible wounds in the defence of the breach. She did not survive. I know she would have been proud of your achievements, indeed as you must be of hers."

"I'm sorry to hear that," said Endor, gently, "she was a fine soldier, a fine woman."

When Endor reached out to grip Lineth's shoulder, there was a tender firmness to it that might have worried Ida, were it not that a sudden truth revealed itself in their profiles. Startling in its clarity, a niggling resemblance that she'd not even acknowledged; they were father and daughter.

Lineth remained silent for a moment, nodding her thanks to the King. Finally she found her voice. "Thank you for your kind words, Sire."

King Malcor saluted Lineth again. "I promise, she won't be forgotten."

Lineth stepped back, tears trickling down her face, and Ida put an arm around her to comfort her. She might be the proudest warrior, but she was still a daughter who had just lost her mother, and likely just gained a father, though clearly that was still to be revealed.

Then, before anyone could stop him, Moleskin stepped forward and held out his hand to the King.

"I'm Moleskin," he said.

Wearing a puzzled expression, the King shook his hand. "Pleased to meet you, Moleskin. What was your part in all of this?"

"I don't know," said Moleskin.

Ida caught Endor's eye, and pointed quickly to her head.

"Sire," said Endor, "I'm afraid he's a little dazed from a blow to the head."

The King nodded sympathetically, and then General Hork leant in and whispered in his ear. "Oh, I see!" The King shook Moleskin's hand enthusiastically. "A very fine effort indeed, thank you!" He turned to Endor. "You'll make sure this fellow gets the best of attention?"

"I will, Sire."

Moleskin nodded and said to the King, "My name is Moleskin. I work for Baron Endor Caffri."

Peter Stamp stepped forward. "Begging you pardon, Sire," he said, and gently took hold of Moleskin's shoulders, guiding him away from the King.

"What of Otric?" said Endor, "I hear he was injured?"

The King looked to Hork.

"Oh, he'll survive," Hork winked at Endor, "but I'm not sure my wine cellar will. Though it's a small price to pay for his fine rearguard action in the retreat from Sollas." He nodded towards Peter Stamp. "Your man Stamp and him did a grand job there."

Ida was glad Otric had survived; his wife Lizbeth still had a husband, and his son Grant a father. She was also proud of Peter, and in fact of all in their militias. They had done their duty, and more.

The King extended his hand. "I'll shake your hand too, Mr Stamp. You and your men, and women, deserve our thanks more than once it seems."

Peter Stamp presented himself, saluting and kneeling first before accepting the King's hand.

"Is that everyone?" said the King.

"No, Sire," said Endor, "there was a man called Bort, a big fellow with the strength of a horse and the heart of a lion. He pulled that bombard single-handed halfway across the country."

"I am sorry," said the King.

"No, Sire, he survived, but he, ah... had to leave. It's difficult to explain."

A distant rumble filled the air, and Ida's eyes turned to where the bombard still sat, just visible over the grassy lip of the plateau. A cloud of dust hung over a mound of rubble in front of the tunnel mouth. Endor gave Ida a knowing look, confirming her own thoughts; there was little doubt that the tunnel was now sealed and impassable.

The King looked puzzled, and Ida felt a moment's panic as Endor stammered out an explanation.

"I'm afraid," said Endor, glancing at Ida for support, "that, ah..."

"...we had to remove some of the tunnel supports to get the bombard out," said Ida. "All this shaking from the steaming must have weakened it further, it's finally collapsed. It wasn't really that safe to start with."

"Tunnel?" said the King, confused.

"Yes." Endor sighed. "It's a long story, Sire."

Ida didn't relish the task of concocting a story to satisfy the King; and wished that, just this once, they could make use of Moleskin's dubious skills.

The King stared up at the dispersing dust cloud for a few seconds, and then looked around their small party, sensing their unease. He took pity on them. "Once we have buried our dead, it's a story I'd like to hear." He raised his arms and in a clear voice shouted out, "A cheer for the Silvermeadow and Cadford militias! Hip... hip..."

The response was near deafening, and tears welled into Ida's eyes. Unexpectedly, she was thrust into the air, and she, Endor, Lineth, and even Moleskin, were carried shoulder high up the ramp and into the city. All around, a sea of cheering faces kept pace as they climbed through the city streets. Ida knew there were many other heroes in that day, but for a time it did no harm for their little band to be the focus of attention. It was rightly a time of celebration.

34

Ida heard a knock on the front door of her cottage. She opened it to find Endor staring down anxiously at the snow covering the toes of his boots. He was smartly and sensibly dressed for the cold; quite the handsome country gentleman, and leaner and fitter looking than when he had left for the conflict.

Since their return to Silvermeadow they had both been busy. Mostly offering support to families that had lost husbands, wives, sons and daughters to the conflict; Ida consoling and comforting, and Endor finding the means to provide pensions and financial security for their futures. Little enough compensation for their losses, but a responsibility Endor took very seriously. It all confirmed what she knew about him, how honourable and caring a man he was.

His chin came up and he took a deep breath. "Good morning, Ida."

Ida shivered and pulled her shawl up around her shoulders. "Good morning, Endor. What brings you out on this fine winter's day?"

Endor presented a folded and sealed note. "I'd like to deliver this."

Ida's breath caught in her throat as she suddenly guessed the reason for his visit. She took the note and stared at it.

"Best you open it," he said, rocking slowly from one foot to the other.

"Very well, Endor."

Her fingers shook as she carefully broke the seal. Under Endor's constant scrutiny she read it through, and as she read her heart warmed and beat faster.

My dear Ida,

I have come to regard you as the finest woman of my

acquaintance. Further, having observed the many splendid

aspects of your nature, your compassion, bravery and

intelligence, to name but a few, I would appreciate the opportunity to spend more time in your company.

To this end I wish to invite you to join me as my guest at the Winter Fair celebrations. Should you agree, I hope it will be the first of many such occasions. I further hope that in time you will find in your heart a fondness for me that matches my own for you.

Your most ardent admirer,

Endor Caffri.

Ida felt tears welling into her eyes. The letter was a little stuffy, but terribly sincere. Exactly, in fact, what she would have expected Endor to produce. Still, she couldn't resist prolonging and enjoying the moment. After dabbing the tears away, she made a show of rereading the letter.

"Endor," she said, finally, "I'd be pleased if you would join me for breakfast. There are elements of this... communication that I wish to discuss with you."

"That is splendid," said Endor.

Ida smiled and stretched out her hands to pull him close. "Yes, Endor, it is quite... splendid!"

THE END

NOTES

Though clearly more complex, I imagined the **Palace of Visions** and other viewing rooms as using an extension of a simple technology known as the camera obscura, or pinhole camera. These were very popular during Victorian times. Camera obscuras can still be found all over the world, gathering images through a pinhole 'lens', often sited at the top of a tower, and projecting them via a mirror onto a flat table below.

The **steam bombard** drew inspiration from an entry in one of Leonardo Da Vinci's notebooks. Da Vinci describes *The Architronito*, a real and functioning weapon built from fine copper and invented by Archimedes. It operated using the same basic steam principle described in the novel, and threw iron balls with *"great noise and fury"*.

Printed in Great Britain
by Amazon